Duel of the Heart

a novel by
Rose Moore Tomlin

EVENINGPOSTBOOKS
Our Accent is Southern!
www.EveningPostBooks.com

Published by
Evening Post Books
134 Columbus Street
Charleston, South Carolina 29403

Editors: Bonnie Grossman, John M. Burbage, and Holly Holladay
Designer: Gill Guerry
Dust jacket portrait: Collection of The New York Historical Society
Author photo: Grace Beahm

First printing 2013
Printed in the United States of America.

A CIP catalog record for this book has been applied
for from the Library of Congress.

ISBN: 978-1-929647-14-9

DEDICATION

For the

keepers of my heart,

my granddaughters:

Sarah, Kendel, Courtney,

Kate, and Morgan

ACKNOWLEDGEMENTS

Heartfelt thanks to:

John Burbage — for taking a chance

Bonnie Grossman, John Burbage, and

Holly Holladay — for expert editing

Courtney Hynes — for tireless research

Betsy Clawson — for reading the first draft

and for her encouraging words

Dick Côté — for steadfast cheerleading

Peter McGee, Nic Butler, and Carol Jones — for information

on the St. Cecilia Society, The Jockey Club, and

the landscape of Charleston in the early 1800s

Don — for absolutely everything else

FOREWORD

Theodosia Burr Alston would be considered an outstanding woman in any era, but in the time she was born, she was extraordinary.

Her father, Aaron Burr, insisted on the highest possible education for his only child. Many young girls of her time learned French and music, but Theodosia was also taught Greek and Latin and was expected to read the classics in these languages. To that end, she had a private tutor, a privilege reserved for young men in the late 1700s.

Some criticized her "masculine education," but there was no young woman more graceful and charming than Theodosia Burr. She excelled in mathematics, English composition, and was a classically trained harpist. Motherless from age eleven, she inherited the job of hostess at Aaron Burr's New York estate, Richmond Hill. There, she entertained notables, some from abroad. At fourteen, she was presiding over formal dinners and discussing politics with dignitaries.

In telling her story, I have held hard to historical facts, though I confess to flights of imagination in the yawning gaps where research material is non-existent. Theodosia's scrupulously kept journal has never been found, so I composed her entries, relying on a number of factual resources and taking some license in improvising what she might have penned.

I also paraphrased often from a wellspring of letters between Theodosia and her father. Their poignant exchange of ideas and opinions populate my imagined journal entries as well as some of the novel's most lively dialogue.

As the story opens, Theodosia has only a hazy memory of a promise she made to her dying mother as a child, but she believes it put her in charge of restraining her unpredictable father — an overwhelming assignment for a child.

Move forward a few years, and Theodosia has lived a lifetime, traveling a hero's journey, though perhaps not in the traditional sense. Sometimes the highest form of heroism is the act of surviving with courage and dignity, circumstances that would defeat a less brave heart. Theodosia's story juxtaposes a woman determined to make her mark and the reality of sometimes unbelievably difficult circumstances.

Rose Moore Tomlin, January 2013

THE CAST

Theodosia Bartow Prevost — Theodosia's mother.

Peggy Gallatin — Slave woman in Burr household.

Alexis — Slave man in Burr household.

Mr. Leshlie — Theodosia's tutor.

Aaron Burr — Theodosia's father and Vice President of the United States.

Natalie Delage — French émigré, Theodosia's "adopted sister." Married Thomas Sumter.

Washington Irving — Perhaps the first American best selling author, he was best known for *The Legend of Sleepy Hollow* and *Rip Van Winkle*. His home was Sunnyside, N.Y., on the Hudson River.

Dolley Madison — Wife of the fourth President of United States, James Madison.

William Peter Van Ness — Close friend of Aaron Burr who accompanied him to the duel, acting as his "second." He became a federal judge in New York City.

Thomas Jefferson — Founding father and third President of United States.

Joseph Brant Thayendanegea — Chief of the Mohawk Nation.

Jerome Bonaparte — Youngest brother of Napoleon I; later King of Westphalia.

Louis Philippe — Exiled from France, he later became King Louis XVI.

Bishop Charles Maurice de Talleyrand — Some believe that he was among the most skilled diplomats in European history.

Joseph Alston — Theodosia's husband. South Carolina rice planter, Governor.

Alexander Hamilton — Founding father, first U.S. Treasurer; killed in duel with Burr.

Colonel "King Billy" Alston — Joseph Alston's father, one of the richest men in the world in the early 1800s. Owner of Clifton, a Waccamaw River rice plantation near Georgetown, S.C.

Mary "Motte" Alston — Joseph Alston's stepmother.

Joseph Alston's siblings — John Ashe Alston, wife, Sally; Algernon Alston and wife, Mary; Lady Maria Nisbet, sister.

Tilda — Theodosia's slave servant, a gift from the Alstons.

Peet — Slave man at the Oaks Plantation in South Carolina.

Aaron Burr Alston, "Gampy" — Theodosia and Joseph Alston's son.

Nathaniel Pendleton — Friend of Alexander Hamilton; and his "second" in duel.

Harman and Margaret Blennerhassett — Owners of Burr headquarters on the Ohio River.

Luther Martin — Burr's defense lawyer at his treason trial.

Journal Entry

Washington, District of Columbia, March 7, 1809

I now know that my "independence" is an apparition. I am transparent, a witless prisoner no more in command of myself than a slave.

I have been captive to a promise given long ago, hazily and only partially remembered and, until now, misunderstood. My past appears to me as a wasteland, and my future may be equally bleak.

But as I write this, it becomes quite clear what I must do. I will end the war within me that has rendered me useless to him whom I have so long loved, and if there is forgiveness for me when I ask, it will suffice. If there should be love left, my heart shall swell until it fills my ears with the sound of its beating: Joy! Joy! Joy!

CHAPTER 1

New York City, May 1794

"Theodosia, my beloved girl. Look at me. I have prayed to be healed. But God cannot grant me this wish. You will be all your father has. This is why you must do this for me."

The child strained to hear her mother's murmured request, then asked: "Mama, how do I do that?"

Peggy, a wiry little woman with a dark and wizened face, stood quietly in the hallway. She could barely hear her mistress' voice.

"Theodosia, give me your word. You must!" Theodosia's mother continued.

"Took the child right out of that girl," Peggy muttered, shaking her head and moving slowly down the hallway. "Got woman's work now."

Since her mother had become too frail to breakfast in the dining room, Theodosia gulped her porridge each morning then hurried to the room and nestled with her on the high poster bed. She wriggled beneath an arm that was barely more than a shard of bone with veins threading the pale flesh like blue yarn.

Peggy had plumped the thick pillows and propped her mistress to a near-sitting position. She'd changed her into a fresh gown, too, and brushed her brittle hair, lank and gray now, a pallor that spread to her face. Once handsome, that face was hollow, more creased than Peggy's. The slave woman was sad, knowing that Mrs. Burr longed to hold Theodosia as she once did but was barely strong enough to listen to her child prattle.

"Papa will be here within the week! He writes that he'll be so happy to be back again. He loves the Senate but Philadelphia is too far away. It's boring there without us, he says. He wants the three of us to sit and have teacakes like we used to do."

Her mother's lips trembled as she tried to smile. *So restless and driven, is my dear husband. Now my life slips away by the hour, and I can give him no comfort.*

There were once good and bad days. Now all were painful and full of sadness. "Cancer," the doctor had said, staring at anything but her sunken eyes. She had been both hopeful and wary of his new treatment — hemlock.

"Is this not a poison?" she had asked.

"A very small dose, at first," the physician reassured her. "We increase it only slightly, and very slowly. It will poison only the toxins in your body, you'll see."

She had felt worse since taking it, but the doctor seemed sure it would result in a cure, and renewed hope brought back some of her husband's good humor. *Oh, Burr, so confident you will have me whole and well beside you again.*

She hated to disappoint him and the doctor. She had not the energy to protest the treatment anyway. So she remained silent, knowing their efforts now were driven by desperation, nothing more. The hemlock was their last hope, and the end of hope would be the most painful loss of all.

When awake, she ruminated about her daughter, about how Burr was consumed with preparing the child for great things. Theodosia's wishes, her mother knew, would not always mesh with his. His nature was to be in command. She wanted Theodosia to know what to do to appease Burr. She had kept him occupied. When he was engaged, she could pursue her own interests; when he became agitated, she soothed him with lively conversation.

Aaron Burr and his family had recently moved from a modest townhouse to Richmond Hill, an elegant mansion used briefly by General Washington during the Revolution. The Ionic columns rose high above its more modest neighbors — townhouses that dotted the shore of the Hudson River like soldiers at attention. The bustling village of New York encircled the structure on three sides but its second-floor portico offered a clear view across the river to the high hills of the New Jersey Palisades.

Burr had 26 acres of gardens, orchards, housing for animals and riding trails. He needed little encouragement to search for fine books and furnishings and show off his estate to politicians and dignitaries. Each coveted an invitation to dine at Richmond Hill. As his wife's strength ebbed, she encouraged his involvement in politics.

Her illness had struck quickly. At first, she forced herself to function in spite of worsening pain and nausea. But the cancer brought her down.

Her body purged itself many times every day and shed flesh rapidly. She became gaunt and listless in just a few weeks. Gnawing pain made it impossible to concentrate or engage in any but a short conversation. The doctor gave her laudanum whenever she asked, but she was reluctant to be less than fully aware during her final days with her daughter and husband.

"Theodosia, my precious one. Remember how we rode together along the river?"

"Oh, yes, Mama! When might we go again?"

The woman, silent for a long time, holding her tears, chose her words carefully.

"Theo, I am not well…."

"But, Mama, the new medicine. Papa says it is a miracle. We shall ride again! But first, we will walk. Just slowly round and round in the garden, perhaps?"

Theodosia put a hand on either side of her mother's face.

"Mama, look at me!"

The woman's heart lost its rhythm for a moment and she glimpsed her husband's expression in Theodosia's dark eyes. Burr's intense stare convinced, commanded, criticized. It could destroy an enemy's bravado or charm a snake.

Their daughter's eyes, deep-set in a delicate pastel face, resonated energy, extraordinary intelligence, curiosity and mischievousness.

"You can lean on me, Mama. I will help you."

The woman rested her head on her child's bright auburn hair. Despair drained her last bit of energy.

Even if I had the strength, I have not the words to tell Theo that I will never walk in the garden again. So much I want her to know. But today is not the day. Perhaps I will be blessed with enough strength another time.

She forced herself to think of what had brought her joy. The garden! A tapestry of roses — whites, reds, and pinks — with perfume so luscious she had longed to capture it and saturate her house with the scents. She remembered days she could walk among the flowers and how she tried to bring the heady aromas inside, crushed the velvety leaves and wrapped them in cheesecloth that she tucked in with her folded clothes and beneath the cushions. But sweetness dwindles too quickly, so she threw the shriveled petals away.

Theodosia felt her mother's arms slacken, her head resting heavier on her own.

Mama will get well, she thought. *She always has. She'll rest for a while and then she can go riding with me. Or we'll cook something. Oh yes, that will be so much fun! Peggy and Mama and me. We'll make little teacakes to surprise Papa when he gets back home.*

The sun tilted toward the Jersey shore, weaving gold into the rumpled darkness of the river. Theodosia slipped from beneath her mother's arms and moved silently from the room in search of Peggy, who knew the recipe for teacakes by heart.

CHAPTER 2

The next day's first light cast a sheer yellow coverlet over the Hudson. May's mild weather awakened the trees and shrubs — some full-flowered; others heavy with fruit.

Peggy tiptoed into Theodosia's room, circling the shivering flame of a candle with gnarled fingers. She set the candlestick down and opened the drapery to a blossom-scented breeze. She chose a housecoat from the linen press. Before waking her young mistress, she stopped and watched the child in peaceful slumber. *My precious, pretty baby. This will be your last sweet sleep for a very long time.*

She knelt beside the bed, traced the girl's cheek with the tip of her finger.

"She askin' for you, Missy Theo."

The child awakened quickly, expecting the intrusion. She arose in an instant, ignored the proffered wrap, and rushed past Peggy across the hall and into her mother's bed.

"Mama? Don't leave me."

Her mother tried but could not speak. *But I must tell her again.*

She willed herself. *I have to.* "Theodosia. Remember what I asked of you?"

The child burrowed into the softness of her mother's gown. "Yes, Mama, I will do it."

Her mother surrendered at that moment. As Theodosia stretched out her arms, her mother slumped toward her, pleading even in her last breath: "Promise?"

"Mama-a-a-a!"

Peggy came quickly to the little girl who was now her mistress and held her close, blotting their mingled tears.

CHAPTER 3

᷒᷒

Peggy tied the ribbon of Theodosia's dark blue hat under her chin and put on her own somber black straw.

"Peggy," the girl began, her chin trembling. "If Papa wanted to do something that I thought he should not, how could I stop him?"

Peggy grimaced.

"You try, Missy Theo. Do your best. But if you can't do it, what happens then is not your fault."

Theodosia frowned.

"You understand?" Peggy asked.

"No. Mama said...."

"Your mama meant you should try, that's all. You a daughter, not a mother, not a wife. Put on your coat now. The carriage is here."

Outside a footman boosted them into a high carriage where Aaron Burr waited. The coffin was already inside the first carriage, covered with a black cloth and pulled by dark horses. Burr; Theodosia; her two half-brothers, Frederick and Bartow Prevost; Peggy and Alexis, the butler, filled the second, and a long line of other coaches waited behind. The driver of the lead carriage slapped the reins, and with the clank of tack and squeak of wheels, the solemn line moved forward around the large circular drive and began its sad, slow journey to the ferry, which took them across the Hudson River to New Jersey.

The crowd around the graveside was large, even though the trip had taken most of the day. Several ferry crossings were needed to transport the mourners across the river. Burr stood beside the coffin as it crossed the choppy waters, steadying the box as it pitched and shook.

"Ashes to ashes," chanted the solemn priest.

Mama, how can you be just ashes?

As the coffin was lowered into the ground Burr nudged his daughter, dispersing her thoughts, and led her to the edge of the grave. No one told her that the two of them were expected to shovel in the first spades of soil.

The newly turned earth, the mourners, the branches of trees that towered above the cemetery swam before Theodosia's eyes. Small rocks thudded against wood and she blinked hard, determined that her tears would not get away from her.

As the mourners walked back to the carriages, many stopped and offered condolences. Peggy returned to the coach, and father and daughter stood alone as several men surrounded the grave shoveling in the rest of the dirt. Theodosia cried as the coffin was covered.

"Papa, once I heard you tell Mama that she brought you more happiness than all of your successes combined. What will happen now?"

He gently cupped her chin and raised her tear-streaked face to his.

"You must remember the words of your fine mother as well, my child. Do you recall her asking, 'When Aaron smiles, shall Theodosia frown?'"

She nodded.

"Good! What do you see?"

"You are smiling, Papa."

With his thumb he gently smoothed out the crease between her eyes.

"No more frowning then. We shall buy a pretty little chariot with matched horses to pull it. And I shall commission Mr. Stuart to do a fine portrait of you for the mantel. Would that please you?"

Theodosia smiled, wiped away her tears with the back of her glove. "Yes, Papa."

He stooped and tucked the hair that had escaped from her bonnet behind her ear.

"Then we shall not speak of this again."

CHAPTER 4

Soon, Theodosia resumed her studies, and Burr returned to the Senate. Theodosia settled into a routine of lessons with her tutor, but she could not ignore the raw ache that consumed her from the loss of a mother forever gone and a father absent, answering the call of duty. She missed both parents and anticipated Burr's return.

Theodosia rode her mare, Wind, like a seasoned equestrian as fast as she dared through the cobblestone streets, her red-gold hair streaming behind her. She had not taken the time to saddle the horse. She loved the feel of the mare's heat and sweat against her bare legs, modestly hidden beneath her petticoats and skirt. Because holes and puddles pockmarked the roadway, maneuvering the spirited animal bareback was no small accomplishment.

In straddling position, she could squeeze her knees, keep a safe seat and let Wind reach maximum pace. People blinked with disbelief as the young rider passed them. Some shook their heads in disapproval. The less inhibited smiled.

Earlier that day, Theodosia had presented her tutor, Mr. Leshlie, with the impossible challenge of holding her attention.

Tap, tap, tap. The timid staccato of his ruler did little to diffuse her excitement.

"Theodosia! You must listen!"

Lessons were taught in a library full of rare books as well as fine French furniture and Oriental carpets. Gold-fringed tassels held back the heavy embroidered draperies, ceiling to floor, nineteen feet, top-to-bottom.

Theodosia returned over and over to the window that faced the Hudson and pulled aside the drapery for a better view. Mr. Leshlie, increasingly exasperated, rapped his ruler faster. His tiny spectacles kept sliding down his beak-like nose, and his lack of authority embarrassed him. He could not keep the whine from his voice.

"Theodosia. We mustn't displease Colonel Burr now, do you agree? Please come here, sit down, and learn."

His thin fingers fluttered helplessly toward a table laden with books, pens, and stacks of parchment. Reluctantly the girl turned from the window.

"I have read 280 lines of horrible old Horace already, Mr. Leshlie! Papa will be arriving from Philadelphia soon."

She turned once more to the window and spotted the ferry, its sails luffing as the captain tacked and angled its snub-nosed bow toward shore.

"He comes now!" She cried. "Good-bye, Mr. Leshlie!"

The man shrugged, pushed at his glasses, gathered up his tools of learning, and stuffed them into a worn leather valise. Exiting the room, the girl almost collided with Peggy vigorously sweeping the hallway. The tutor blushed when he saw the woman, ashamed that he was powerless to stop his pupil's escape.

"Not your fault, sir. She always watchin' out for her Papa. I tell her she better watch out for herself."

Theodosia turned at the front door.

"Oh, Peggy, I am far ahead with my lessons. Papa's making everything possible for me; educating me as he would a son. Knowledge makes me strong, he says, and I can be remembered for important things! He wants me to be independent. So you see? I have studied hard today and will go to Papa now! He wants me there."

"Well, wait for me!" Peggy cried.

But Theodosia had already gone.

Theodosia quickly dismounted when she reached the busy docks, her bright, dark eyes focusing only on the ferry. She barely heard the clank and screech of chains holding fast the many ships, the shouts and curses of men as they unloaded heavy crates of merchandise from across the sea. Two drunken sailors argued heatedly about how many bottles were in a large container of wine.

"No more'n I could drink in a fortnight, b'God," shouted one.

"Yeah, and they'd cart your arse off to jail. Wouldn't be the first time, neither."

A disheveled man lifted a harmonica to his shaggy face. Theodosia winced at its raw wail and listened as a balladeer joined him, strummed a battered dulcimer, and sang:

Oh, the stormy winds do blow
And the raging seas o'er they flow.
While we poor sailors are toiling in the tower below

And the landsmen are lying down below
And the landsmen are lying down below.

Three times around sailed our gallant Ship,
Three times around sailed she,
And when she was going the fourth time around,
She sank to the bottom of the sea, the sea.
She sank to the bottom of the sea.

Theodosia shuddered as others clapped their approval. She had always been wary of the sea. Forcing her attention back to the ferry, she searched for her father, wrinkling her small nose against the sour smell of rotting fish on warm cobblestone.

The lower tip of Manhattan throbbed with activity. Those who came from the Old World seemed infused with a contagious vitality. One had to be robust to survive in New York, and those who did became strong leaders and eager followers. The young city expanded as its energy grew and exploded into the economic and entertainment center of the world.

Theodosia felt its pulse. When she escaped her rigorous lessons, she rode in the streets, oblivious of foul odors, ignoring the raucous behavior of vagrants who turned to the taverns for solace.

As the ferry clunked against the dock, Theodosia heard a hard wheezing at her side. Peggy had caught up with her.

"Thank the Lord, girl! Didn't you hear me, tellin' you to wait? You not supposed to come down here by yourself. And look at you! Hair blowin' all over, and I saw you straddlin' that horse like a *man*."

"There was no time, Peggy. Look! Papa is here!"

"Well, you s'posed to take time, Miss! Your mama'd somersault in her grave if she saw you not wearin' a hat!"

"Oh, Mama never cared about hats."

Theodosia stood on tiptoe and, spotting her father, lifted a tiny hand as high as she could and waved.

"Papa! Papa! Over here! Here I am!"

"No gloves either," Peggy growled.

Theodosia hoped Burr could see her from the ferry. When he walked down the gangplank, she jumped up and down, much to the consternation of Peggy, who grabbed the girl by the wrist.

"Slow down, Missy. Stay on the ground."

Theodosia slipped her grasp and ran toward her father.

Burr looked about as soon as he disembarked and saw his daughter. Only a slight smile revealed his pleasure as he walked toward her in his usual dignified way — indifferent, haughty. But Theodosia was not fooled.

She hugged him fiercely. He lifted her high off the ground and whirled her about, then set her back on her feet and stepped back to better see her face.

"You are home!" she cried.

"How goes it, Miss Prissy? I trust no event other than the arrival of Papa would remove you from your lessons."

Theodosia pouted.

"Horace, Papa. So much Horace."

"Heigh-ho for Terence and the Greek grammar tomorrow."

"But, Papa, you have just arrived. I wish to show you how well I am riding. Peggy hates for me to ride alone. Go with me! Please?"

"Perhaps, if there is time. But I have a surprise for you. Mayor Livingston has requested your presence aboard that French frigate yonder."

He pointed to the warship docked nearby, riding proud and high on the flood tide.

Burr continued, touching her lips to squelch the squeal of delight he knew would come.

"The Mayor was explicit," Burr said. "'Tell your Theodosia not to bring any of her sparks with her, for we carry ammunition aboard, and we should all be blown up!'"

They turned at the sound of Peggy's huffing. She could barely gasp out her greeting.

"Welcome home, Colonel Burr."

"Thank you, Peggy."

Burr took the horse's reins and put his other arm around Theodosia. Peggy fell in behind and listened to Burr's pronouncements.

"Within the year you must know German as well as French. I insist on a most perfect education for you, Theodosia. It will strengthen you."

Peggy stumbled and muttered.

"All that learnin' better make her strong. Soon enough, she be needin' all the strength she can get."

CHAPTER 5

Theodosia had waved her father off to the Senate many times, but now that she was motherless, she missed him with an intensity that sometimes was intolerable.

Often in Philadelphia, Burr was also lonely but he relished his appointment, knowing it was a stepping-stone to bigger opportunities. He cared little for socializing, but one evening he had agreed to meet several fellow senators who had been insisting he join them at a tavern.

The gathering was all male, loud and ripe with the scent of cigar smoke and the acrid chewed tobacco that floated in shining brass spittoons. Barmaids smiled demurely as they raised their skirts to expose their ankles. Breasts strained against precariously suspended bodices.

A fiddler slumped in a corner, rising to ply his art when energized by a pint of free ale. The instrument screeched, as though protesting its owner's lack of skill. One of the senators raised a palm, a stop signal aimed at the music maker. With his other arm he hoisted a mug of ale.

"I propose a toast! To Senator Burr. A fine addition you are, sir! Finally we are given the chance to welcome you to Philadelphia. To your political victory...and those to come!"

Burr nodded.

"Thank you, David."

Another senator spoke.

"A sweet victory, eh Aaron...especially being chosen over General Hamilton's father-in-law. How did he take the news?"

"I am told that the good General Hamilton indulged himself in one of his famous tantrums," answered Burr. "And after all of this time, he still has not come 'round to congratulate me."

He was silent then, gazing into the distance. After a moment his mood lightened, and he chuckled softly.

"Do you suppose, gentlemen, if I affect him so gravely, the world may be too small to hold both Aaron Burr and Alexander Hamilton?"

His companions glanced uneasily at each other, then David answered Burr's question with one of his own.

"Why is General Hamilton so determined to be your enemy, sir?"

"Oh, it is simple. I am liked by his Federalists as well as the Democratic-Republicans. Quite simply, I threaten his power. He stoops to ever-new lows to discredit me."

He allowed his words to sink in a bit before he spoke again. It was not time, he knew, to have them know just how much he hated the Federalist gadfly who dogged his every move. Not yet.

"How so?" asked one of the senators.

"The General has a penchant for seeing in me what he fears to look at in himself — political impotency and a propensity toward, ah, certain temptations. Gentlemen, there is no need for subtlety among colleagues. The very things Hamilton attacks me for — intemperance, marital infidelity. Well, his behavior is public record, is it not?"

His companions nodded, spellbound by his confident demeanor and articulate speech.

Burr raised his mug again.

"Well, let us drink again. To men who win with grace, and those who lose not so gracefully!"

The others followed suit, whacking their mugs together with such zeal that dark ale splashed onto their stiff white cuffs.

Burr stood suddenly, dabbing his lips with a spotless handkerchief.

"Thank you, gentlemen. And now, I must purchase a journal for my daughter, Theodosia. I feel it is time she begins to record her thoughts, and she agrees. I dare not return home without one made of the finest eel skin. It will not be easy to find."

"I hear she is a great beauty, sir," spoke one of his colleagues.

"Beautiful, yes. But more importantly, she reads so much I am challenged to amuse her. Fairy tales and such nonsense abound, but these will never do. Her understanding begins to be above such things. Within the year she shall be writing and speaking German as well as French."

"Amazing! For a girl."

"Why are women taught from infancy nothing is important but beauty?" Burr replied. "Why are they kept in ignorance under the name of innocence and told they must seek the protection of a man?"

"Why indeed?" asked another senator. "I have pondered these things myself, Aaron. This so-called 'innocence' assigns women to a perpetual state of childhood."

"All the better, I say!" David cheered. "There is not space for more than one great mind within a family."

He laughed as he spoke, looked to his companions for approval. There was none.

"Typical thinking!" Burr snapped. "I believe it may be possible for a wife to be a friend to her husband. And for this reason, I insist on a challenging education for my Theodosia! It will strengthen her body ...form her heart! Most importantly, it will render her self-sufficient."

"Is this independence wise, Senator? A woman who is self-reliant is thought to lack feminine charm."

Burr leaned over until his eyes were inches from his companion's face.

"You would find Theodosia more charming than any young woman you have known. But, more importantly, the world will soon know of her accomplishments. I supervise her education, and it leaves me little time for frivolity. Good day, gentlemen."

The men rose to acknowledge Burr's abrupt departure and watched him tip his hat to the tavern keeper with a flourish and disappear. The inebriated fiddler resumed his scratchy melody, and another imbiber stood weaving, singing along, his raspy voice wavering as he tried to stay on key. The senators settled back into their chairs and continued their discussion.

"He may find himself with leisure time soon enough! If his daughter becomes what he wishes, she will go her own way."

"Ah, if she were anyone else's daughter, I would agree. I think Aaron Burr's way must be her way if she's to keep her senses. Don't envy her that."

"Well, I will take my women dependent," David said with a wink. "I like them to need me."

A busty barmaid appeared, and he grabbed her skirt.

"Come closer, Nellie. You know what I need!"

Nellie sat on his knee, nibbled his ear, and rolled her eyes provocatively toward the other men as they laughed.

"Not now, Nellie. I need another ale! Another round!"

He slapped her on the buttocks.

"And be quick about it!"

Nellie flounced off, crimson lips pouting in protest. For the moment, her "feminine charm" had let her down.

CHAPTER 6

Richmond Hill, New York City. September 1794

Papa instructs me to write daily in my new journal. Ten or twelve pages, he says! Does he truly believe that my mind contains ten or twelve pages of knowledge, thoughts, feelings, worthy to be captured forever on this splendid paper every single day?

I do try my best, as Papa commands. And only here on these pages do I allow myself to release my sentiments. Not to speak of sadness feels like choking.

Gone. Mama is gone. I cannot yet believe it. The bed is empty. Her gowns are in the press. Her bottle with the medicine is by the bed, just so. But she is not with me anymore.

Where are you, Mama? I need to know how I can do what you asked. I do not understand, so it seems impossible to do as you wished.

You said that Papa was spirited. That I must be his tether. How can I hold back a grown man?

There were other things you said. I can't remember them all, Mama. Something about holding on to myself, too?

Oh, Mama....

The girl put down her quill and blotted the tears that smeared her words.

Why did you leave me? I miss you so.

Papa goes about the business he must do and he acts the same as always. Is he, too, not feeling that something huge and full of misery is stuck in his chest?

Peggy and I find it hard to be cheerful, but we do not speak of Mama often. Sometimes Peggy says something like 'She would be proud of you.' But mostly she goes about her work the same as always.

I heard her and Alexis talking the other day about the hemlock. 'It killed her for sure,' Peggy said. I wanted to scream. Alexis was upset, too, but he told Peggy that he thought Mama had a bad sickness before she took the hemlock. Peggy agreed, but she said she thought Mama could have lived longer and had many more good days if it had not been for the medicine.

I have been so much sadder since their conversation. Peggy would be upset if she knew that I heard, so I do not speak to her about it. There is no one to talk to and sometimes I think I will just shatter inside.

Could this happen to me? Could my heart and mind just break and make me someone else altogether? Papa says to always look ahead, but it frightens me to be so alone. I asked Mama about so many things, and she always gave me answers.

We loved riding together; riding alone now brings me no joy. Does Wind know? Can she tell by the way I sit on her and hold the reins that I am different now?

And the garden! I no longer go there now that the flowers she loved have drooped and their petals have fallen to the ground. It is because the summer has ended, of course, but I sometimes think they miss Mama, too.

We used to bring some of the plants inside for the winter, but I don't know which ones need warmth for the cold season and which will live outside. I don't ask the gardeners though I know they would have the right answer. It's not their voice I want. I am writing it all here, hoping I will not weep in front of Papa.

I have not yet. But I cry into my pillow at night sometimes. I have a nightdress of Mama's that smells of her, clean like the soap that Peggy makes from the lard and ashes, sweetened with something she picks from Mama's garden. I keep it under my pillow and Papa does not know. Peggy does, of course, because she makes up my bed. But she never says anything. She would not, I know.

CHAPTER 7

B urr had intriguing news for his daughter when he returned to Richmond Hill.

"Discord in France is serendipitous for us, *ma petite amour.* Crude revolutionaries destroy the French countryside, and nobility must flee for their lives. They go all across Europe, even to Russia.

"My French friends told me of a Madame de Senat, a governess, who has accompanied a young girl of nobility to America for safety."

Burr became silent, increasing Theodosia's suspense. He drew her to him, smoothing her hair, but she ruined his grooming with one vigorous shake of her head.

"Go on," she begged, "tell me more, please."

"Madame de Senat wishes to start a fine school here in New York but had no place to do so. I have offered to share our Petition Street space with her," he said, walking to a window and gazing across the rooftops to the chimney of his townhouse. His family had lived there prior to his acquiring Richmond Hill. Now the building housed only his office.

He frowned when he spotted a young driver leap from a carriage to soothe his skittish horse. The young man was nimble and secured the reins in seconds. Burr relaxed as he saw the passenger fumble through her purse and produce a large vial of what he assumed was smelling salts. But instead of passing it beneath her nose, she held it to her lips and swigged mightily.

Burr laughed.

"What is funny, Papa?"

Burr turned from the window.

"I am happy that we are so lucky. The most prominent families are vying to enroll their children in the new school. Of course, you are already assured of a place. But wait, before you begin to jump about, there is more."

"Tell me, Papa. Please!"

"So-o-o-o," he continued, "I have invited the young French girl to live with us. She is just nine months older than you."

Theodosia clapped her hands then grew solemn.

"But what of her family, Papa?"

"Her mother, the Marquise de Lage de Volude, is, no doubt, missing her daughter terribly, but she hopes to travel to America and join her, perhaps this year."

"Such a long time," Theodosia mused. "But we shall cheer her up, Papa! She and I have...."

She was about to say that they, both without mothers, had much in common but caught herself in time to honor her father's admonition on the day of her mother's funeral: *We shall not speak of this again.*

"*And...,*" Burr resumed, "it is possible you will meet Marie Antoinette's son, Louis Charles. It is rumored that he has escaped to America."

A few days later, he escorted his "adopted daughter" into her new home where Theodosia waited eagerly. He had prepared an introduction, but the lively French girl jumped ahead.

"I am Marie Louise Stephanie Beatrix Nathalie de Lage de Volude."

Theodosia laughed. "Your name is that long?"

The girl giggled and answered in precise English. "Yes, is it not ridiculous? Here in America I shall drop all of the pretension."

"What will you be called from all of your choices?"

"Simply Natalie, spelled the English way. That is the prettiest of the lot, do you agree?"

Theodosia concurred, and from that moment the girl was Natalie Delage, her lifetime friend.

The motherless girls' friendship grew as companionship slowly displaced the loneliness they had suffered. They rode horseback, learned the art of hosting Burr's extravagant parties, teased Peggy, and spent hours engaged in the exchange of confidences that have filled young girls' conversations from the beginning of time.

Having Natalie in residence solved the problem of Theodosia's isolation while the Senate was in session. Burr refocused on political life. Still, when each day ended and he retired to his lodgings, he wrote Theodosia demanding she study hard and interact with only those people of whom he approved. The distance disappeared as Burr lost himself in his work as well as his desire to create the ideal woman of his time. Fine-tuning would pay off, he believed. Failure was not an option.

CHAPTER 8

Richmond Hill, 1797

Theodosia had been watching for the carrier all morning. When the dogs began to bark, she bounded down the stairs of Richmond Hill and out onto the lawn to receive a packet of letters from her father.

Fourteen years old and emerging into young womanhood, she now wore sophisticated clothing. Her hair was swept from her face and held with tortoise-shell combs sent to her by Natalie's mother. Soon she sat at her desk and read:

Philadelphia, 24th February 1797
Your letters are important to me. They are improving in style, in knowledge of French and in your handwriting. When you finish a letter, read it over carefully and correct all the errors. It is necessary I should peruse your letters with an eye of criticism. You have misspelled some words.

She slapped her forehead with the heel of her hand and continued reading:

You improve much in journalizing. But pray, when you are up to 200 lines, why do you go back again to 120? Strive never to diminish. Do not forget the intrepidity, the self-possession, the pursuit of knowledge that Lord Chesterfield lived by. As a woman, you have every right to choose these goals for yourself. Do not strive for admiration and flattery from men.

Theodosia walked to her dressing table and studied herself thoroughly before the mirror. She pinched her cheeks, pulled the bodice of her dress off her shoulders, pleased with the look of her high, small breasts. Returning to her desk, she lifted her skirt a bit higher than she might have in public as she sat and continued to read.

You are maturing in a more solid way. You are concentrating on more important things.

She giggled. *Ah, yes, Papa, more important things!*

You spell with an 'i' when it is supposed to be an 'e.' Either can sometimes be proper, but with an 'e' is the most usual and the most proper. Mr. Leshlie will explain to you how to make a perfect and elegant sentence. Continue!
Thine, A. Burr.

She pondered his assertions and wrote in her journal:

You always tell me that, when I set about it in earnest, I can accomplish wonders. You think I can be all that you wish. You write that my music seems to leave little time for any other study. But I love the harp so. I am fond of the journal, too, but it becomes less of a joy when I imagine you creasing your handsome brow if I tell you how much I have written and it contains fewer pages than you wish. At least you do not ask to read the words. I would simply refuse to allow it. But you count the pages.

"Almost 400 pages in your journal, all in one day," she mimicked him aloud, using her most commanding voice, then sighed and closed the journal.

It is growing more difficult to please him because I have wishes that are my own, she thought. *I do not want to always obey as I did as a child. Today I want to enjoy the company of Natalie without worrying about my lessons.*

She decided that her father would have to excuse her this time. He had assigned a huge endeavor to Natalie and her, and there was much activity in the house. She had not written even close to 300 lines this time in her journal. Suddenly she raced to the kitchen holding her skirts high above her feet.

CHAPTER 9

Peggy was presiding over her staff as they chopped and julienned carrots, onions, and turnips and polished silver vases, platters and flatware when Theodosia arrived.

"Peggy, the day is finally here! I am so full of butterflies that there is no room for any lunch."

Theodosia reached for a bowl of pudding and, perching on a high stool, stirred vigorously with a large wooden spoon. The back door opened and a slave from the market heaved in a large side of meat for her inspection. She examined it, running her fingers over the red flesh and lowering her head for the crucial smell test.

"The venison seems quite prime and very fresh. Oh, Peggy, did I make the right choice? I want the dinner to be very special. Chief Brant, after all, may live in the woods and eat venison three times a day!"

Peggy shuddered. "I know nothing about Indians, Missy, other than they take the hair off your head, scalp and all! I don't want to be here during this dinner. Why your papa won't be here to take care of us is beyond me."

"He is too often absent," Theodosia answered wistfully, but she quickly turned to optimism.

"Peggy, nothing bad will happen. The Bishop of New York will be here, too! Since Papa can't protect us, I've seen to it that the Lord will!"

"No blasphemy, Miss Theo, or we'll deserve to lose our scalps!"

All was ready for the dinner later that evening. Peggy jumped at the loud knock at the door and shouted for the butler.

"Alexis! Where are you?"

She wiped her hands and started reluctantly toward the door. Theodosia and Natalie opened it for her. Peggy stifled a scream when she saw two large men with spears.

Theodosia was frightened, too, but forced herself to curtsey as a third man stepped forward between his bodyguards. Chief Brant was handsome, impeccably dressed in English-style finery except for a crown of brightly colored feathers that fanned up and around his ruddy face. He took Theodosia's hand, bowed, and brought her hand to his lips.

"I am Chief Joseph Brant Thayendanegea of the Mohawk Nation. You are Miss Theodosia Burr?"

"Lord help us," Peggy gasped but not loud enough for the men to hear her.

Theodosia straightened her back, met the chief's gaze fully and curtsied again.

"I am Theodosia Burr, Chief Brant. It is my pleasure to welcome you to Richmond Hill. I am pleased you could come."

She then turned to Natalie and introduced her as "my French sister."

Senator Burr's daughter wore a simple dress of cobalt blue, and her auburn hair was held at the nape of her neck with a matching ribbon. A tiny cameo at her throat was the only jewelry she chose for the evening. She was slim, graceful, poised, and self-confident.

The dinner went smoothly from one succulent course to the next, and Chief Brant was astounded at Theodosia's knowledge of the issue he had hoped to discuss with her father.

"I have heard of your efforts to convince our government you don't wish to fight with us ever again," she told him, "but I also know your tribes have been encouraged by the French and Spaniards in Mississippi to take up hatchets and other arms against our citizens. What is your plan now?"

Brant studied his hostess carefully before responding. "I am thinking of writing to your governor to see if I might secure a large tract of land in Ohio that could serve as a refuge for some of the tribes that are inclined to go to war. I think that, with this land, the governor and your father might be able to create a new territory for our nation, a nonviolent neighbor governed by peaceful chiefs."

"Ah, yes, Sir, it seems to me that land has always been at the center of life for your people. Surely you fear that some day there will be none left for you. This pilfering must stop!"

Chief Brant left Richmond Hill convinced his ideas were so completely understood that a meeting with Senator Burr might not be necessary. "Amazing girl," he said to his assistants. "Although perhaps too precocious for her time. A pity if that is so."

CHAPTER 10

Theodosia and Natalie loved reading and discussing the books Burr assigned to them. He thought them old enough for Mary Wollstonecraft, who had caused a stir in her native England with her feminist writings. Burr had shared her ideas with Theodosia's mother, and both had concurred with Wollstonecraft that women have souls.

The girls sat on the veranda at Richmond Hill surrounded by a day swollen with spring. Buds strained toward full bloom and birds that were finished with the dances of courtship were building nests with twigs and stray bits of cord and cloth. Theodosia and Natalie chatted more than read. The *Rights of Woman* was impacting them with ideas far more provocative than Burr had anticipated.

"Listen to this, Nat. Mary Wollstonecraft decries Rousseau, and I agree with her. Such rubbish he wrote! She quotes him here: 'A woman should never, for a moment, feel herself independent.' Can you believe that Rousseau could espouse such a thing?"

"Of course, Theo. Most in America seem to feel this way. Keep reading."

"'She should be governed by fear to exercise her natural cunning,' he writes. Governed by fear — an insult! And listen to the rest of it. 'She should be made a coquettish slave in order to render her a more alluring object of desire, a sweeter companion to man, whenever he chooses to relax himself.' Natalie!"

Theodosia trembled, clasping the book to her breast.

"Natalie! Does this speak of...of sacred relations?"

The French girl howled with laughter.

"Sacred relations? Theo, Theo. Just say sex for goodness' sakes!"

Theodosia choked on the word.

"Well...*sex* then."

"Of course, my shy little sister. Now read on. See if Mrs. Wollstonecraft puts Mr. Rousseau in his place!"

"Well, she says here, 'Youth is the season for love in both sexes, but in those days of thoughtless enjoyment....' Thoughtless enjoyment, Nat! Do you think intimate love takes away all reason?"

Natalie laughed more. "Theo, you are so innocent. Perhaps this book your papa provided is beyond your tender comprehension. Here, give it to me."

Theodosia held the book firm against her bosom. "No, no!" she protested. "Papa insists I read it. He says Mary Wollstonecraft's ideas will teach me to breathe the 'sharp, invigorating air of freedom.' He used those very words!"

"Well, continue then."

"Okay. 'Provision should be made for the more important years of life, when reflection takes place of...' uh, 'when reflection takes place of...sensation.' What do you make of that?"

Natalie answered without a trace of embarrassment.

"She believes, as do I, that friendship is as important as sex in marriage."

"Yes!" Theodosia agreed as she shuffled rapidly through the pages.

"Here she says, 'Weakness may excite tenderness and gratify the arrogant pride of man, but the lordly caresses of a protector will not gratify a noble mind that pants for the respect it deserves.'"

The girls grew silent, allowing the words to sink in.

"I think," Theodosia said, "she believes the mind of a wife must have room to unfold and that it is possible for her husband to enjoy her mind as well as..."

She blushed, and Natalie finished her sentence.

"Her body! Theo, sex is not a shameful word!"

But Theodosia, on uncertain ground, continued: "Natalie, Mary Wollstonecraft writes of education, too. She thinks many men wish to tyrannize their sisters, wives, and daughters. These men are terrified that if women are educated it will end their blind obedience."

Natalie nodded. "Indeed, it would!"

"Tyrants want slaves, and sensualists want a plaything! Which will you be Natalie?"

"Neither! Nor will you!"

They laughed heartily, and then Natalie grew serious.

"Think of this, Theodosia. A slave. I mean a true slave, like Peggy, like Alexis. If they, and others like them, obtained the power of literacy...."

"Oh, but they have it, Nat. Both were taught to read as soon as Papa purchased them. He insisted upon it."

"I believe they are the exception. I understand that in other regions, where a person might own hundreds of slaves, it is against the law to teach them to read."

"Oh, I cannot fathom such a thing!" Theodosia said.

"It is true, I am certain of it. When slaves outnumber white people, they are kept ignorant for the safety of their owners."

The girls hurried to the library. Burr had instructed them to look for knowledge in his book collection, often saying ignorance could never be excused if answers are readily available. He made certain his library was always an up-to-date source.

They soon found proof of Natalie's belief that in many states slaves were kept illiterate by law. Although not as fascinating as sex, the right of a person to read was, for the time being, a more comfortable subject for Theodosia.

"I would never tolerate such a thing," she declared. "I would break such a law and be proud of it!"

The girls wandered back outside. An ardent squirrel chased his intended mate, snapping his tail rakishly. *Squit, squit,* the suitor implored, but the object of his affection ignored him, leaping onto a branch so fragile that he dared not follow.

Natalie giggled.

"She rejects him, Theo. Will she have a change of heart do you think?"

But Theodosia, again engaged by Mary Wollstonecraft, continued walking, careful to stay on the stepping-stones of the pathway. Sparks of excitement glowed in the deep blackness of her eyes.

"Natalie. Listen to this. 'When the husband ceases to be a lover... and the time will inevitably come...her desire of pleasing will then grow languid or become a spring of bitterness. Love, perhaps the most evanescent of all passions, may give place to unhappiness.' Do you think that is true...that the husband will cease to be a lover?"

"Passion will subside somewhat, Theo. But I have observed my parents. They have a tender regard for each other I would hope to have in my marriage. And, I must add, this respect exists because my mother and father are equals, just as Mary Wollstonecraft believes it should be."

"I suppose," Theodosia mused. "But the passion, Natalie...I am intrigued with it. And I shall try and be, like you, more willing to speak of it and learn from you."

Natalie lowered her eyes.

"Well, my sister. You must understand I can speak only of what my mother has told me."

"Of course!" answered Theodosia with a knowing smile. "Even in France, you would still be considered too young to be in love."

Feeling mysterious and powerful, Natalie was not about to give up the edge her superior knowledge on the subject of love gave her.

"Well, perhaps. But girls mature early in my country. Some who are my age are already married."

"Poor things!" exclaimed Theodosia. "Mary Wollstonecraft thinks it unspeakable many women feel they have arrived at their life's goal when they obtain a husband."

"Well, I am in no hurry, but I do wish for love, of course, and also for children," Natalie said. "And a home I can make a beautiful haven for us all. And for travel and adventure."

"Oh, yes!" Theodosia agreed.

"And who shall it be for you, *mon amie*? Will it be our charming Mr. Washington Irving? You would be mistress of Sunnyside, a reasonable ride to Richmond Hill. He is in love with you, it is obvious."

Theodosia tossed her head.

"I have much to do before marriage, Natalie. And now … do you think we have studied seriously enough to please our Papa?"

"I have been as serious as I wish to be today," Natalie answered. "I am pleased with myself, and you should be also."

Now that they had given themselves permission to play, they agreed without words what they would do. Spring fever was rampant and their mares, not yet bred this season, were watching for them, eager to run free rein, releasing their skittish energy on paths rimmed with sweet new grass.

CHAPTER 11

B uffed mahogany paneling and well-oiled leather-bound books glowed in candlelight inside Richmond Hill as Theodosia received her guests in the library. At fourteen, she was an accomplished and confident hostess, and with Natalie's help, she had planned an elaborate meal combining the cuisines of France and America.

The guests would dine on a first course of fresh fish in a rich wine sauce, followed by an assortment of game birds, roasted potatoes, fresh vegetables from the garden, and a variety of French pastries. Burr had hired a steward to serve a different wine with each course and to ensure every crystal glass was full throughout the evening.

The house was decorated with great bowls of fruit from the orchards of Richmond Hill, and flowers from its gardens spilled from vases of silver, brass, and porcelain.

Burr introduced his daughter and Natalie with pride.

"Gentlemen, I present to you my daughter, Theodosia, and my adopted daughter, Marie Louise Stephanie Beatrix Nathalie de Lage de Volude."

The girls rolled their eyes at each other. They knew Burr loved using Natalie's complete French name to impress his guests — most of them escapees from France. The nation remained a dangerous, desolated place for members of nobility as the Revolution unfolded. But the upheaval was fortuitous for Burr, providing him with a steady stream of French guests in his home.

"Theodosia, Natalie. This is Jerome Bonaparte of the esteemed Emperor's family."

Bonaparte bowed and kissed the girls' hands.

"And Bishop Charles Maurice de Talleyrand."

Talleyrand followed Bonaparte's example, bowing slightly as his lips grazed their fingers.

"May I present Louis Philippe, certain to be the next King of France when this nasty business is resolved."

Theodosia curtsied and took his arm.

"Your unfortunate circumstances have caused us much concern," she said, steering him toward the dining room.

Natalie slipped one arm through the Bishop's, the other she offered to Bonaparte, and the party proceeded to such a splendidly laid table that the men were eager to raise their goblets in a toast to their hostesses.

Conversation was always lively under the sparkling chandeliers of Richmond Hill. Tonight, Philippe, not a subtle man, introduced the provocative topic of the evening.

"Word has it abroad that Mr. Jefferson will run against President Adams, Colonel Burr, and that you have your sights set on the Vice Presidency. What do you say?"

Theodosia answered before her father could.

"The Federalists have had their chance, and now it is ours."

Burr pretended to admonish her.

"Theodosia!"

The young Bonaparte rose to her defense.

"She knows of what she speaks, Colonel Burr. New York is likely to determine the election, don't you agree? And it is said you are the best man to swing this state."

Bishop Talleyrand raised his goblet.

"More power to you."

"*Merci*, Your Eminence," said Burr. "I shall need it. And luck, too!"

CHAPTER 12

⁓⤳⤳⤳

A few months later, Burr, valise in hand, bid his daughter goodbye in the entry hall. Theodosia tried to ignore the waiting carriage.

"Papa, must you go again?"

Burr disliked lingering goodbyes and was especially impatient for this trip to get underway.

"It is not every day in a gentlemen's life he is called to Monticello! I shall return soon, possibly in a fortnight. Save a whole day for a ride with me."

He embraced her.

"Study. Write to me, and in your journal. Daily."

He left her with no further words. She watched him as he reached the carriage and stepped inside, brushing off the driver's attempt to give him a boost. She hoped he would turn to wave to her, but he did not. The carriage jumped forward with a start and around the circular driveway smoothly as the matched pair of horses hit their stride. Theodosia's shoulders slumped slightly. Before her was another time of hard study and the pain of Burr's absence.

By contrast, the next few days were full of promise and distinguished company for Burr. After dinner, he and Thomas Jefferson walked together in a wooded area on the grounds of Monticello. A lush late summer surrounded them with daisies, hydrangeas, and wild roses, though the visual feast was lost on two men of the same party gripped in the intensity of political planning.

"So what say you, Aaron? Do you agree with most of the nation that I am a wild-eyed radical?"

"Long ago, sir, I gave up indulging myself in fantasies regarding the opinion of others. Wild-eyed radical is mild when compared to Hamilton's descriptions of me."

Jefferson chuckled and stopped to pinch off a fading blossom, turned it over, and analyzed its every facet before flipping it to the ground.

"I have heard you have the talent of attaching men to your views, Mr. Burr. Much of what I hear, except when it comes from the lips or pen of Mr. Hamilton, is highly complimentary."

"Ah! Mr. Hamilton worries me least of all, Thomas. He has accused me of being as unprincipled and dangerous a man as any country can hold — and he calls you, by the way, an atheist and a fanatic in politics. Do we listen to the likes of him, or do we act? What do you wish me to do?"

"Sway New York City for our party, if you can, sir. If we have New York, I believe we have the Nation!"

Burr stared intently at Jefferson.

"We, sir?

"We, Aaron — you and me. President and Vice President! I can arrange it."

Thomas Jefferson and Aaron Burr faced each other and grasped hands. Affirming their alliance with a long, firm shake, neither could have guessed how rare such accord would be.

CHAPTER 13

Two years later

Theodosia and her father cantered at high speed along the wind-whipped Hudson River on a small path that held tight to the shoreline. Burr allowed her to abandon the awkward sidesaddle and straddle Wind when they rode alone. She was sixteen, no longer the charming child but an exquisite young woman, slim and vibrant.

A wine-red ribbon restrained her long hair. The two drew up their horses to enjoy the view of the river and the sailing ships making their way in both directions.

Just as the heart is the manager of human life, the tides of the Atlantic Ocean control the rhythm of the lower Hudson River. When a flood tide crests, the swift-running water slows and snuggles languidly into the crooks and crevices of the west side of Manhattan, relaxed like a spent lover. It seems to stop and hold its breath before exhaling into the ebb cycle.

Flowing toward Tappan, the Hudson meanders from the north in no hurry to get anywhere. But as it rolls closer to Manhattan, it becomes tide-driven, alternately thrusting through churning water and pulling toward the heaving sea. Theodosia found the constant change exhilarating.

Now she was especially heady, feeling carefree and excited to have this entire day with her father. Breathless, she leaned forward and felt the energy in the heat of her mare's neck, untangling the animal's damp mane with nimble fingers.

"Heaven must be like our special place, Papa. Perhaps I will never be able to leave the Hudson."

"We need not think of it now, Theodosia. Today is ours — yours and mine."

"But the election is ever in my mind, Papa. Think of it. You may be the next Vice President!"

"I shall be, Theodosia! Jefferson and Burr will win in December."

"I fear General Hamilton, Papa."

"He will fight me every step of the way, of course. Indulge himself in fits of temper."

Burr looked off into the distance, his eyes narrowed, and his lips a thread of scorn.

"What do you think, my Theodosia? Can General Hamilton and your papa co-exist in a world as small as this one?"

Theodosia heard her mother's words once more.

Listen, my dearest. Your father. A brilliant man. You can be proud always to be the daughter of Aaron Burr. I have loved him. But he can be erratic, like a high-strung horse. Spirited, needing a tether. I have been that for him, Theodosia. Now it must be you.

There was more, she knew and she strained to remember, but no more came to her. How could she do as she had been asked? She looked to the high hills across the river for strength.

"Papa, that is foolish talk. I will not listen."

She turned Wind and galloped away. Burr watched her disappear down the path, and for the first time had misgivings about the freedoms he had allowed her.

Perhaps it is time to rein her in a bit. He hoped he had not waited too long.

CHAPTER 14

In addition to newspapers, privately printed pamphlets proclaimed the promises and accusations of politicians. Their supporters distributed the leaflets in the streets and public gathering places.

Theodosia held her skirt above the dirt of the crowded street but the coarse black grit still slipped into its hem and seeped inside her shoes. She stopped here and there to speak to individuals and small crowds, handing Burr's leaflets to all who would reach for them.

A blacksmith stopped his work, tied his horse and approached her. "There are many of us who support your father's party, Miss Burr, but we are unable to vote because we own no land."

Theodosia was shocked. "There must be a way, sir. I will give it much study, and when the matter is resolved, you will vote, and I shall thank you for your support."

The man bowed to her, and she surprised him by curtseying, an unexpected gesture of respect for a common worker. She continued on her way dispensing her pamphlets.

After dinner that evening she approached Burr with an idea.

"Papa, the law says that a man must own property to vote, but it does not say how much. Could not a man buy a share in a large tract?"

He was ecstatic. "By God, Theodosia. It could be done! We will make landowners of the masses. My bank can even lend the money!"

"No, Papa. That is going too far."

"It is perfectly legal."

"But honorable?"

Burr thought for a moment. "Some will say no, but every man likes his own opinion best. As far as I am concerned, they may indulge in any opinion they choose."

For the second time in as many days, Theodosia defied him. "Honor is all, Papa. I will not allow it!"

He shrugged, acquiesced. *There is truth in what she says. This time, I will give the girl her head.*

CHAPTER 15

❧

The election was held on April 29, 30, and May 1, 1800. Theodosia was again on the streets, staying close to the building where voters came and went, holding the placard she and Natalie had carefully lettered:

Senator Burr urges you
To vote
DEMOCRATIC-REPUBLICAN

Men milled about, talking excitedly. Alexander Hamilton, red-faced and agitated, pulled his white horse abruptly to a halt when he spotted his adversary's daughter.

"Gentlemen," he shouted. "Use your reasoning. That parchment you hold is just a piece of paper. It is nothing, and it will get you nothing. Do not forget the Federalist Party. It is your party and the party of your fathers!"

An old man on his way to vote challenged him, his voice acrid with sarcasm.

"Well, it's General Alexander Hamilton, showing his face to the common man. How's it that the Federalist Party is my party, but we ain't met 'til now?"

A younger man yelled at the old man, "And you've never been voting 'til now neither, Patrick!"

Most in the crowd laughed. Hamilton lost control.

"Damn you, stupid men! Our lawmakers were right when they denied you the vote!"

He quickly changed his demeanor, forcing his sneer into a smile.

"Gentlemen," he purred. "Do you not live well? Are your families not sufficiently fed?"

The blacksmith raked his grimy hands through his hair.

"All I know is, General Hamilton, I never owned much more'n the shirt on my back. Never could vote to do nothin' 'bout it neither."

Hamilton's fragile control gave way once more.

"Enough of my good time wasted on men who will not, or cannot, understand. I intend to visit every polling place, and may God help me if I meet with no better reasoning than yours. Good day, gentlemen. May God help you."

He tightened the reins, and the white horse reared and whirled, bringing his rider face-to-face with Theodosia. Again his lips curled with contempt.

"A disgrace! A young woman of your station in the streets, where is your pride?"

She pulled herself erect and the hint of a smile played about her lips as she answered with exaggerated sweetness.

"I am proud to be here, sir. But you have nothing to fear, General. Even a woman of my station has no vote to cast for your opposition."

Hamilton's crop whistled as it sliced the air and the horse nickered loudly, bolting away at full speed. Spinning happily in a dusty cloud, the men laughed and cheered, holding their deeds high in the air.

"We feel privileged to be part of this, Miss Burr," the blacksmith said. "Thank you."

"It is only your right, sir," she answered. "It is the Democratic-Republican Party that is privileged."

She kept a vigil until the results were in. Giddy with the news, she skipped over the cobblestones, her long hair escaping from its coil and spinning wildly in the wind from the river.

Careful not to slam the door at Richmond Hill, she grabbed Peggy around the waist, trying to engage her in a dance. Failing, she hugged her until she winced.

"This is good news, Peggy! We have won in New York! Now Papa and Mr. Jefferson will surely get the nomination. Then on to Washington!"

"Washington," Peggy muttered. "Don't hear much good about that place: Roads all muddy, people rough; hardly any houses; lots of taverns...."

"Oh, be happy for us, Peggy," Theodosia interrupted. "We have planned and worked so hard."

"I'll try, Missy Theo."

Silent for a moment, Peggy looked skyward as she often did when troubled.

"When you sees happiness in this world, you better grab on to it, hold it tight. It's got a way of running away from you...."

Slowly, Peggy's wizened gray head waggled up then down, as she slowly agreed with herself. *Sure does.*

CHAPTER 16

⤳⤲

Music resonated through Richmond Hill at the celebration of the Jefferson-Burr alliance in 1800. Two chamber orchestras on opposite ends of the grand ballroom played in unison. Roses, brought in on ice from Virginia, graced every table. Guests dressed lavishly in starched collars, powdered wigs, and hand-sewn silk dresses. Diamond jewelry, set afire by candlelight, spun prisms across gilded ceilings.

Bejeweled and animated, Dolley Madison conversed with Theodosia, Judge Van Ness, and Washington Irving. She waved her arms and rolled her eyes as she spoke, her dark curls bouncing on plump shoulders.

"What a wonderful celebration, darling! We shall all be so happy to have you in Washington at last."

Theodosia was dressed in a lemon-yellow gown tufted with saffron bows, cut daringly low at her cleavage. She wore no jewelry, declaring it "useless paraphernalia."

"Thank you, Mrs. Madison," she answered. "Please tell me about Washington. I hear there is no hotel in the city, only boarding houses, and rather primitive ones at that."

"I do find life in our capital a bit on the rough side, my dear. What is your opinion, Judge?"

"Well," Van Ness began, "the city has a long way to go. But I dare say that Miss Burr's presence will do much to make it more palatable."

Theodosia smiled. "Thank you, Judge, and we can all thank General Hamilton for agreeing to move our capital from New York to a swamp on the Potomac."

Dolley was intrigued. "How so?"

"General Hamilton wanted the government to pay our Revolutionary debts, Mrs. Madison, and the South was against the idea. But they conceded when promised the capital."

Van Ness nodded. "She speaks the truth, Mrs. Madison."

Dolley frowned, contemplating recent deprivations. Her ringlets danced in protest as she shook her head. "Well, I often wondered why we were made to leave the comforts and culture of New York City for what is still a mud hole. I am infuriated! Theodosia, dear, how did you know this?"

"Politicians gather here at Richmond Hill, Mrs. Madison, and I have sharp ears. Of course, Papa keeps me well informed, too."

The conversation ended when Irving invited Theodosia to join the minuet. Soon they slipped into a column of dancers and blended into the graceful movements.

"I am pleased to be favored with your first dance, Theodosia."

"My pleasure, Washington," she answered.

The childhood friends were silent, awkward with this unaccustomed formality. Theodosia knew many watched, considering them a possible match. Irving was already becoming well known in literary circles, and Burr would be pleased with a union that kept his daughter in New York.

She suddenly broke the ice.

"I am still the same Theodosia, Washington — your fastest riding companion; the one who swam with you in the Hudson. Oh! Remember how cold it was? And Peggy. She was so angry she told you never to come back. Of course, the next day she sent for you."

Burr ended their chatter. "I apologize for interrupting your dance."

Annoyed, Theodosia protested. "Papa, Washington and I...."

"Theodosia, I would not insist if this were not important."

She was about to argue, but Irving stepped back and placed Theodosia's hand in her father's.

"We shall dance again, Theodosia, and I daresay, enter into more devilment."

Burr gave the young man a less-than-cordial look, took Theodosia's elbow, and guided her quickly from the room.

"A messenger has brought me word that an important visitor from South Carolina travels nearby. I should like a place set for him at our dinner table."

Already peeved, Theodosia did not feel accommodating. "Papa, the table is arranged. Surely you can invite him to join you later for port?"

"Theodosia, use your head! South Carolina will be a key state in the election. They hold eight electoral votes."

Weighing this information for a moment, she acquiesced.

"Of course. We shall have the gentleman from South Carolina."

She left the festivities and hurried to the dining room where a long banquet table was set for the formal dinner. She began preparing the additional place herself. Peggy, who had received the news of the extra guest, bustled in with a plate and silver goblet.

Joseph Alston arrived at Richmond Hill in a high-wheeled carriage painted wine-red, trimmed with gold, and pulled by his bay geldings, Peacock and Prince. A few guests spied the fine vehicle approaching the house, and small groups began to gather on the veranda for a better view.

The driver jumped to the ground before the horses had come to a full stop. They snorted, their sides heaving, spewing white foam from their nostrils. A young man stepped from the carriage, and Burr hurried to greet him, followed by Alexis. Joseph Alston was only slightly taller than Burr, solidly built and formally dressed, the ruffles on his shirt gleaming white in the darkness. His face was clean-shaven. Coal-dark sideburns defined a strong jaw line. A gusty wind tumbled his dark hair over a high forehead. Burr hustled him up the stairs and into the ballroom, steering him straight to the center.

"Ladies and gentlemen," he announced with great flourish. "Your attention please. It is my pleasure to present to you an esteemed guest. This is Mr. Joseph Alston, counselor and rice planter from the Lowcountry of South Carolina."

The guests applauded and began to form a line to greet the stranger. Theodosia re-entered the ballroom, adjusting the shoulders of her gown. She was flushed from her hurried preparations in the dining room, and her cheeks darkened from pink to crimson as she watched him smiling, shaking hands with the men, raising the ladies' hands to his lips.

When Burr saw her, he abruptly ended the receiving line and steered Joseph toward her.

"Theodosia, I present our guest from South Carolina, Mr. Joseph Alston."

She saw pleasure in his dark blue eyes, and it so delighted and terrified her that, for the moment, she could not speak.

Burr was irritated but controlled his peevishness. "Theodosia?"

She managed a curtsey. "Forgive me, Mr. Alston. I was preoccupied for a moment. Welcome to Richmond Hill."

Later amid snatches of conversation, the clink of silverware, the ring of crystal and soft background music, Theodosia sneaked looks at Joseph without being conspicuous. Once he caught her staring at him, and she quickly lowered her eyes, feeling her lips tremble with the effort of sending him only the slightest smile.

Halfway through the meal, Burr rose and raised his goblet.

"My honored guests. We are together tonight to celebrate the election of our beloved Democratic-Republican statesmen. I also wish to toast our visitor from the state of South Carolina, Mr. Joseph Alston. May his visit to New York be pleasant, and may he make fruitful alliances!"

The guests at Richmond Hill that early fall evening were full of rich food, fine wines, and enthusiasm for their candidates. A few voices were raucous as goblets were held high.

"Hear, hear!"

They filed from the room — the ladies into the parlor, the men upstairs into the inner sanctum of the drawing room, papered in damask the color of the port they would enjoy with their "seegars."

Theodosia was too restless for idle talk and excused herself, moving onto the veranda where she stayed until the last of the guests were leaving and she could hear her father bidding good night to Joseph. She spoke quickly from her dark corner.

"We are honored you could join us this evening, sir. We hope you will call before you return home?"

Joseph felt Burr's eyes on him and was uneasy. He bowed to the dark silhouette in the shadows and hastily bid them both a good evening.

When Joseph had boarded his carriage, Burr derided her for not standing with him when he bid good night to their guests.

"President and Mrs. Adams asked where you were, and they were only two of many."

"It was your party, Papa. A beautiful evening, but it was, well, taxing. I was fatigued."

"You seemed able to rouse up a bit of energy here at the last, Miss Prissy!" he teased her.

"Yes, so I did."

She took his arm and they walked past servants who carried away the dinner plates, rolled up the linens, and swept up crumbs.

Theodosia dismissed Peggy, announcing she needed no help in preparing for bed. But she was angry with herself for not gleaning more information from Joseph. She found herself restless when she blew out the candle and tried to sleep.

Why did I not ask him how long he would be in New York? If he were leaving soon, surely he would have told me when I invited him to call.

Would he come? He ignored my invitation altogether.

The sun was well up when Peggy softly knocked and, not waiting for an answer, burst into the room knowing her mistress would not mind when she heard her news.

"Messenger just came with note from your Mr. Alston!"

"*My* Mr. Alston?" Theodosia cried, snatching the paper.

"Yes, yours. Or you might like him to be. You don't fool me, Missy. Never could. What does he say?"

Theodosia read: "I would be pleased to call this afternoon at three." She was out of bed in a moment, penning her answer.

"I am telling him not to come, Peggy," said Theodosia as she dipped her quill into the ink. "Urging him to make his way back to South Carolina and wishing him well."

"How many times you going to try and fool me, girl?"

Theodosia did not respond. Smiling, she spritzed the paper with her perfume atomizer before sliding it into an envelope. Shaking her head, Peggy took the note.

"What gown you want me to get ready? The green one looks the best on you, and it won't be too hot for today. The one with the parasol that matches."

Peggy heard Theodosia's song before she reached the front door with her envelope. It made her feel good, because Theodosia sang when she was happy.

I gave my love a cherry without a stone.
I gave my love a chicken without a bone.
I told my love a story that had no end.
I gave my love a baby, with no crying.

The melody reached as far as the stable, where the groom curried Wind's coat until it shone, bright as the July sun.

48

CHAPTER 17

July 15, 1800

I am here all alone, dressed and ready to go downstairs as soon as Mr. Alston calls.

Peggy was fussing over me, making me jumpy.

"You'll get your dress all wrinkled up," she said, and I told her I'd sit very carefully. She helped me and then took Natalie off to the butcher's. Papa had a meeting at Tammany. I am glad because I want to be alone to calm myself.

My heart feels like it is beating in my throat. I hope my words will not again get stuck there! And I hope Mr. Alston will look at me as he did last night. It seemed to me he liked me and wanted to know me better. Or did I just imagine it? No. I could feel his eyes upon me many times during dinner.

Poor Judge Van Ness. I had seated him to my right. Several times I would be telling him something or answering his question, and I would feel Mr. Alston looking at me. My voice would just trail away, right in mid-sentence.

He once asked me if I was feeling well. And I said, "Of course." Inside I was just shouting: Oh yes. I am feeling well. Very well indeed!

As usual, Peggy was right. The green gown was the best choice. Theodosia's figure was developing a little too slowly to please her, but the dress helped. It accented the curves of her hips and pushed her small breasts high.

Alexis took Joseph's hat while Theodosia stood just inside the door.

"I am pleased you could come, Mr. Alston," she said.

He heard his own quick intake of breath and hoped his pleasure was not too obvious. Her sophistication intimidated him; he did not want to appear as undone as he felt.

"My pleasure, Miss Burr."

She hid her hands behind her, lacing her fingers to still their trembling. She spoke quickly, needing to be in motion.

"Would you like to see the gardens, Mr. Alston?"

"Oh yes, that would please me very much."

Peggy hustled after the two.

"Missy. Your parasol."

Theodosia whirled it slowly behind her head as she walked, knowing that the soft green silk enhanced the darkness of her eyes and the glow of her auburn hair.

"The summer has wearied most of our flowers. But in just a few weeks the maples will turn to splendid colors. Reds and golds. Perhaps you will be here to see?"

"My plans are uncertain," he answered. "I have been traveling throughout the country for two years and am eager to return to the lowlands of South Carolina."

"Do tell me of your Carolina, Mr. Alston. I hear the ladies there are not generally as handsome as those of the Northern states."

Was she teasing him? He couldn't be sure.

"Perhaps this is true. But most are quite well informed and accomplished." Theodosia picked a small chrysanthemum and tucked it in her hair. She sat down on a garden bench, and Joseph was quick to join her, feeling quite breathless. *I have never seen a more beautiful woman*, he thought.

"I have been told the men and women associate very little in Carolina, Mr. Alston, that the men employ themselves in business or in hunting, horseracing and gaming; and the women, poor things, meet in large parties composed entirely of themselves to sip tea and look prim."

He jumped to his feet.

"Why, Miss Burr, these are merely amusements for leisure time! South Carolina has a claim to superior refinement. A woman of your imagination and taste can easily imagine the beautiful and romantic place I call home. The fair and fertile land interspersed with groves of the orange, the lemon and the myrtle."

He stretched his arms wide.

"Oh, and the tea olive! It flings its healthful fragrance to the air...."

He swiftly waved a hand, and Theodosia stifled a giggle as a covey of startled quail burst into the air, surprising him.

Embarrassed, he sat down.

"Forgive me, Miss Burr. I became carried away."

"Not at all, Mr. Alston. Love of one's homeland is a virtue, I believe. I myself cannot imagine living anywhere other than Richmond Hill.

But I suppose I shall. My father expects me to be an adventurer, a seeker, a learner."

"He has my complete agreement, Miss Burr, and you, my utmost admiration! You appear to be all that he has hoped you would be."

"I have my own hopes as well, sir."

This impressed him. He was, in fact, awed by everything about her. He reached for her hand, and they continued their walk, returning to lighter conversation. She told him how the fading plants would look in the spring, before turning the conversation back to him.

"Has not your family been saddened by your long absence, Mr. Alston?"

"We have kept in touch as best we can. The mail is often slow, and when one is traveling, the letters cannot always catch up."

"I would like to know about your family."

"I have four full brothers and sisters and six much younger half-brothers and sisters. My mother died when I was nine."

"Oh!" she cried. "I lost my mother at age eleven. It is quite hard to find oneself motherless at such a young age, do you agree?"

Joseph concurred. "I wept every night because I thought it weak to give way to my sorrow when anyone could see. My stepmother is fine enough, but I shall never forget the tenderness of my mother. No other can love quite as completely as a mother, I believe."

Once more they were in accord. She had never told anyone but Natalie about the pain of grieving alone in the night, but it was somehow important to her that Joseph knew as well.

"My father forbade me to speak of Mother after she was buried," Theodosia said.

"That seems rather harsh," said Joseph, quickly adding, "but everyone must deal with grief in his own way. Or hers."

He decided to change the subject. "Do you have brothers or sisters?"

"My mother was a widow when she married Papa. I have two half-brothers, Frederick and Bartow Prevost. I adore them and would like very much for you to meet them. Will you be here for some time?"

The question hung suspended between them. Joseph had planned to return to South Carolina soon, but now nothing seemed important except being with this woman.

"My father suggested I travel to complete my education. I finished college at seventeen and was admitted to the bar at nineteen. But I knew little of places and people outside of South Carolina. My father believes the best way of strengthening one's judgment is to allow it to be constantly exercised. He has always expected me to think and act like a man."

"And after all of this exercising of judgment, what is it you wish to do, Mr. Alston?"

"One learns much in traveling, perhaps most about himself. I wish to return home now, to follow tradition."

"And what is that tradition, Mr. Alston?"

"To, uh, marry, to have children, to live on the Waccamaw River as my family has for generations. My father has a rice plantation called Clifton, and I have a plantation home there as well, The Oaks. My grandfather left it to me, but no one has lived there in many years and it has fallen into disrepair. I so look forward to restoring it to the comfortable and beautiful home I remember when I was a child."

His fervor stirred her, and she was pleased with all he had described. During the weeks that followed, the two were almost inseparable, riding or walking when the weather was fair, reading and exchanging ideas in the library when autumn's chill kept them inside.

They traveled occasionally in the company of Burr, Natalie, and the servants. They visited Albany and other places upstate where friends and family were eager to entertain them and see for themselves the young man who had won the favor of Theodosia Burr.

Once they rode alone to Frederick Prevost's estate in Pelham, a village fifteen miles north. Some thought their actions improper and there was much gossip about the unchaperoned trip, but the girl was not one to take the opinion of others to heart. She was enjoying herself immensely.

Indifference to public approval ran in the family. Theodosia's parents had once created lively gossip, now forgotten by most. Mrs. Burr's first husband, Lieutenant Colonel James Mark Prevost, had been wounded and died in Jamaica in 1781. Theodosia did not know that her parents had been lovers long before Prevost's death was officially announced.

Joseph was in such an intense state of desire that he found it difficult to eat or sleep. Every hour away from Theodosia was torture. Her interest in him mounted daily, but she was cautious, considering how dramatically her life would change should she decide to marry Joseph. She was confident he would propose to her.

He knew he must leave to maintain his sanity. He went to the docks to inquire of ships that would be making the passage to South

Carolina. He hoped she would beg him to stay, but she did not, so he booked aboard a pilot ship that would depart in December. He did not allow himself to dwell on thoughts of leaving, trying to enjoy each magical day with the woman he loved.

One afternoon an unexpected Indian summer lured them outside to explore the neighborhoods Theodosia knew so well. One of her favorite places to visit was Trinity Church. As they wandered among the tombstones in the cemetery, she kept up a running commentary.

"My mother married her first husband in this church. And look at these tombstones — this one almost fifty years old. William Bradford. He is called the father of American printing, but there is a mistake on his tombstone! He was born in 1660; the tombstone says 1663."

The couple then wandered the few blocks to Broad and Pearl Streets.

"A very rich French Huguenot built this as his home, oh, at least 60 years ago," Theodosia continued. "Then Samuel Frances bought it and opened it as the Queen's Head Tavern. This is where George Washington said farewell to his officers."

Joseph stepped out into the street to better view the building. "It certainly does not resemble a tavern now."

"You are right. The United States Government moved in. The departments of Foreign Affairs, of War, and of the Treasury run the business of our Republic right here."

"My Theodosia," Joseph took both of her hands in his while carriages bumped noisily along the two intersecting streets, and pigeons mumbled as they pecked for food between the cobblestones.

"Watch out below!" someone screamed.

A woman leaned from a window overhead and heaved a bucket of grimy water onto the street a few feet from where they stood. Geese, seeking warmer climes, honked overhead. But Theodosia and Joseph heard nothing but the beating of their own hearts.

"Is there anything about New York you do not know?" he asked her.

"A great deal. On all my outings, I see something new."

"Show me more."

Theodosia giggled as they began to walk again. "Aren't you forgetting something?"

She pointed to the sidewalk behind them. "Peggy would be upset. We are about to leave our picnic!"

Silently he scolded himself. *I cannot seem to concentrate on anything except her.*

Sensing his embarrassment, Theodosia changed the subject. Or thought she did. "Look at the sky, Joseph. Look at the geese. They are flying..."

She bowed her head and Joseph had to strain to hear the end of her sentence.

"...South."

CHAPTER 18

Richmond Hill, New York. November 1, 1800
Mr. Alston. Joseph. Oh, I love his name. Joseph. It is strong and honest, like him. And how deeply he cares for his home, his family, and the importance of deep roots in a place one loves.

I know little about my family beyond Mama and Papa, and, of course, dear Bartow and Frederick. But Joseph ... his family has been on their Waccamaw River and in Charleston for generations. They grow rice and sell it all over the world. It has made them very wealthy, but riches have not spoiled my Joseph.

He is unimpressed with the splendor of Papa's fine furnishings and objets d'art. Oh, he is appreciative of things that are fine, but what is important to him is what he finds in someone's heart. He is troubled because of the dangers Natalie's family must endure. He joins me in my concern for Papa's impulsiveness.

We find so much to speak about and do together. I have been proud to travel about introducing him to family and friends. But now the weather has turned foul, and sadly, early snows have ended the ramblings we have so enjoyed.

There was one more place she felt she must take him. The foliage had enjoyed a last fling at beauty, but surrendered to winter, leaving the countryside light-starved and bare except for an occasional spruce or pine. But the view along the Hudson did not disappoint Joseph and Theodosia. The reflection of the near-black Palisades and a cold pale sky danced on the water, black shadows etched with silver.

Perched primly sidesaddle, Theodosia could still feel her mare trembling with contained energy. We must behave ourselves, she thought, smiling to herself and holding Wind in pace with Joseph's gelding. After a time, they stopped to bask in this beautiful day.

"I wished you to see this, Joseph, my special place."

He looked up and down the river. "It is magnificent, Theo."

He hesitated. "Do you think you might learn to love my river as well?"

He dismounted and helped her from her horse, took both of her hands in his. He removed her riding gloves and kissed each palm.

"You asked me what I had learned in my travels. I knew nothing that mattered until we met. Now I know I wish to spend all my days with you. Marry me, Theodosia."

Trembling, she fought for composure, forcing herself as she had been taught to be rational.

"I care for you deeply, Joseph, but there is much to consider. I must be here for the election. And then, there are so many miles between New York and Carolina.

"I promise we will make many journeys, my Theo!"

"I am honored, Joseph. But I must have more time."

He was disappointed, having hoped she would give her word immediately, but he smiled as he helped her mount. He would want her all, without reservation, that was certain. He was willing to wait for that.

His departure day arrived too soon for them both. A harsh winter wind blew a bitterly cold breath over the Hudson, twisting the debris along the wharf into grimy funnels. Theodosia and Joseph shivered as gusts clawed into their heavy garments.

They held each other for warmth as much as solace. Both were uncertain if they would be together again. Theodosia frowned as she looked beyond him to the sailing vessel ready to take him from her. Dark clouds knotted the sky to the west.

"I fear a storm, Joseph,"

"She is a fine vessel, Theo."

His answer did not comfort her.

"It is not a rational feeling, I know. She looks quite seaworthy, but I am anxious just the same."

"My concern is not for the journey, Theo. I leave you with such a heavy heart. If I had an answer to my question, I should leave with a lighter one."

"I seem not to know my own heart, Joseph. I had never planned to marry at seventeen! Even Aristotle says that a man should not marry before he is six and thirty."

Her humor did not please Joseph. "Do not speak so lightly, Theodosia. It is with such sorrow that I leave you here."

She reached for him then, boldly slipping her arms beneath his cape and feeling, for the first time, the rippling of his muscular back as he strained against her. Longings she had not known before seized her and she trembled, wanting more of him. Her voice was husky and breathless.

"My dear, dear Joseph. Would that I never cause you suffering. You shall hear from me soon, and often."

They broke apart as the first mate shouted, "Anchor comin' up. Lines away!"

Joseph's voice was thick as well. "I must leave you."

He kissed her lips, her hair. "Adieu, Theodosia. I feel I shall not laugh again, or even smile, until once again I hold you."

"Safe journey, Joseph," she whispered.

CHAPTER 19

December 1800

The beech trees cast stark, angular shadows on the snow outside the dining room at Richmond Hill. Theodosia and Burr breakfasted together, reading the newspaper as Peggy hustled in and out bringing fresh rolls and hot coffee.

"Ha!" cried Burr waving his paper high in the air then slapping it soundly on the table. "It goes well, Theodosia! It appears that Mr. Jefferson and I will emerge victorious, unless South Carolina does something unpredictable."

He stared at her for a silent moment. "Oh, but I am not using my head. Perhaps I have overlooked something. Possibly, I have the world's most informed citizen on the state of South Carolina, and, I might add, the state of some of its residents, right beside me."

She would have sparred with him a few weeks ago, but now lowered her head, determined not show her discomfort as he continued to watch her.

"So what does Miss Prissy say?"

She smiled as their black eyes — piercing mirror images — locked.

"Of what, sir? The state? Or the state of its residents?"

"First things first. South Carolina is the only state whose electoral votes are not in. What do you think is happening in Carolina?"

If I can amuse him, he will not pressure me, she thought then said, "Oh, much is happening there, sir. Their electors have not been able to resist the Jefferson-Burr ticket. And now they celebrate!"

She leapt to her feet, danced, and whirled. "The men have forgotten the hunt, the race, even their seegars! They have declared a holiday! They dance the reel in the streets of Charleston."

Burr doubled over with laughter. Peggy appeared with the coffee service and watched, shaking her head.

Theodosia lifted her skirt. "The women show their ankles!"

Burr wiped away tears of laughter. "Stop, stop. Enough, *ma fille*, or your Papa shall surely have apoplexy! But we still have not addressed the state of the residents of South Carolina."

He rose abruptly, ending their giddiness. "Spare me, Theodosia. I leave you and your preoccupation with South Carolina. Adieu!"

She was momentarily hurt but relieved the discussion was over. When Burr was out of sight, she rushed to her bedroom where she took a thick envelope from her desk.

Charleston, South Carolina. December 1800

You informed me that Aristotle says a man should not marry before he is six-and-thirty. And then you write: "Pray, Mr. Alston, what arguments have you to oppose such authority?" Hear me, Miss Burr....

One can object to early marriage only if there is lack of good judgment or fortune. Some may never have good judgment at any age, and wealth is considered differently by many. But suppose, for instance, that a young man, two-and-twenty, already of the greatest judgment and with an ample fortune, were to be passionately in love with a young lady almost eighteen. Do you think it would be necessary to make him wait for fourteen more years? This is unthinkable!

At that moment Theodosia looked up and thought about the Hudson River. She never tired of the familiar vista: Great sailing vessels skimmed in both directions on the Hudson, well distanced from the great chunks of ice that floated near the shore.

Then she read the balance of Joseph's words aloud:

"Is it not better that persons should marry young so each might absorb the other's passions, habits, and ideas? Enough of this topic 'til we meet."

She smiled, made her decision, dipped her quill in ink, and began to write.

CHAPTER 20

Politicians and the public were accustomed to suspense in 1800. News traveled slowly, and circumstances such as weather and the availability of messengers and horses, made it impossible to predict when bulletins would arrive.

Voting for those who would serve in the U.S. Electoral College took place over several months. Each state voted separately. Although the waiting was uncomfortable for Burr, he went about his daily schedule with no complaint, writing wills and presiding over the closing of properties.

Finally the news was in: South Carolina — in spite of being home to Charles Cotesworth Pinckney, a Federalist candidate and the man President Adams hoped would be his Vice President — voted Democratic-Republican. Adams and Pinckney had won sixty-five and sixty-four electoral votes, respectively, while Jefferson and Burr each won seventy-three.

Burr ran from his office on Petition Street to Richmond Hill and threw his hat to Alexis as he shouted for his daughter.

"Theodosia! Theodosia! God in Heaven, where is she?"

Alexis scurried up the staircase. "Upstairs, sir. I get her."

Burr paced until he heard the rustle of her skirts.

"I am coming, Papa!"

He gripped her arms when she reached him.

"What is it, Papa?"

"The most astounding thing, Theodosia!"

"What, Papa? Did we win? You look pleased, but...."

"Yes, the Democratic-Republicans won!"

Theodosia clapped her hands and squealed like a child. But she was puzzled. This was not his victory stance.

"Papa, what is wrong?"

Burr guided her to a chair, pulled up another for himself, and sat facing her.

"The country has gone Democratic-Republican, Theodosia, but it has not elected a president. Mr. Jefferson and I are tied."

Shock silenced her for only a moment.

"But Papa, how can this be?"

"As you know, the Presidency goes to the nominee with the highest number of votes, the Vice Presidency to the second in line, regardless of party. Jefferson and I each got seventy-three electoral votes!"

"So what will happen now?"

"It goes to the House of Representatives next month."

She looked away, biting her lip, searching for the courage to tell him. Finally her words came out in a rush.

"There will be quite a bustle in the month of February."

He waited for her to continue, her reticence irritating him. "How so?"

She went eye-to-eye with him then, her back straight, her voice steady: "I have just posted my promise to Mr. Alston, Papa. I expect him to arrive for our wedding in February."

Stunned, Burr clenched his jaw and his eyes turned flat and hard. "Have you lost your senses?"

"To the contrary. I have taken many weeks to make my decision."

He jumped to his feet. "I did not nurture your mind to have it molder in a swamp! I hear the damned place is paradise only in the spring. Then it turns to a summer hell and in the fall, an infirmary. There is nothing for you in South Carolina, Theodosia."

She rose quickly. "Nothing indeed! My future husband is there, an important man in that state, I might add! We shall have our own plantation, mingle in intelligent society. I shall teach our slaves. Perhaps write a book like your beloved Mary Wollstonecraft!"

She headed toward the stairs, but turned before she started the climb. "Mr. Alston values my independence and education. And he wishes me to be his friend, not his property! Can you say the same?"

They faced off for a very long time. She had struck home, and he knew the importance of a judicious answer.

"Your happiness is all that has ever mattered to me, Theodosia. I do not believe you will have it in South Carolina."

It felt like a curse, a prediction of certain misery, and she was momentarily frightened. Regaining her composure, she climbed the stairs slowly.

Peggy and Alexis were eavesdropping just outside the room. Alexis shook his head. "I've known him all his life. He got to own what he loves."

"Well, he owns me, but he will never own my heart," Peggy declared, thumping her chest with a bony fist. "Right here? This is mine. But, Lexis, I'm scared for Missy's heart. Who has it now?"

CHAPTER 21

❧❧

February 2, 1801

Guests filed into the Dutch Reformed Church in Albany, N.Y., honored to have received an invitation to the wedding of Theodosia Burr, the daughter of the future Vice President, even perhaps, the President of the United States.

The Rev. John Johnson took his place in front of the church as all turned to see Theodosia and Burr in ostensible harmony, walking in measured steps toward the groom. Washington Irving was among the guests, as was Judge William Van Ness. Natalie, Alexis, and Peggy enjoyed front row seats.

Few noticed the pause following the Rev. Johnson's question, "Who giveth this woman to be married to this man?"

Even fewer knew that Burr gave no answer to the question. He placed Theodosia's hand in Joseph's and turned quickly to take his seat, his face devoid of emotion.

"I, Theodosia, take thee, Joseph, as my lawful wedded husband."

She spoke her vows with conviction and sufficient volume to be heard on the last row. "To love and to cherish from this day forward...."

Her eyes brimmed with tears.

"Until we are parted by death."

Later at a festive reception guests lined up and presented themselves to the bride and groom. Theodosia had insisted the servants who accompanied them on the journey from Richmond Hill be dressed as formally as the guests. Peggy wore a gown of silver-grey silk and pearls that had belonged to Theodosia's mother.

When Washington Irving reached the bride, he held both of her hands in his and looked directly into her eyes. "I wish for your happiness with all of my heart."

She kissed him on the cheek and whispered, "I shall never forget you."

As a string quartet began to play Mozart's Don Giovanni, Natalie took Washington's hand and led him directly beneath the chandelier in the center of the ballroom. They spun about silently, not wanting to speak of how much they would miss Theodosia Burr, now Alston.

Theodosia already had her fill of socializing and was impatient to leave. Her husband had arrived only four days before, and they had enjoyed little time together. She was eager for the intimacy that would follow.

The erudite Natalie had coached her eager student. "I cannot believe the attitude about love that people have in America," she had told Theodosia.

Her student had become less and less reticent. The longer the two of them talked, the more comfortable Theodosia became and the more specific her questions.

"I seem to be absorbing the French way of thinking," she had cheerfully informed Natalie. "This expression of love between a man and a woman, does it just take place naturally?"

"Sex is a very natural thing," Natalie had said, "yet for some strange reason, American women are reluctant to say it is also enjoyable."

Theodosia wanted more information. "That is very true," she had told Natalie. "Peggy told me it was a bothersome thing. But you say sex is for a woman to enjoy as well as a man?"

"Oh yes! It is a very important part of marriage. If the man is kind and patient, and if both of you truly love each other, you will discover wonderful feelings."

Then Natalie had lowered her eyes and smiled. "That's what Mother said, anyway."

As often as the young ladies had spoken about sex, they still enjoyed a giggly secret. Theodosia knew Natalie was chaste, and Natalie knew Theodosia was as well. But they kept up the charade — Natalie as tutor, Theodosia as the rapt novice.

Later, Theodosia took her friend's hand and squeezed hard. "I must find Papa, it's time for good-byes."

Theodosia found him in a small back room having a cigar with Judge Van Ness.

"Papa, we leave now," she told him, kissing his cheek. "It was a perfect wedding."

As impatient as she was to be away, she already worried about her father alone at Richmond Hill. "When will you join us?"

"Within a fortnight. At Richmond Hill."

"Then on to Washington for the inauguration!" she cried. Then frowning, she added, "Yet we know not whom we inaugurate."

Burr was adamant. "It will be President Jefferson, Miss Prissy. Uh, excuse me, Mrs. Alston. I have never campaigned for the presidency. You will be the daughter of the Vice President, and that will suffice."

He did not join the family and guests who assembled outside and braved the winter weather to see the young couple off. Instead, he retreated up a winding staircase to an upstairs room where he sat by a window, watching the start of a gentle snow.

There was a knock at the door.

"Come in," said Burr, his voice heavy and flat.

It was Judge Van Ness, who touched Burr's shoulder as he sat beside him. "Ah, Aaron, our children are not our children, after all. We give them our love, but their lives are their own."

Burr did not answer immediately. He simply lowered his head momentarily, and with a leaden voice responded. "You cannot know, William. Theodosia is my life."

"You have much reason to be proud of her, Aaron."

"Damn! I encouraged her to charm Mr. Alston. We needed South Carolina. But I never imagined she would be charmed as well."

Van Ness was silent.

"But I shall go forward in good faith, William, knowing she will come back."

Van Ness was alarmed. "Good God, Aaron, you have given her in marriage!"

Burr stood quickly, his agitation rising. "She is my earth, and if there is such a thing, my heaven. She stands for all my tender hopes. William, Theodosia will come back to me."

The newlyweds climbed into their carriage as their guests cheered. Alexis and Peggy clapped as the horses began to move, their nostrils spewing bursts of steam in the frosty air. As the carriage pulled away, Theodosia, radiant in anticipation of her new life, turned and waved through the window.

"She free now, Peggy," Alexis said. "Got her own dreams."

"She think she free," Peggy answered.

The old servant was the last to go inside. She focused hard on her thoughts, hoping they might reach Theodosia. *Hold that thinkin', girl. Be strong.*

CHAPTER 22

❦

A blustery wind lashed the primitive capital city. Horses pulled carriages in streets laced with ruts and puddles. A group of drunken men gathered outside a tavern and sang, very badly:

Calumny and Falsehood in vain raise their voice
To blast our republican's fair reputation:
But Jefferson still is America's choice,
And he will her liberties guard from invasion!

Slurring his words, a dapper young man asked no one in particular, "How long you think we'll be without a president? Makes a man feel confident, eh? Safe and sound!"

"Thirty-five ballots were taken," another answered. "Only 35! While the politicians are rattling their papers, do you think they really care if we sleep at night?"

"How many ballots? My God, I've lost count!"

Coarse laughter followed and the men began to sing out of tune again.

Calumny and Falsehood in vain raise their voice....

Unknown to them, their shenanigans were being observed by distinguished citizens — Thomas Jefferson and his fervent advocate James Madison — on their way to the half-finished Capitol building.

"Pull over," Jefferson told the driver.

Jefferson and Madison watched and listened to the activity in the streets. They might have been amused had they not felt so responsible. Since there had been a tie between Jefferson and Burr in the Electoral College, the decision as to who would be President and who would be Vice President fell to the House of Representatives.

On February 11, the House of Representatives assembled to elect a president, resulting in fifty-five votes for Burr and fifty-one for

Jefferson. Burr would have been president except the Constitution required that victory not be based on individual votes, but by states. Nine states had to agree on a winner. Eight states had voted for Jefferson, seven for Burr. But in the next six days, thirty-five ballots were taken and nothing changed.

"I feel the nation's anxiety at my very core," Jefferson told his colleague. "Or is it just my own?"

"You have nothing to fear, Thomas. Colonel Burr is not attempting to influence the vote in any way. He says the people unmistakably want you for President, and he honors their wishes."

"But to be so close to the Presidency and not reach for it! The Federalists prefer him, there's no doubt," Jefferson chuckled. "All but Hamilton that is!"

Madison nodded his agreement and returned his gaze to the street. "What a mess this is! I'm told they are sleeping fifty in a room on the floors of the taverns, waiting for the results."

"I would value your opinion, Jemmy," said Jefferson. "We have weathered many a political skirmish, and I trust your judgment on this matter."

Madison laughed quietly and took his time in answering.

"Tom, my opinion is tainted. I dare not express it, even to you. For you do know, do you not, that my very happy existence is due in great measure to my marriage to Dolley. And it is for this that I am in debt to Aaron."

"Oh, yes," Jefferson replied. "I had forgotten that she owned a boarding house after her husband's death. Aaron was a resident there. He was the one who shot cupid's arrow, am I not correct?"

"He aimed accurately, Tom. He was a very good shot."

The driver, given permission to resume the journey, plodded toward the Capitol, trying his best to give his passengers the smoothest ride possible. Still, the carriage rocked as its wheels sank into crevices and rolled over fist-sized stones.

As they pulled up to the building, the men watched in amazement as a man was carried inside on a stretcher.

"By God!" exclaimed Jefferson. "It's Joseph Nicholson from Maryland, being taken in to vote. I've heard he's very ill. He should not be out in this weather."

Madison shook his head. "He refuses to miss a single balloting. There's a chance this will kill him, it is said."

Later that day they watched the frail Congressman Nicholson as his wife sat beside his stretcher, pressing her handkerchief to his feverish face.

"We will now take another ballot," the Speaker's voice boomed. "This is number 36."

Nicholson's wife put a pad in one of his hands and a pencil in the other, as the Speaker gave another directive: "Please have them ready for collection."

Mrs. Nicholson then prodded her husband several times before his shaky fingers closed around the quill, and he slowly wrote a name — "Jefferson." Wearily, he sank back, exhausted with his effort.

His wife grabbed the paper with its spidery letters and handed it to the vote collector.

CHAPTER 23

❧✦

M r. and Mrs. Joseph Alston lay together in the four-poster bed that was Theodosia's all of her life, their legs wound about each other for warmth in the chill of early morning.

"When do you suppose Papa will arrive?" Theodosia asked.

"Not, I trust, in the next few moments."

"Papa is no prude, Joseph. Already he speaks of grandchildren."

"Nevertheless, I am not in a hurry for him, or anyone, to intrude upon our honeymoon."

He kissed her, and they cuddled contentedly. Later Theodosia asked, "Do you think there is a chance he gets the presidency, Joseph? He swears he will not."

"I have spent much time thinking of it. Theo, if he had lifted one finger, he could have had it. The Federalists are tremendously frightened of Jefferson."

"Papa believes that most of the country wants Jefferson for President. They had an agreement."

"Still, among the Federalists only Alexander Hamilton stood against your father. If it were not for his fierce negative campaigning, Aaron could have won on the first ballot, fair and square. Such a deluge of slanderous pamphlets. Lies, all."

"Well, Joseph, we shall know soon enough, I suppose."

Theodosia slipped under her husband's arm, pressed her cheek into the hollow of his chest.

"A man in my bed! I never thought it could be!" she said.

"Not until we met, and then you thought of it often!"

"You flatter yourself, Mr. Alston."

"I do indeed, and may I have the honor of flattering you, Mrs. Alston?

He traced her features with his fingertips. "You are the most beautiful creature I have ever seen. I cherish you, all that is you."

She pulled him closer, pressing herself against him. "My dear husband."

Richmond Hill, New York. February 28, 1801

I awakened early, and now I sit beside my window watching the waters of the Hudson tangle as the tide changes. How many times in my life have I done this? Did I ever think that I might sit here at my writing, enjoying the view while my husband sleeps beneath my canopy? Never!

Though I was reluctant to leave Joseph's arms, I wanted to be up early to record my thoughts. My flowered coverlet lies lightly over him. The sight of his strong, hard body surrounded by pink and yellow blossoms makes me want to laugh out loud, but I do not because it is such joy to watch him without his knowing. His lips turn up ever so slightly. Is he dreaming that he is with me just the way he was last night?

In spite of the travel, I am invigorated and want to be outside. Perhaps we shall ride today for I am sure that Wind has missed me, as well as the gelding that became attached to Joseph before he left in December.

I hear hoof beats. Could it be Papa so soon? He said within a fort-night, but it seems he has hurried. I will write more later....

Theodosia raced to her armoire, grabbed her peignoir and dashed toward the stairway.

Burr burst through the massive front door suddenly.

"Hello-o!! Rise and shine, you shameless animals! Still in your nightclothes though the sun is high! Pack your bags! We go to Washington!"

"It is over, Papa?"

"Over, at last, my daughter. After 36 ballots, six days! Pack, you hussy, you and your brazen consort. You go to see your Papa inaugurated as Vice President of the United States!"

Later that day, Burr's carriage, followed by Joseph's, left the city for the journey to Washington, D.C. Theodosia looked back at her beloved Richmond Hill, wondering when she would see it again. But she smiled. There was no reason to think life would not continue to bless her.

March 4, 1801 dawned bright and breezy. Already a large crowd milled about the chunky new Capitol building. Bands played. Children darted about, shouting to each other.

The Capitol rose starkly plain above a street pocked with mud puddles. The crowd cheered as Thomas Jefferson and Aaron Burr took the podium. Jefferson raised his hand and placed it on a Bible. Burr, in a rare moment of sincere submission, escorted him to his chair after his swearing in.

In the audience, Joseph Alston clapped and the Vice President's daughter smiled as she watched Burr take his seat. Joseph took her hand in his and offered his own vow: *I must make her happy. I will.*

CHAPTER 24

⁓

In the young United States of America, a coach journey through three states was never a smooth trip. The Alston carriage rocked along the primitive roads, bearing the newlyweds to their South Carolina home.

The expanse of the Chesapeake Bay had to be circumnavigated, adding days to the journey. Narrow roads snaked through forests where tree branches slapped the sides of the carriage, splitting the leather. Cold wind knifed into the openings and chilled the passengers to the bone.

Theodosia remained cheerful, reflecting on the inauguration. "Ah, he was so elegant, Joseph. So gallant."

Her husband agreed. "Yes. If he was disappointed, there was no hint of it."

"Nor would there be. Papa does not believe in dwelling on defeat of any kind!"

"I daresay, my love, that his disappointment over losing you far outweighs any distress over the election."

Theodosia smiled, nodding her agreement. "But he will turn it to his advantage. Now there are two futures to direct."

That idea alarmed Joseph, although he forgot it quickly, reaching for the hand of his bride, looking forward to the next tavern and a warm bed with Theodosia in his arms. The carriage rolled and pitched on the uneven road.

In the third week of their journey, Theodosia noticed a change in the terrain. Black soil yielded to sandy loam and tall pines lined the roadside. Wild flowers bloomed in abundance. Twisted vines strangled and stunted scrub oaks.

The rolling hills of the Piedmont gave way to land so flat she could see white-tailed deer in the roadway a mile ahead. The graceful animals observed the approaching carriage with calm eyes, their jaws moving precisely as they savored tender new grass.

At Clifton Plantation, on a narrow peninsula between the Atlantic Ocean and the Waccamaw River, Joseph's brother William Algernon Alston was unable to soothe his wife, Mary. She leaned over the rail of the porch — or "piazza," as it is called in the Lowcountry — and peered down Clifton's alley of live oaks with increasing frequency. She was red-haired, her saucy face peppered with freckles.

"Where did the messenger say they had spent the night, Algernon?"

"Only about 15 miles north. What an impatient one you are, Mary, my love!"

"Forgive me. I pass so many hours alone, and now someone my own age to talk with!"

Algernon saw the carriage first. "Your wait is over, eager one. I believe your new sister has come."

Mary jumped and clapped her hands like a child, as did Joseph's youngest sister, Charlotte. Another brother, John Ashe, and his bride Sally, newlyweds themselves, rushed to the piazza's rail. Joseph's sister, Maria Nesbitt and her English husband, Sir John, stood slightly apart from the others. Maria, the unconventional sibling, aspired to an acting career and had married into British royalty. She reveled in the Alstons' fascination with her bold choices. She turned her back to the driveway, fanning herself.

As the carriage approached the plantation house, members of the family spilled out onto the lawn and shouted greetings. From the slave street behind the big house, a gray-haired gentleman, too old to join the festivities, participated as best he could, drawing a bow across the strings of a fiddle in a lively melody.

Theodosia had been asleep when the driver made the turn between two great gate pillars and moved forward through the alley. The oaks' ancient branches, laced with long strands of gray moss, drooped and rested on the earth. Her head bobbed on Joseph's shoulder. She was travel-worn, her clothing wrinkled.

Gently he awakened her with a running commentary on the surroundings, beginning with the chalky pillars that stood like sentinels.

"These are made of tabby," he explained, "a combination of lime, sand, and oyster shells. The shells are burned until they turn to lime. Then salt has to be removed and the sand washed to make a cement."

Theodosia tried to listen, but she was more concerned with smoothing the wrinkles from her clothes. She tried to tidy her hair with one hand while searching for a comb with the other. "What will they think of me? I look a sight!"

"A sight you are, my love. A beautiful sight." He cupped her chin and gently turned her head. "Look. Another sight, no more beautiful, but almost as dear to my heart. There is my father's home — Clifton — your home until our own is ready."

She drew a quick breath.

Lofty piazzas graced both floors of the gleaming Greek Revival structure, tall and white before her. Corinthian columns, larger and more ornate than Richmond Hill's plain pillars, bore up the imposing verandas.

The land that comprised Clifton Plantation began at the shores of the Waccamaw River and stretched four miles east to the Atlantic. On windy days, whitecaps on the ocean were visible from the highest piazza across diked lowland that yielded rice known around the world as Carolina Gold.

As the carriage drew closer, Theodosia saw people assembled on the first-floor piazza and on the manicured lawn.

Theodosia smiled to herself. *Here are the men I imagined, ready for their hunting and horseracing. And their women, the prim tea-sippers!*

Mary could barely contain herself as the carriage stopped and the driver jumped down to open the door. Theodosia immediately commanded everyone's attention as Joseph stepped down and gave her his hand. She emerged with poise and smiled without a hint of self-consciousness. No one noticed the wrinkles in her dress, only its fashion, and the beauty and grace of the one who wore it.

Joseph's relatives could clearly see how proud he was.

"My dear family, meet my wife, Theodosia — Mrs. Joseph Alston!"

There was much embracing and exclaiming, which stopped suddenly as Colonel William Alston, Joseph's father, and wife, Mary Motte, whom her husband called "Motte," walked out onto the piazza. Someone signaled to the old musician to cease fiddling in recognition of the family head — called "King Billy," ruler of Clifton — tall, handsome, and elegantly dressed every day. Today he had taken extra time with his morning preparations. He was determined to be immaculately attired and groomed for the newest family member.

Colonel Alston was the wealthiest rice planter on the Waccamaw River, and in addition to Clifton, he owned a huge Georgian house in Charleston. His wife stood slightly behind him, curious but apprehensive. Colonel Alston unhurriedly stepped forward and visually appraised his son, then his new daughter-in-law. Everyone was silent until he broke into a warm smile, walked briskly down the stairs, embraced Joseph, and took both of Theodosia's hands. His voice was deep, his speech slow.

"Welcome to your new home, my daughter. May you come to feel the pride and love for Clifton that is part of the Alston heritage. Your heritage now!"

Theodosia curtsied and smiled.

"It is not often, sir, one is so fortunate to claim two illustrious legacies. I greet you with affection, and bring you salutations from my father, the Vice President of the United States."

Someone handed Theodosia and Joseph silver tumblers of red wine, and the introductions continued in earnest.

Mary and Charlotte, their heads close together, spoke quietly to each other.

"She speaks strangely," Mary whispered.

"Yes," agreed Charlotte. "But with such...what is it? Confidence?"

Maria joined them. "She is not like us."

"For Heaven sakes, Maria!" Mary snapped. "There is much in this world that is not like us, and thank God for it!"

The fiddler resumed his music as family members lined up to embrace Theodosia. When greetings were complete, the women eagerly steered her across the piazza and into the grand entry hall. Theodosia complimented the Alstons on the fine English furniture and splendid artwork in the parlors and the formal dining room. At the rear of the entry hall, she gazed across the lawn at a brick building with gray smoke snaking from fat chimneys on each end.

"That is the kitchen house," Mary explained. "The servants do all the cooking there and bring the hot food to the main house. There are often unintended fires in the kitchen, which we put out before they spread.

Theodosia nodded, smiling when she saw a lithe and agile woman scurrying across the lawn toward them. Mary Motte guided the slave girl toward Theodosia and introduced her.

"This is Tilda, our very finest young girl. She is our gift to you, Theodosia."

Theodosia held out her hand.

"I am so pleased to meet you, Tilda."

The girl, not knowing how to respond, lowered her eyes, ignored Theodosia's outstretched hand and answered in a small voice thick with Gullah tones.

"Miss The'dosie."

Theodosia shrugged and laughed.

"We shall be good friends, Tilda."

Mary Motte fanned herself, an activity that, as Theodosia would learn, was common to Southern woman who were miffed, baffled, or shocked.

"Friends? Mercy!" Mrs. Alston said.

Charlotte snatched the fan. "Mamma! She does not yet know our ways. But isn't she beautiful? And the dress!"

The woman agreed. "I have never seen silk of that color."

Theodosia struggled to converse with Tilda. "Would you like to show me to my room?"

"Yes'm."

Theodosia looked to Charlotte for help.

"She says 'yes'."

"Off we go, then. You first Tilda."

Theodosia followed the girl up the steep circular stairway and into a bedroom that rivaled hers at Richmond Hill. Tilda scurried across the room to the long windows and threw open the heavy draperies. Azaleas blazed across the lawn.

"Tilda! It is so beautiful! Tell me, what do you call the red flowers?"

Tilda stared at the floor. "Don' know nothin' 'bout no fla'wah."

Theodosia gently lifted the girl's chin and looked into her face.

"Tilda, help me to understand. Look at me. Speak distinctly."

Frightened, Tilda said nothing.

"Oh well," Theodosia prattled, "I will learn your way of speaking and can teach you French! *Voulez-nous etre mon amie?*"

Tilda remained silent, head bowed.

"We will help each other, Tilda. Right now, I need some help unpacking. Let's see, where's the best place for my bonnets?"

Clifton Plantation, March 1801

Here I am at home, Papa. The family is so kind. The idea we have in the North of the reserve and coldness of the Carolina women is ridiculous. But there are differences.

CHAPTER 25

⟋≈⟍⟋

"Almost day-clean, missus."

Startled, Theodosia sat up in her bed and reached for her gown before realizing it was Tilda.

Her voice sounds like a harp, Theodosia thought, sinking blissfully back into her pillows. Joseph had long before left their bed.

"It be day-clean," Tilda repeated.

"Pardon?"

The women, neither understanding the other, were reduced to staring. Theodosia felt laughter bubbling up inside her, but kept a solemn face. "You said 'day something?' What is it that you said?"

"Day-clean, Missus. Be full light ob the mornin'."

"Day-clean?"

"Yes'm."

"What does it mean?"

"Mean sun done up and day start fresh. Ebery mornin'. What hab ben day befo' done gone. Cock, he crow, new day, start over."

"Oh!" Theodosia said. "What a delightful idea!"

She was out of her bed and to Tilda's side in a moment, but the girl stepped back and turned away.

She is uncomfortable with proximity, Theodosia thought, giving her space and changing the subject.

"Tilda, I wish to see the Waccamaw River. Will you show me?"

Solemnly, Tilda led her mistress to the hall where, looking west, they saw at some distance a wide channel. Its lazy water looked thick and dark as tar. Ricefields stretched from the big house to the river-bank, and on its far shore long-leaf pines cradled huge cones in their lustrious green needles. Between the pines and the house, hovering over the muddy ricefields, mosquitoes and dragonflies swarmed.

Theodosia wrinkled her nose at the odor of decay. Tilda removed a fan from an apron pocket and waved it slowly, drying a thin glaze of sweat on her mistress's face. Theodosia smiled at her, but Tilda's gaze dropped to the floor.

"Tilda, I was expecting...well, I thought the river would be wide and clear; that it flowed quickly; that I could hear it rush by.

Tilda smiled and ventured quick eye contact, proud that she could offer hope to her new mistress.

"You like big water? Marse' Joseph fetch us to the Castle."

"Where is the Castle?"

"On big water. You see. As' him."

Theodosia waited impatiently for her husband to return for the elaborate dinner the family had each day at 2 p.m. She disliked trying to consume large quantities of food in early afternoon so soon after a multi-course breakfast. Although an early riser, she pretended to sleep through the day's first meal.

She looked out the bedroom window and saw Joseph approaching on horseback and ran out to meet him. Several family members sitting on the piazza fanned and rocked and shook their heads as they watched her race headlong into the warm day while batting the bugs from her hair.

Joseph smiled broadly when he saw her. *She is so beautiful, and I, so fortunate.*

"Tell me, Joseph," she begged as he dismounted. "Tell me about this place called the Castle, please!"

"Oh, that is the family's strange little house on the ocean. On DeBordieu Island, a few miles south," he said pointing.

"The ocean? Oh how lovely! I saw a bit of surf beyond the ricefields this morning but have never seen the ocean up close."

Joseph, still smiling, hugged her.

"All of your life you lived only a few miles from the shore and no one ever took you to the ocean? My poor neglected one. We shall go this Saturday. The cooks will prepare food, and we will sneak into Father's wine cellar and slip out with a bottle of his finest Madeira!"

"Would he approve?"

"Oh, yes. My father is known far and wide for his very fine imported Madeira. He would be offended if you did not sample it."

Theodosia's sadness left her. Joseph was with her again, and she had an adventure in her future. Her father had spoken of the shore many times. The idea of the pounding surf, the calls of seabirds, and the cooling winds that blew constantly fascinated her.

Best of all, there would be a whole day alone with her husband. In the meantime, there was still unpacking to do and a family she wanted to know better. But whenever she passed a west-side window, she turned her face away from the Waccamaw River.

CHAPTER 26

The Castle, DeBordieu Island, South Carolina. April 5, 1801

My journalizing has suffered during the past few weeks as Tilda and I unpack my trunks, interrupted as we are hourly, it sometimes seems, by relatives and friends from neighboring plantations who want to make my acquaintance.

However, I am now happily ensconced in a bare, clean room over-looking the ocean, a view that fills me with joy each time I look outside. Except for the servants, we have been alone, not just for the one night I begged for, but three!

The beach excursion did not begin so happily. Joseph announced our plans at dinner with the family, and immediately several relatives decided that a day at the Castle was in order for them as well.

In all, 12 adults, almost as many children, and several dogs traveled overland by carriage eastward and slightly south on the next Saturday morning. There were baskets upon baskets of hot and cold food and precious bottles of wine, placed flat, carefully wrapped and padded so that they would not break. Valises contained changes of clothing and swimming apparel and toys for the children.

An hour's bumpy ride brought us to the edge of a tide-swollen creek and marsh where all had to be transferred to boats that took us across to the beach that is called DeBordieu.

The wait was torturous. Gnats swarmed around me, invading the bosom of my dress and nesting in my hair. The sun beat down relent-lessly, and I regretted refusing to wear a hat. I hate hats. They make my brow perspire and are always tilting to one side or the other. I was the only Alston woman not wearing one and tried hard not to appear uncomfortable, although I convinced no one of that. Tilda fanned me vigorously, but hot air did little to comfort me.

Finally, the carriages were transported onto barges for the short pas-sage across the creek. Once we reached the island, the entire procedure had to be repeated.

I was sunburned, itching from bug bites, and exhausted with trying to appear unruffled. Our carriage finally stopped beside an awkward, eight-sided wooden structure, its porches sagging in one direction and the tin roof in another.

I exited the carriage quickly, pulling on Joseph's arm.

"The ocean, darling. How do we get there?"

He laughed at my impatience, guiding me on a path that encircled the house and crossed over gently rolling dunes topped with sea oats that whispered softly in the wind and rippled like the tails of young colts.

"Oh, Joseph. Oh!" I cried.

I gazed for miles in both directions, seeing nothing but snow-white sand and ocean that caught the sun in its waves and hurled rainbow foam onto the shore. Gulls screamed and glided with the wind; tiny sandpipers darted along the edges of the waves, poking their needle-like beaks after fast-burrowing sea animals. I was giddy with the vast open space, the fresh salty smells, the brilliance of the sun and sea; and too exhilarated to allow my usual fear of the water to ruin the scene.

"Joseph," I gasped when I finally retrieved my voice. "Could we live here? Here by this magnificent ocean?"

He pulled me to him and pushed back my wind-whipped hair with his hand.

"A bit far for me to travel every day, my love, but you may spend as much time here as you wish; or as much time as you can bear to be away from me."

I threw my arms about him.

"Oh, Joseph, after the crop is in, could not we come and stay then?"

He gave this some thought.

"That could be September, Theo. We have never used the cottage that late in the year."

"But we could!"

He was silent.

"We could," I repeated. "Could we not?"

"I suppose," he answered. "I have never considered it before. The house can be very cold and drafty, and decent firewood is scarce."

"We can manage," I answered firmly. "It is so beautiful and refreshing. I feel so free! I cannot imagine being unhappy here."

He kissed my forehead and looked over my head at the rambling and unpretentious beach cottage, snuggled against the dunes.

"It seems to be right where it wants to be," I said, and that made Joseph smile.

Later, as the family prepared for their return to the mainland, I begged him, "We could spend the night here, Joseph. Please?"

At first he seemed unnerved by my request. But we stayed and have been deliriously happy. If only we could stay all summer.

Joseph thought himself finally attuned to his whimsical bride, but she astonished him once more.

"We have no nightclothes here, Theodosia," he answered when she begged to stay at the Castle.

She laughed at his prudishness and reminded him in a whisper.

"Joseph, we have slept without nightclothes before."

He thought this over and the idea became more appealing. He pictured the two of them in this house alone, lying close, holding each other, and listening to the gently pounding surf. He smiled, and she knew they would stay.

Tilda remained at the Castle, too, as well as Peet, a strong field slave who would drive the carriage and ford the creek on the return journey. Family members said little until they had left the newlyweds, waving goodbye to them in the doorway of the cottage, but there was conversation aplenty on the trip home. Joseph had married a most unusual woman. Was this to be a blessing or a curse?

CHAPTER 27

Theodosia was eager to see her own plantation house, so Joseph planned a ride to The Oaks—fifteen miles north. She was adjusting somewhat to the South Carolina heat and enjoyed riding the black gelding that he had given her for her eighteenth birthday.

She considered naming it Wind for her beloved mare at Richmond Hill, but decided on Storm because she was intrigued with powerful squalls that often roared in during the late afternoons. Lightning would pierce the dark skies, whipping the languid Waccamaw into a frenzy.

No gale brought relief from the heat this day, and she reined in Storm, wiped streams of perspiration from her face, and slapped at the halo of ever-present gnats and flies that hummed about her head.

"The heat, Joseph."

"Yes," he answered, stopping beside her. "It's almost time to get away."

"Away?"

"A deadly fever comes from the steaming marshes in summer, so we go to Alston homes in the mountains. It's safe up there. And on occasion some of the family summer at the Castle. The ocean breeze keeps them well."

Theodosia had already deduced from family conversations there would be no privacy for her during the summer at the beach cottage. They had had several excursions there since her first one and, although she loved the bustle, such close family living had little appeal for her. The children were plentiful and noisy; the slaves did all the work. Hours were spent in idle chit chat, an unaccustomed activity for Theodosia.

Of the ubiquitous Alston women, Sally and Mary were her favorites. But early on Theodosia discovered they preferred sewing to riding, gossiping to reading. She realized she was ill prepared to be a plantation housewife.

"Oh, Joseph, I should like to go to New York. We can move about in the out-of-doors without risk of illness, visit friends, go to the opera."

"There is opera in Charleston, Theodosia. We can go all winter long."

But Theodosia had already begun to see herself at Richmond Hill where it was cool at night, and the wind from the water brought the scent of fruit trees instead of the stench of marsh mud.

"Please, Joseph. We shall summer at the shore or the mountains next summer, I promise."

Joseph, eager to please her, agreed.

"Make plans then, Theo," he said, "and soon. We must be off the river within the month for the sake of our health."

He slapped the reins lightly on his horse's neck and the two moved forward.

"First, we must complete plans to restore The Oaks and leave instructions for the servants. It will take many months to prepare it for us."

"Oh, Joseph, I shall be so happy when we are settled! Your family is most civil, but they do think me strange. They disapprove of many things I do, I fear."

"I approve of everything about you," he answered. "So you need no other endorsement."

She decided to bring up a controversial idea.

"I would like to teach Tilda to read, Joseph. I am concerned about how the family might react."

"It has never been done here, Theo. There are laws against teaching slaves to read, you know."

Oh yes. Natalie and I know all about that, and I am entirely prepared to totally ignore it, she thought.

"Joseph, did you know Papa introduced a resolution in the New York Legislature to free all slaves?"

"No I did not."

"It was not passed."

"Well, darling, I want you to know that, even though I am a lawyer, I will not prosecute if you teach Tilda how to read and write."

She blew him a kiss.

Around the next bend, Theodosia had the first view of the dilapidated Oaks mansion through a tangle of vegetation. Joseph quickly dismounted and surveyed the condition of his inheritance, slapping at insects as he thrashed through looping wild-grape vines that had woven themselves tightly into the overgrown shrub oak and myrtle.

He took measurements and scrawled hasty notes with a quill he carried in his saddlebag.

Theodosia sat astride her horse for a long time, her jaw slack. The Oaks was a tiny house with wood siding, barely thirty-two feet deep and forty-two feet wide. A crestfallen kitchen house behind leaned precariously, and a small row of slave cabins in bad repair stretched toward the east.

"Joseph, I cannot see the river," she shouted.

"You will when all of this is cleared away," he answered, wiping his brow. "There is a creek just there, and the Waccamaw is not far beyond."

Theodosia looked where he pointed, and saw nothing but rotting trunks of fallen trees so covered with vines and moss they appeared to be piles of debris. The sun had sucked everything dry — the green from the grass, the color from the sluggish river.

"We will clear that all out," Joseph said, seeing her dismay. "Our little creek is full of shrimp and clams, and we will dine like royalty."

She forced herself to smile. She shaded her eyes and watched two vultures circling. They were so close, she could see the yellow glow of their eyes as they soared, searching for a meal.

The couple walked a few feet to an old cemetery and pushed open a rusty gate. Surrounded by a wall of old bricks, smooth and velvety with green moss, Theodosia read engraving on the stones as she pulled away weeds.

"Oh!" she stood quickly. "How sad; a little girl. Listen to this, Joseph: 'All that could die of this beautiful child, lies here.'"

"It is the summer fever I spoke about," he answered. "It is merciless. It must be cured quickly or it quickly kills. The young are especially defenseless. Sadly, many are lost."

Theodosia shuddered. She flattened a mosquito against her neck and a rivulet of bright red blood mixed with her sweat.

"This an ominous place, Joseph. It saddens me and frightens me, all at once. I must never be here, Joseph. Never!"

"But this is the family burial ground, Theodosia. It is our place."

She pulled away from him. "It can never be my place. Promise me, Joseph, please. Promise me I will not lie here!"

Lost for words, he made no promise to her, and in her eagerness to get away she did not exact one.

That night she poured her disillusionment into a letter to Burr.

I cannot see how I can make a home in this little wreck of a mansion. It is but a story and a half and has no view of anything inspirational.

The pragmatic Burr responded with little sympathy:
It is best not to start with splendor. To descend with dignity is rare.

Theodosia would soon know that the dignity for which Aaron Burr was famous would be sorely tested.

CHAPTER 28

❦

Summer had not arrived at Richmond Hill, although flowers abounded and birds were returning from their southern winter. The air was crisp and Aaron Burr felt energized as he surveyed his estate and awaited the post. When he saw the carrier approaching, he abandoned his usual dignity and rushed to meet him.

"Good day, sir."

The postman handed him an envelope. "And a good day to you. I've guarded this 'un with ma' life, I have!"

Burr tipped his hat and ripped open the letter. "They come, they come!" he shouted hurrying back into the house. "Alexis, Peggy! The fatted calf is not nearly good enough! Order venison, the ripest fruit, and the finest nuts! Theodosia is coming home!"

Within the week the Alstons' carriage was at Burr's door. Theodosia burst out before the horses had settled to a full stop and leapt into her father's arms. Natalie, Peggy, and Alexis eagerly waited for their turn. She hugged one after the other, over and over.

"My dear hearts, how I've missed you!"

Joseph stood silently until Burr greeted him.

"A great day for me, my son," Burr said.

"We have anticipated it with pleasure as well, sir. I promised you, Theo would not summer in the Lowcountry."

"A good thing. Your marshes are malignant! How you live is a miracle! But please come inside. I have many plans for your holiday!"

Theodosia's excited chatter echoed in the almost-empty entry hall and she gasped.

"Papa, what has happened? The furniture...."

"A temporary situation, I can assure you. A few restless creditors."

He hurried her toward the dining room where most of the furnishings remained intact, but Theodosia gazed sorrowfully over her shoulder at the bleakness behind her.

"Come," Burr urged. "Dinner is waiting. I have much to tell you."

He seated Theodosia and Natalie, and the four of them settled down to the elaborate feast he had planned.

After dinner, Burr and his son-in-law took a brisk walk along the edge of the water at the tip of Manhattan Island.

"Ah, they pursue me unmercifully, Joseph!" Burr lamented. "Let this be a lesson. Never find yourself on the wrong side of the press. They do not forgive or forget."

"What do they say of you, sir?"

Burr tipped his hat and nodded to an acquaintance then said to his son-in-law:

"First you have to understand that Jefferson is paranoid. He will always believe I schemed against him to get the Presidency."

"Had you tried, sir...."

Burr interrupted. "I know. I could have won, and that drives Hamilton mad. He is determined to ruin me. Calls me a womanizer; says I am bankrupt! And the press prints it all. As a result, Jefferson does not consult me on any matters of state. I doubt he will support me for Vice President the next time around."

"This is distressing news, sir."

"Well, we shall see. If my sun sets, yours can rise! Get involved in your state's business, my son. Rice-planting uses none of your talents."

"But, sir, it is what I know best."

"Nonsense, Joseph! It is your Africans who know of rice planting. You only give orders. Your minds are turning to mush! Theodosia is pale but a few days here will put color back into her face."

"Sir, I disagree. Theodosia has been charmed with the society of Charleston. She has, however, found plantation life somewhat trying."

"Not just trying, boring. Too many servants."

"Sir, my apologies, but you are mistaken."

"Perhaps I overstated my case. But you store yourselves too often in the swamps with too much family. Her mind is keen, Joseph. I have raised her to believe occupation is necessary to give her command over herself."

Joseph countered. "We will travel to Charleston for the winter, sir. Charleston society will occupy her totally. She will be well-received at all of the St. Cecilia concerts."

"This is no surprise to me!" shouted Burr. "She has led the society of New York for years and served as Richmond Hill's hostess since she was fourteen years old."

Burr turned toward the harbor and both men rested against the railing. A small sloop tacked toward shore, a white train of noisy gulls trailing behind. One of the sailors emptied a wooden bucket of fish heads and entrails over the stern and the birds screamed their delight, circling the little boat in a feeding frenzy.

"Your concerns and Theodosia's are the highest, the dearest interests I have in this world. All others are insignificant," Burr continued. He waved his arm in a grand gesture over the water. "The world can be yours! You have a spotless reputation, a wife who loves you, no quarrel with any man. South Carolina is close to your heart, and she needs you. I only ask you to investigate what your state has to offer, and how you may best use your talents to serve her."

"I may, sir, but The Oaks comes first."

"Before your wife, Joseph? Good God, are you mad?"

"Sir, you are twisting my words. Nothing is more important than Theodosia! But my home and my occupation as rice planter take precedent over political aspirations."

Burr, always the diplomat, assented. "Of course," he purred. "I know her happiness is all that matters to you. For what else and for whom else do we live? Which brings me to mention one excellent idea Mr. Jefferson has. He feels the energies of our men ought to be principally employed in the multiplication of the human race."

He grinned broadly, clapping Joseph on the shoulder. "The ladies, yours included, I am sure, have promised ardent and active cooperation. I know you need no urging on that score, Mr. Alston!"

Burr took Joseph's arm. "We must go back now. We have much planning to do."

He turned abruptly and Joseph followed, lost in thought.

He confuses me. I have a response ready, then suddenly the game has changed, and it is not the proper maneuver after all.

They turned toward the Hudson as Burr kept up an exuberant monologue. "I wish you to visit Chief Brant and his Mohawk nation upstate. Theodosia entertained him with great aplomb at Richmond Hill four years ago. Then you must see Niagara Falls. Have you heard of the talented young artist, Vanderlyn? I have told him the falls are worthy of a painting, and I wish to know what you think. I will accompany you for part of your journey."

But Joseph, deep in contemplation, heard none of it.

Theodosia's happiness is my highest wish. But is it truly Colonel Burr's, as he says? For whom else do we live? Does he live for her or through her? Many times it seems to me he puts his expectations above her happiness. I fear for her, but I know no way to help her save retreat. We must go home soon.

CHAPTER 29

Clifton Plantation, South Carolina. November 12, 1801
My Dearest Papa,
November and it is still humid. Did it all take place as I remember
— the cool air and our long rides at Richmond Hill? The parties with
friends?

Theodosia pushed lank wisps of hair from her damp face, struggling to answer her father's letter. She read it for the fifth time.

"My dearest Theodosia. Vanderlyn has painted your Niagara so
beautifully that the beholder of his picture could almost hear the roaring...."

She closed her eyes, and the sound of Niagara came to her — turbulent, frightening, and exhilarating all at once. Her skin tingled with chill bumps remembering how the air had picked at her garments with icy fingers until it found the gaps and touched bare skin. She had shivered then, too, but could not pull away from the sight and sound of the falls plunging over the high precipice and smashing onto the rocks hundreds of feet below.

She had been mesmerized by the power of the white cascade. She could hear it roaring throughout the night, and it stirred her deeply. She was positive now that she was pregnant, and she wondered if she had conceived at Niagara.

Happily, she relived their travels, remembering their visit at Chief Brant's magnificent house deep in the woods of the Mohawk Valley. When her father knocked on the door, Brant opened it himself, flanked on either side with the same spear-bearers that guarded him at the entrance to Richmond Hill. She knew her father wouldn't flinch, and he did not. But she held Tilda's hand and giggled when they saw Joseph gulp and step back.

She continued reading Burr's letter.

You made more conquests on your northern tour...King Brant among them. He has written me two letters on the subject and sends moccasins for you and your husband. It would not have surprised me if he had scalped your husband and made you Queen of the Mohawks!

She sighed, hoping her depression was due to pregnancy but feared it was the result of too little to occupy her active mind. Each morning, servants swarmed over Clifton. "Dayclean!" Tilda would announce when she brought Theodosia's morning tea. "Day be clean ebbery mornin'," Tilda reminded her. "New start. Bad be wash away in de night."

Theodosia longed for such a transformation. For her, daybreak was the start of a frantic search to find something meaningful to occupy her until the evening when she and her husband would dine with the family then retire to their room and talk until bedtime.

Joseph and Theodosia had little time to celebrate their impending parenthood together. For weeks the rising rice crop required his presence in the fields most of the day. Theodosia did not protest. Her husband was a full-time planter now, and she knew that one day's neglect of the crop could spell disaster and disgrace. Occasionally he took time off to hunt or to travel to Charleston for the horse races. She longed to go to the races, but the trips were strictly all-male and considered too boisterous for ladies with child.

The rice harvest began in August, and the slaves were still working at fever pace when Theodosia and Joseph returned from New York in the fall. She was troubled about the health of the slaves and took her concerns to her father-in-law.

"Sir," she began, "yesterday, twelve men and women were brought in from the field suffering from heat exhaustion. Today I have seen some of these same people returned to the field. I fear for them."

William Alston abruptly ended her plea. "My dear, it has been my custom to treat my slaves with the utmost liberality. They have dwellings of the best description. They are clothed well, and my wife attends to their health and comfort. I would suggest you find some other activity for your sympathetic nature."

He pushed back his chair, bowed slightly and left the room before Theodosia could protest. Her anger raced like lightning through her body until it tingled with energy that had no place to go.

"You would do well to discover a 'sympathetic nature,'" she growled, knowing her words merely echoed among the vast shelves of books and the gun cases in Colonel Alston's study. But then she cocked her head. *Do I hear the ubiquitous swish of a protesting fan in the next room?*

She smiled. *Oh, there is humor in every situation, I suppose, and I pray I am always able to find it.*

CHAPTER 30

⚜

To Theodosia's relief, the Alstons traveled to Charleston for a long stay just before Christmas. She had spent her life in lavish surroundings, but she found the Miles Brewton House, her father-in-law's King Street mansion, astounding.

"Come, daughter," Colonel Alston's invitation contained the hint of a command. He gave her a brief and affectionate kiss on her forehead as he took her elbow and introduced her to his in-town dwelling.

"The original Mr. Brewton came here from Barbados. His son, Robert, had a daughter who was a heroine in the Revolutionary War, but more of that later. One of Robert's sons was named Miles, for his grandfather."

Theodosia was enjoying herself. *Miles the first, then Robert, then Miles again. My Joseph, his grandfather Joseph, and all of the Williams, first, seconds, and thirds.*

"Sir," she began, "Joseph said you dropped an 'L' from your last name to distinguish the immediate family from your cousins'. Was he only trying to amuse me?"

"No, my dear," William replied. "My father was Joseph Allston, with two 'L's. Your husband, my first-born son, would be Joseph the Second, but it seemed foolish to crowd the family tree with so many of the same names. So I took care of that."

Theodosia bit her lip, determined not to giggle. *It all seems foolish to me. Why not some new names? Michael? David? Adam? Aaron! Now there is a name any Alston should be proud of, one "L" or two.*

William continued. "Miles owned eight seaworthy vessels, a number of plantations, great works of art, and a library like no other," Colonel Alston continued. "He was only thirty-four when he began work on this house."

The two entered a room wallpapered in a rich turquoise gilded with gold. Everything sparkled — the wavy windows, the crystal prisms on the chandeliers, and the sconces. Theodosia noticed that the decorative plates on the mantel and the fireplace tools were meticulously dusted and polished.

"Now Rebecca...," Colonel Alston continued as he huffed and puffed up the steep staircase to the attic, "... she moved into the house at the beginning of the Revolutionary War when she inherited the house from her brother. Shortly afterward, the British took Charleston, and the commanding officers made this house their headquarters. Rebecca's husband died during the occupation, but she steadfastly refused to leave her home."

Theodosia's attention wavered. She gazed out over the backyard. She could see the entire estate. The slave quarters, stables and gardens, full of scurrying people — picking fruit, feeding chickens, currying horses, carrying food from the kitchen house to the main dwelling.

Colonel Alston took her arm and turned her toward him.

"Well, daughter, if I may have your interest once more."

When her eyes met his, he could not look away, feeling strangely bewitched. *Black as midnight*, he thought. *Yet so much energy shines through.*

He forced himself to focus elsewhere to stay on track. "In this garret, Rebecca kept her three daughters locked up — yes, confined in this very space. For many months they did not leave, so afraid was their mother they would harmed by the soldiers downstairs."

Theodosia had a rare moment of speechlessness. No sound penetrated the thick walls. Although she felt the vibration of feet as servants performed their duties in the rooms below, the garret was deathly quiet. Colonel Alston, sensing her awe, guided her to the steps, this time going before her as a buffer, should she fall.

CHAPTER 31

～⟡～

Colonel William owned an impressive stable of thoroughbreds that brought the Alston colors glory on the racetrack.

"I would so like to have seen Betsy run," said Theodosia referring to Betsy Baker, a mare that had created much excitement on the track before she was retired for breeding.

Theodosia loved visiting the stables at the Miles Brewton House and would often pick up a currycomb and groom Betsy until her black coat shone like patent leather. Theodosia called the mare's newest foal Bitsy. When the filly was a year old, she trained her to the halter and gently led her to the edge of Charleston harbor to snack on the green grass that grew at water's edge.

She wished someday she might ride Bitsy at full speed through the cobblestone streets of Charleston, and snickered at the thought of an Alston seeing her astride the animal. Would the thrill be worth the sniffs and quivering fans that would follow? *Yes! Most definitely yes.*

Few women were regular attendees on the racing circuit, but February's Race Week, the culmination of a year's preparations by the Charleston Jockey Club, was an event they were expected to adorn. Theodosia spent the better part of a morning at the milliner's selecting a bonnet to wear to the races. She smiled, remembering the admonishments her father regularly gave her against vanity.

She indulged herself, so thrilled about going somewhere, anywhere, to a bustle of activity, excitement and involvement. Each evening Joseph described to her in detail all he did: anecdotes about planting, tending, harvesting, hunting and, of course, the horses. But nothing excited her like the thought of being there.

She modeled the hat for her husband but instead of approval, he frowned at her. "You don't like it, Joseph? Is it the color? I thought red and green...."

He took her hands. "Sit down with me, Theodosia. I never dreamed...."

"Joseph!" She touched his lips with a finger. "Whatever is wrong?

It is only a hat. I can have another made."

He could hardly meet her eyes. "Dearest, you are only three months away from giving birth. It would never do."

"Joseph!" her words burst from her, high-pitched and tight with anger. "Do not tell me this. Are you saying that because I am carrying your child I would not be welcome at the races?"

His shoulders slumped. "It is not considered proper, Theodosia. Perhaps in New York, but not here."

She rose quickly, wincing with the effort.

"What you are saying," she began evenly, "is that it has never been done. The devil with that. This year, Mr. Alston, it shall be done. I will go. My dress will hide what seems to shame you so!"

"Theodosia, you know I have no shame. Please."

"Be proud then. Be proud that you — we — are producing yet another Alston. I shall go to the races, Joseph, and I will go to Mrs. Middleton's ball afterward. If I should faint, I trust you will be there to catch me. If anyone else should faint at the sight of me, well, I hope there will be someone to catch them as well!"

She left the room.

And she did go to the races, and stood and clapped and cheered for the Alston horses: Raven, Hawk, Bold Billy, Miss Mary. She helped carry the large silver trophies to the carriage in which they were taken to the Miles Brewton House to join the gleaming display in the library. Later, she danced at Mrs. Middleton's ball.

"Theodosia," whispered Sally as they sipped champagne. "Mary and I are proud of you. We hope because of your courage, ladies who are with child will no longer sit home and weep during Race Week."

Theodosia hugged her Alston sisters and thought, *You will if your husband permits it, and if you care not a whit what people think. Those "ifs" may be far more formidable than you, sweet Sally.*

"I will cheer you on every step of the way," she promised Sally, having little hope her support would make the slightest difference. Insurgency was lonely work.

CHAPTER 32

〰〰

While Theodosia challenged social norms in South Carolina, her New York family faced changes of their own. She learned of Natalie's adventures through frequent letters from Burr and her beloved "sister." Napoleon was in charge in France, and it was safe for the émigrés to return to their homes. Natalie was preparing to set sail for France after almost eight years in America. There was not sufficient space on the small ship for Madame Senat and her daughter to make the trip with Natalie, so the talk in New York was that she would be traveling alone.

"She will make an ocean voyage unchaperoned!" Theodosia exclaimed to her husband, hoping she kept envy from her voice. *The freedom! Imagine walking about alone, dining with strangers. Arising, retiring at one's will!*

She purged the delicious thoughts quickly and felt a familiar torpor descending, weighing her down like a dark heavy cloak. She realized this was happening too often. *I will gain better control*, she resolved.

Actually, Chancellor Robert Livingston, the new head of the legation to France, was watching over Natalie. The newly appointed secretary to Livingston, another young South Carolina gentleman, Thomas Sumter Jr., traveled with the party.

Natalie had met Sumter at a farewell gathering hosted by Theodosia's half-brother, Bartow Prevost, and his wife, Frances Ann. Natalie was immediately attracted to Sumter, and her fascination dispelled any anxieties she might have had about the voyage.

They boarded the frigate *Boston* on October 15, 1802. Due to communication problems, Natalie was not reunited with her mother for another two months. By that time, her heart was thoroughly joined to Sumter's.

He was devoid of one drop of noble blood and fourteen years older than Natalie. Her mother was determined no marriage would take place. The young couple was equally resolute in their commitment to each other.

Burr kept Theodosia informed of the saga all along the way as news traveled much faster to New York than to South Carolina. Revived by the excitement and suspense of Natalie's situation, she cheered her on in her heart, writing letters to her, encouraging her to be steadfast in her efforts to allay her mother's resistance.

She wished for Natalie's happiness, but she barely let herself think of the joy the union would bring to her lest she be disappointed. If Natalie married Sumter, she would live in South Carolina, in Stateburg, just a two-day journey from the coast.

She hoped Natalie received her strong thoughts. *Hold fast, my dear sister. Remember our many talks. Love is the most important thing of all.*

When she knew for certain Natalie would be married in March, she had to fight another time of discontent with plantation life. *I could be in France*, she thought, imagining a new gown of simple linen, dyed the exquisite azure the local indigo produced. *Tiny crystal buttons from nape of neck to waist, and a hat that will catch every eye. Blue, of course, to match the gown, but with glossy black feathers, curving sensually over one brow. A large pocket in front, large enough to hide my belly. The skirt would be so full my precious babe should not offend even the sharpest eye.*

CHAPTER 33

⁓⁓⁓

The excitement of February's Race Week melted into memory, and Natalie was blissfully married when the Alstons returned to Clifton in March. Theodosia was once more restless in the long empty hours of the day.

She asked her husband to take her into the ricefields where she had been watching the slaves level the soil for many weeks. Joseph explained to her that all sections of the fields must have equal irrigation so the new growth would be uniform.

In April, seed trenches were laid about a foot apart over the hundreds of acres that made up the fields of Colonel William's plantations. It was backbreaking work and the slaves' labor saddened Theodosia. But in a month the bright green slivers of new rice plants broke through and brought her fleeting joy.

She missed Charleston, where there were people everywhere, and she could ride out in a carriage with no company except for the driver and walk almost any place she pleased. On the Waccamaw, it was not considered safe for a white woman to be alone away from the immediate grounds of her plantation, even with a driver. Theodosia could not ride to the fields to search for her husband or stay by herself at the Castle or spend time with Sally at her plantation, Hagley, a few miles north on the Waccamaw.

Sally was eager to be with her as well but the same constraints kept her bound to her plantation where she had resigned herself to working on needlepoint, embroidery, and cross stitch. Theodosia had never enjoyed handwork and was too restless now to learn. She had no duties, no responsibilities. Tilda anticipated her every need.

"Tilda, go home," she often told her. "Go to your house and help your grandmother with the children. Or just take a walk. Don't you have a gentleman friend?"

Tilda was puzzled. Black people were not referred to as "gentleman," she said.

"Oh, I mean a special man!" Theodosia burst out in exasperation.

Tilda's shy grin answered her question.

"Then go find him. When do you think he will finish his tasks today?"

Clifton operated on the task system. Each slave was given a set amount of work each day; when that was completed, his or her work-day was over.

"Soon, Missus. Peet fast worker."

"Then go wait for him. I have some work to do myself."

Colonel Alston was reluctant to have another confrontation with his daughter-in-law. He admired her courage even when it approached audacity and envied his son a companion who conversed with him so freely. She kept Joseph's intellect challenged, and the Colonel enjoyed the benefits of her keen intelligence as well.

Theodosia had greatly enhanced dinner conversations at Clifton. Tedious reports of family matters and the day's activities gave way to political debates and rounds of highly charged discussions on a wide range of subjects. The Colonel encouraged her participation, even though he felt an undercurrent of ennui and disapproval among some of the diners. But order and tradition had to be maintained in the Kingdom of Clifton and he felt that Theodosia was much too per-missive in allowing Tilda excessive privileges, so the Colonel decided he must confront her.

"Come with me, please," he commanded one morning after break-fast.

She followed him to his office where he held a chair for her and seated himself behind a desk piled with ledger books and stacks of correspondence.

"I understand your girl Tilda spends a great deal of time unsuper-vised," he began.

"I gave her permission," Theodosia said.

"Do not do this," he ordered. "It sets a bad example for the other servants. In addition, they will begin to be jealous of her leisure and it will cause trouble. Please keep her with you at all times during the day."

"Sir, I do not wish to always be in the company of someone else. I enjoy being alone when I read or write letters."

"That simply cannot be done here. You may send her to the kitchen to prepare something for you to eat or to the garden for flowers. But she may not idle away on the slave street or in the field waiting for that boy."

Colonel William watched Theodosia straighten her back, cock her shoulders and lift her chin as she composed an answer. He knew he had angered her and sensed he may have diminished the spirit he so admired. But no, she had a retort.

"Sir, perhaps Mother Motte could use some help with her mending, or maybe her laundry. I've noticed her servant is often overwhelmed. Please consider asking Tilda to help her."

She turned and left the room, forcing herself to appear confident and proud, but she knew Colonel William had won. Somehow she must accept that she could seldom be alone. And worse, at Clifton it was impossible to create the bustles that energized her. She knew how to prepare French cuisine, but a white woman working in a plantation kitchen was beyond understanding. Slaves prepared all the meals.

Theodosia would not have minded cleaning to keep her busy; she had often helped Peggy with her chores. One day she picked up a silver goblet from the hunt board in the dining room, spit on her handkerchief and rubbed at a spot of tarnish. Mary Motte saw her and pulled a fan from her bosom and brandished it so rapidly her tiny corkscrew curls sprung straight up on her forehead.

She looks as though she has little horns, thought Theodosia, but she held onto her mirth, pressing the handkerchief to her lips to hide a smile that threatened to explode into an unladylike guffaw.

There was a piano at Clifton, but Theodosia's instrument was the harp, so she could not entertain herself with music as she once did. She daydreamed of the beautiful harp at the Miles Brewton House that was richly carved and expertly tuned, and she looked forward to returning to Charleston for the social season, but late fall was a long way off.

She closed her eyes and tried to remember the resonance as she ran her thin fingers over the strings. But her hands were swollen now because of her pregnancy. *Would they be nimble again? If I put my fingers on the strings, would they know what to do?*

Unchallenged and underused, her mind wandered, skimming the tops of thoughts, not taking any substance from them and retaining little. Then she had an idea that excited her. The children in the family knew little about Greek mythology. She loved the fantasies as a child and could read them in their original language.

"I will rewrite the stories so the children can understand them," she told Joseph, who encouraged her. Burr was ecstatic when she wrote him of her plans.

A worthy idea, he responded. *You must do this as the occupation will amuse you and add to your stock of knowledge. I will be your editor and critic. Three weeks after I have received them, they will be in print.*

But concentration had become difficult for Theodosia. She dawdled with pen and paper, found fault with her writing, and soon abandoned the effort.

Sensitive to her difficulties, Joseph decided they would return to Charleston. The family was at first critical of his decision to leave the plantations in spring, arguing he was needed to supervise work in the ricefields. But he had the perfect justification. Their child would be born in the same house where he came into the world. Tradition was all; no one would dare argue with that.

CHAPTER 34

〜∞〜

Theodosia seated herself at the harp in the grand parlor of the Miles Brewton House and, after an awkward moment when she had trouble positioning the instrument alongside her huge belly, she began to sing:

Shepherds, I have lost my waist
Have you seen my body?
Sacrificed to modern taste,
I have become a dotty toddy.

Her actress sister-in-law, Maria, did not care for being upstaged. Leaning close to Charlotte, she whispered, "Bad taste, don't you think? In her condition."

Charlotte pointed toward their father who was nodding and patting his foot in rhythm. The concert continued.

Never will you see me more
'Til common sense returning
My body to my legs restored
To gladness turn my mourning.

For fashion's sake I have forsook
What sages call the belly,
And fashion has not left a nook
For cheesecakes, tarts, or jelly!

The applause was politely enthusiastic except that of Colonel William, who clapped loudly and jumped to his feet before embracing Theodosia.

"Well done, my dear! Wherever did you learn that ditty?"

"I composed it, sir!"

"Ah," began the Colonel, "Joseph, you have married yourself a musician and a poet!"

Maria stood, waving a lace hanky. "I think I have heard it before. Isn't it...let me think. Oh yes, I remember now. Isn't it called 'Shepherd, I Have Lost My Love?'"

"You are quite right," Theodosia answered with a gracious smile. "I must confess that I used that tune. But the words, well, no one but I could be that silly. They are mine."

Upstaged and miffed, Maria pressed the handkerchief to her rather prominent nose and said her good night.

Theodosia found her annoyance with family increasing with the girth of her abdomen, but the weather was agreeable and Burr had advised her to walk, so walk she did. One day, she received two letters in the post and took them with her to her favorite place beside the sea wall to read when she sat to rest.

Washington. April 16, 1802

You must continue to walk a great deal. It is the only exercise you can take with safety and advantage. Get a very stout pair of overshoes, or short boots, to draw on over your shoes. But they must come up to the ankle with one button to keep them on...thick enough to turn water. I wish you to write me that you have them because without them you cannot walk, and without exercise you will suffer much in the month of May.

She looked at the sailing ships. Gulls swooped and glided. She reached up toward an especially bold one who dove daringly close, hoping for food. She had some hardtack hidden in a cloth bag tied to her belt. After she tossed the bird a morsel, a cloud of screaming scavengers surrounded her. Several pedestrians were alarmed until they heard the girl laughing. She walked on, reading her father's letter.

Do not allow any work to be done on your teeth at this time.

My life has no variety and, of course, no incident. To my feelings, your letters are the most important occurrence. Five weeks without hearing from you! Intolerable! Adieu, my dear little negligent baggage! Health and blessings. A. Burr.

She felt multiple Alston eyes upon her as she pulled herself slowly up the steep stairs to the front door of the house. She held fast to the wrought-iron handrail, stopping often to rest. Maria and Charlotte observed her slow ascent as they watched through the bubbly glass of the drawing room window. "Never would I be seen in the streets during a confinement!" Maria declared. "Why does she do it? What does she try to prove?"

"She does it for exercise," Charlotte answered, adding wistfully, "and she wants to prove nothing. Her mind is her own, and she has no need of our opinion."

CHAPTER 35

May 1802

A bright high moon illuminated the rough, narrow road and the trees on both sides, standing guard in their eerie garb of wispy moss. The shrill cry of crickets and tree frogs calling to one another went unnoticed by Aaron Burr, riding at a furious pace. The entrance to Clifton could hardly be missed, even at this hour. The massive tabby columns stood like pockmarked ghosts at its entrance.

The turf had been smoothed and leveled on the alley, and Burr pushed his mount harder. Flecks of white foam flew from the animal's nostrils as he gave his best. No slave waited at this midnight hour to take the reins when he reached the house, but in his hurry he didn't bother to tether his mount. Too exhausted to go anywhere, the horse dropped its head and stood still except for its heaving sides.

Burr yanked impatiently on the clapper of the large cast iron bell at the doorway.

"*Hel...loo!* Colonel William?"

He continued to clang the bell until a sleepy slave in a nightshirt opened the door and beckoned him inside.

"I git 'um, suh. He be sleeping."

"Sleeping? Theodosia's time is near. Someone must stay awake to watch her!"

"Missy Theo in Charleston, suh. Mas' Joseph be with her."

Burr was distraught.

"My God in Heaven. I will never get to her in time."

Colonel William descended the stairway pulling on his robe. He grasped Burr's hand.

"Colonel Burr? Ah, we meet at last! Welcome to Clifton. Come inside. Have a nightcap. You look in need of a good night's rest."

"Thank you, sir. I am pleased to meet you also. But I must not tarry over a nightcap. I have come to be with Theodosia during her time."

"Ah yes, it is her time, isn't it? But it is her work, after all, Colonel

Burr. Women have been giving birth for centuries without us."

Colonel Alston laughed uproariously while lighting a cigar. "Well, not entirely without us, but..."

Burr interrupted. "I cannot share your humor, sir, not when Theodosia needs me."

Colonel William offered a cigar and put his arm around Burr's shoulder, guiding him into the great parlor. "There is nothing to be done tonight, sir. Charleston is sixty miles off. At dawn we shall set out in my curricle. Now you look as though you could use some Madeira, and I'll need a bit of a sleeping aid as well, after such an abrupt awakening. Come!"

Burr drank deeply from the crystal goblet, but the potion brought him little ease. He was up early pacing in anticipation while the Alston carriage was made ready for its journey. The sun was still low in the eastern sky when the two men left Clifton and headed south on the primitive road known as the King's Highway. Ricefields surrounded them, and the air was dank and heavy with the smell of the marshes.

Burr held a handkerchief to his nose. "How do you live here, William? The air seems quite unhealthy,"

Colonel William was a confident man, slow to take offense.

"We manage, Aaron, we manage. But some cannot acclimate, either physically or mentally, and for them life is especially difficult. But I live a charmed life!"

He made a great circle with his arms. "This is my land...as far as the eye can see. This is the rice kingdom, and for the moment, I am King!"

Alston commanded all of his surroundings — realistic and harsh when he had to be and justifiably proud of the empire he had carved from the swamps of the Lowcountry.

"That's my nickname, you know," he said with a hearty laugh, 'King Billy!'"

A group of small birds took wing from a gnarled cypress tree, which twisted upward from the shallow waters of the marsh.

"Bob-o-link!" he noted then frowned at their taunting cries. "Pesky rice birds be damned! A few more of these hungry birds, a bad season, the end of slave labor, and my empire will be over. It is fragile, Aaron, bound to fail. For now, I cannot ask for more, but I pray to God that I will not live to witness the demise."

Burr nodded, still pressing a handkerchief hard against his nostrils.

"Motte and I entertained President Washington at Clifton in 1791," Alston continued then chuckled. "Motte is usually a shy little thing, but she wore a headband across her forehead with big letters that said, 'Hail to the Chief!'"

He offered Burr another cigar, which was refused. Alston lit one and took long puffs, leaning back with a great sigh of satisfaction.

"I must boast. The President said that he had seen nothing in all his travels so justly entitled to be called a fairy land as the ricefields of Waccamaw in the genial month of May."

At Colonel William's Charleston home, polished brass lanterns spread their light into the darkness of King Street. The curricle came to a stop and a man rushed from the shadows to take the horses' reins at the end of the daylong drive. Burr got out quickly and soon rapped at the mansion's huge front door. When a servant opened it, Burr pushed past him into the entry hall.

"Where is she? Where is Mrs. Alston?"

"Which Miz Alston, suh?"

"For God's sake, how many Mrs. Alstons do you have here?"

"Tonight be fo', sir.

"Fo'?"

Colonel William, struggling to hide his amusement, caught up with his guest.

"Four, Aaron, a small number for an average day. Wash up now and I shall find our Theodosia."

"I shall wash later. Please...."

He turned to the slave.

"Send Theodosia's personal maid to me at once."

With a quiet "yessuh," the man turned toward the stairs. Tilda was already halfway down.

"Bad now, she," Tilda said.

Burr sank into a living room chair and covered his face with his hands. "Oh, God. Oh my God."

Colonel William placed a large hand on his shoulder.

"Aaron, Aaron, do not distress yourself so. Let us retire to the drawing room, have a good seegar."

Burr ignored him, interested only in what Tilda had to say. "Are you Mrs. Alston's slave girl?" he asked. "For Mrs. Theodosia Alston?"

"Yessuh."

"Tell her that her papa is here. Tell her to be brave. Tell her, make sure she knows," his voice broke, "that I love her. That she is my life."

Tilda turned to go, and her eyes widened as she realized that Burr was following her upstairs. She ran ahead of him to the midwife, Mariah.

"Man be comin' in fo' the birthin'!"

Mariah rolled her eyes. "Folks from away hab the strange ways."

"Let him in?" Tilda asked.

But Burr was already at his daughter's bedside. He took her hand as Theodosia screamed, and, drenched with sweat, writhed in the four-poster bed. Mariah passed a small fabric sack back and forth across her huge belly.

Theodosia gasped, "I cannot go on."

The midwife placed a cloth on Theodosia's head and resumed waving the bag. "De rosemary and de garlic, dey hep wid de pain. Bear down, Missy, chile be comin' soon."

A full moon cast shadows of the city's rounded chimneys and peaked rooftops onto the walls and the high ceilings in the bedroom.

Theodosia was suddenly silent and still.

Mariah continued to swing the bag, chanting softly.

Tilda whispered, "Be daid, Sister M'iah?"

"No, but bad off, she. Lose her blood."

"Do something!" Burr shouted.

Mariah leaned close to Theodosia.

"Miss Theo. You gotta push mo' now. Give all your strength. Give yo baby life. I need to catch 'um soon, or mebbe we lose yo chile."

Theodosia's eyes glazed and fluttered. A contraction lifted up her body and she strained, falling back.

The midwife held onto the slippery shoulders of the infant until another contraction thrust him into the world in a gush of thick, blood-streaked fluid. He mewed as Mariah swaddled him in a blanket, and quickly his whimper became a howl.

"Be a boy! Puny, but speak up strong, he do."

She placed the child in his mother's arms, and Theodosia pulled the blanket from his face, tracing his features with a finger. Tears and perspiration streamed onto her pillow.

Aaron Burr looked at his grandchild, and for once, no words came. Joseph rushed past him and kissed his wife's face, his own wet with tears. "Theo? Look at me, darling, please!"

Her lips moved slightly. "Never did I behold anything so beautiful. Oh, the flowers. The splendid colors. The Hudson! And look across, the Palisades. So high and dark! It is Heaven to me, Joseph."

"She speaks of Richmond Hill, Joseph," Burr said. "She believes she is at home."

Joseph was still shaken and weeping. "She is home, sir, here with me and our son."

Ignoring Joseph, Burr leaned close to his daughter's ear. "Be brave, Theodosia. You must consider what's best for your boy; he has our blood, our will. As soon as you are able, we will travel to Richmond Hill."

Joseph composed himself. "Sir, she belongs here with me, and I will not go to New York. I cannot hope for a seat in the Legislature if we leave during the campaign."

"You cannot hope for a healthy wife and son if they do not escape your summer, Joseph. Take hold of your senses! You stay, campaign and win!"

Theodosia was twisted in the blood-soaked linens. "Mama!" she screamed.

She heard her mother's voice, a whisper inside her head.

When I am gone, you will be all he has.

"Mama, don't leave me!"

Tilda set down an armful of fresh sheets and gently stroked her mistress's brow. Theodosia, soothed by her touch, slowly returned to reality. Too weak to speak, she begged with blood-streaked eyes, veins ruptured by the effort of thrusting her son into the world.

Joseph, dear God. Tell my father that you will not allow me to go.

"Should I win the election, sir, she and the child can join me in Columbia until the House recesses in December," Joseph told Burr. "But if the child goes to New York, I will not see him until he is seven months old."

"And healthy as a young colt, I dare say!" Burr responded. "When next you see them you will find a strapping child and a wife with roses in her cheeks and a fiery yearning in her heart for you."

Exhausted, Joseph was no match for the formidable Burr. He touched his son's hand. The baby made a tiny fist around his finger.

CHAPTER 36

B urr, as usual, got his way. He would take Theodosia north with
him, but not before she regained enough strength to travel. In
the meantime, he took advantage of the excitement he created in
Charleston.

The news that the Vice President was in residence in Charleston
surged through the port city, and Burr received invitations from its
most prominent citizens. Fine goblets were raised at formal dinners
and zealous toasts rang out into the streets where less prominent
residents gathered in the shadows of palmetto trees, hoping for a
glimpse of the man.

An opulent meal was enjoyed at the Carolina Coffee House, which
began and ended with a rendering of "Burr's March," performed by
the city's most talented musicians and composed especially for the occasion. Joseph Alston walked in his father-in-law's shadow, although
his poise and intelligence did not go unnoticed by Lowcountry voters. A seat for him in the S.C. Legislature became more of a reality
as weeks passed.

The family traveled to Sullivan's Island, a beach community where
comfortable cottages squatted behind lofty dunes, insulating Charles-
tonians from the heat and the fatal fevers that they believed tainted
the night air.

When Theodosia could raise herself enough to write, she began
a letter to Natalie congratulating her on her nuptials and telling her
of her precious baby. Then she began to describe the state of her
health, for Natalie was the only person to whom she could speak
about intimate subjects.

My womb continues low, she wrote, *and the bleeding has not ebbed
in the slightest.*

She described a doctor's treatment of daily doses of steel dissolved
in vitriolic acid, Peruvian bark, and Eanella Alba, which nauseated

her. She tried a vegetable diet and drank herbal teas constantly. Often, her fever brought hallucinations, and even on the best of days she felt irritable and anxious.

But my babe continues to thrive. He was weak at first, but since Heaven has granted him life, I shall never repent what he may have cost me.

She read over her letter and tore up the page that contained the complaints. What right had she to mar her friend's newfound happiness? Slowly she turned, rolled her swollen legs off the side of the bed and tried to stand. Tilda caught her before she could faint and fall to the wide-planked floor.

"Help me dress, Tilda," she whispered.

Two weeks later, she and Burr were at sea headed for Richmond Hill. Cradling the baby to her heart, she lay on the open deck day after day near the stern, hypnotized by the hiss of the ship's wake and the words that she forced herself to repeat in her head.

Look ahead with courage. Burrs do not accept defeat.

CHAPTER 37

Joseph Alston's campaign speech was full of passion. As the election progressed, he had developed into an articulate and forceful orator.

"Elect me to the South Carolina House, and I will enter a bill to alter the present mode of electing members of Congress. At present, some of our citizens are not fairly represented."

The crowd cheered as he smiled, thanked them and climbed into his carriage to return to Clifton. His brother Algernon had made the trip with him, and the two rode silently for a time. No sunset was visible through the dense swamps but later a moon lit their way as the terrain flattened out.

"I think the speech was well-received, brother." Joseph was too preoccupied to hear him, thinking of nothing but the last letter he had received from Theodosia.

The time of our reunion draws nearer, my darling. Your letter, which I received yesterday, delighted me all the more, as it was unexpected. I did not imagine a letter from Charleston would reach here on the eleventh day. How anxious I am for tomorrow...perhaps I shall hear from you again. How goes the campaign?

I know you have Algernon with you, but he cannot, like your little Theo, watch you in your sleep. Your son, too, would charm away your cares. His smiles could not fail to soothe any pain. You cannot perceive this until you see him.

My ailment, about which feminine modesty forbids me to speak, does not improve. The great misfortune of this complaint is that one may vegetate many years in a sort of middle state between life and death, without the enjoyment of one or the rest and peace of the other.

"Joseph!"

"Forgive me, Algernon. My mind was miles away."

"I know you have private concerns, my brother. Talk, if it will help."

Joseph continued. "Damn it all! I travel from town to town, reciting words that seem to me empty, while my wife needs me. Her body has not recovered from childbirth. Our climate has not agreed with her, and now she does little better in New York. And Mr. Burr, he keeps her mind in turmoil. I scarcely know what to make of him. At times I feel that he is not a rational man."

"This is shocking, Joseph."

"I know. Only Theodosia can appease him, restore his sensibilities. But she pays a perilous price. She needs me; my son needs me. I should never have let them go."

"You must think of your reunion, now not so far off," Algernon said. "We will be able to quit the empty words and unceasing travel when you win, which most certainly you will."

Joseph shook his brother's hand and smiled as they steered their horses to yet another town.

CHAPTER 38

$\approx$ ✧ $\approx$

At Richmond Hill, Theodosia convalesced slowly, propped with pillows in the library, the baby beside her in his wooden cradle. She had been briefly energized when she heard of Joseph's election victory, but it was difficult to share his joy from such a distance. She felt removed and disconnected, barely noticing summer sneaking into fall.

But one day she awoke from dozing and saw the New Jersey Palisades before her in a blaze of autumn color. She called for Peggy to help move the baby outside, and she sat beside him, removed her slippers and wiggled her bare toes in the cool grass.

From his upstairs quarters, Burr saw her and could not resist joining them.

"Ah, does Aaron Burr Alston sleep?"

He rocked the cradle, smiling into the tiny face.

"Gathering energy for great things! Think of it, Theodosia, next summer I'll teach him his letters. And then we shall place a pen in his hand."

Theodosia fanned herself and was slow in answering.

"Ah, Papa, he is not yet five months old. You exhaust me with talk of such activity."

"All thought of activity appears to exhaust you, my Theodosia. A bustle used to bring you such joy."

He went to her, cupped her face in his hands. "I have never seen more dispirited young people than you and your planter husband. Had I not persuaded him to seek public office, he would be content only to sit and watch your rice grow."

Burr began to pace. "You must study, be active, or you will lose your head."

"I fear that has happened already, Papa," Theodosia answered, but she smiled, straightening her back and tightening her belly. "It seems that my head as well as my body are in ruins!"

"Nonsense, Theodosia. I will not listen to such drivel. The same strength that drives me is also in you."

He pulled up a chair to sit beside her. "I have my trials, too."

"What do you mean?"

Burr rose and paced again. "Mr. Hamilton. He speaks; the presses print. I was faithless to my party, he says. I negotiated behind Jefferson's back for the Presidency. He hints that I am a shameless womanizer."

"But...."

"You know the truth as well as I, but Mr. Jefferson believes Hamilton. I have no job at present other than presiding over the Senate. Mere child's play. A man's honor is his most priceless possession, Theodosia. I will defend mine at any cost."

She winced as she stood. "No, Papa! Please, I beg you. Leave politics. When your term is over, you can return to your law practice."

She took his hands, felt his tension subside.

"I will consider it, but you will have to extend your visit. We must explore all options."

She turned her head so that her father would not see her irritation. Just yesterday she had written to Joseph:

New York, October 30, 1802

Oh, my husband, when will we be reunited? I feel that we have lost so much of our life together. Where you are, there is my country, and in you are centered all my wishes.

I bathed in the waters of Ballston and Saratoga, and they did not heal me. But thoughts of being with you again do much to mend me, and I try each day to write and study. Please be well for me. Your devoted, Theodosia.

"Theodosia, did you hear me?"

She sighed. "I heard you, Papa. Perhaps I will extend my visit for a short time. But by Christmas, I must be on the Waccamaw."

CHAPTER 39

 ∽◦ ◦∾

Weeks of preparation preceded Christmas at Clifton. In the center of the grand parlor, a giant cedar tree blazed with hundreds of candles. Servants took shifts guarding it in case it caught fire. Galax leaves and turkey pine vine had been brought in from the upcountry and all the mantles and staircases wore festive green attire.

Gleaming silver bowls of long-leaf pinecones garnished with ribbons and stick candy adorned tables that were polished to a mellow glow every day. The slaves sought this job above all others. Busy hands that buffed the furniture could easily slide a sweet into a pocket, but there was no shortness of candy, and no one was admonished.

Theodosia had arrived in mid-December, thrilled with the news that her husband had been elected to Congress but bitterly disappointed that his new duties kept him in the capital city of Columbia.

On Christmas morning she was despondent. He still had not come home. She tried to appear happy as she joined the family around the tree and awaited the arrival of the house servants. According to tradition, if the servants could say the words "Christmas gift" before their owners, those gifts would be given out sooner. In the Alston household, the family had strict orders from Colonel William to be silent until the servants had shouted their greeting.

The massive doors to the grand parlor were closed, but the family could hear the shuffle of eager feet and the excited whispers on the other side. "Sh...h...h...."

Mothers held tightly to children who wiggled and bobbed with excitement. Finally, as anticipation built, the servants and their children burst into the room.

"Christmas gift! Christmas gift!"

"Ah," cried Colonel Alston. "'Christmas gift' to you all!"

The servants formed a line and received new clothes, shoes, and candy. Later there would be dancing and music on the slave street as the field hands and their families celebrated. Hogs and sweet potatoes would roast over pits of hot coals while collard greens boiled in great cauldrons, filling the air with their acrid scent. Everyone received a gift, and there were special treats, enjoyed only on holidays — candies, pies, nuts, and fruits.

Theodosia stood slightly apart from the Alstons, crooning to her baby. As the excitement abated and the room became quieter, the family paused in their celebration, hearing the sound of a horse and rider. The front door flew open, and Joseph burst into the room, his cheeks chilled crimson. He was greeted with hearty cheers. He nodded quickly to everyone as he hurried to Theodosia and held her and his infant son as tightly as he could.

"My Christmas gift! My Joseph! Thank God!" Theodosia cried.

Colonel Alston kept a polite distance until the couple released each other, which was, in the mind of some family members, not nearly soon enough.

"Ah, our new legislator!" the Colonel said. "Welcome home, and Merry Christmas, my son. We hope you bring us much news from the session."

"In due time, Father," Joseph answered. "In due time I'll tell you all about it. My wife and I have been long separated. We wish you joy in your holiday. We shall leave you to enjoy ours." He took the baby into his arms and escorted his wife out of the room and up the staircase.

Only Colonel Alston, Mary, and Charlotte were amused. Charlotte could no longer hold her mirth and exploded with a giggle. Mary Motte, her mother, grabbed her wrist, saying, "Do not lose your self-control, daughter."

To Maria she declared, "We must set an example, young ladies. Let us go now to the back street and do our duty. The gifts are on the dining table. Everyone please take a basket."

The family filed out onto the grounds. Joseph and Theodosia were grateful they were busy and distracted. Spirited music had already begun. Homemade drums throbbed with African rhythms, and the slaves' near-delirious voices rose and fell joyfully, praising the faith of their owners that they had come to embrace as their own.

But homecomings and holidays provided only temporary relief for Theodosia. Soon her days and nights continued to be tedious and lonely. When her husband returned to Columbia, she had little congenial company. Receipt of her father's letters was the only bright spot in the cold winter days of 1803.

The day after you left us, though the weather was mild, not even a frost, the leaves of the trees about the house began to fall. In three days' time they were as bare as in mid-winter, though you may recollect that you left them in perfect foliage. I shall respect these trees for their understanding; their sorrow and regret was in harmony with my feelings. Truly, all was dreary. Richmond Hill seemed no longer home. But let us think of our next meeting.

Adieu, ma belle. A. Burr.

CHAPTER 40

⚬⚭⚭⚬

The windows in the library at Clifton rose almost to the 19-foot ceilings, and the bottom of their frames touched the wide heart pine floors. Theodosia had a panoramic view of the fields and the slaves who tended them in the bitter cold. She saw a honey-colored girl, a shawl pulled tightly about her, slip across the lawn toward her quarters on the slave street.

Theodosia moved to another window where she saw a drained rice impoundment being plowed while several men hoed the mud, leveling the field. Another plowed behind an immense ox wearing rawhide boots called mule shoes, which provided the animal traction in the black ooze.

She sat at the desk and picked up a quill. When she wrote to Burr, she felt his presence.

Clifton. March 17, 1803

Since my last letter to you I have been quite ill, totally unable to write. Often I had no appetite and at times, quite forgot to eat. I became weak and unable to rise from my bed. The whole family had begun to think pretty seriously of my last journey. Fortunately I have had the pleasure of keeping them up a few nights and drawing forth all of their "concern," without giving them the trouble of burying and mourning!

I exert myself to the utmost, feeling none of that pride, so common to my sex, of being weak and ill. I encourage good spirits, try to appear well and am sometimes rewarded.

But I am so often alone, Papa. The work at our plantation goes slowly. Heaven only knows when we may move in. I do so miss a bustle! What a charming thing it is. Oh dear delightful confusion! It gives a circulation to the blood, an activity to the mind, a spring to the spirits.

Tilda tiptoed in, glancing behind her furtively. Theodosia smiled and held a finger to her lips. "Sh-h-h-h-h!"

She motioned Tilda to follow her, and the two left the library and quietly mounted the stairs. Safely inside her bedroom, the two giggled like schoolgirls. Theodosia locked the door, and they settled side-by-side.

"This is by Horace," explained Theodosia, opening a book. "Originally written in Latin. Remember, I told you that Latin was once spoken in Rome, a city across the ocean in Italy?"

Tilda, an eager student, nodded then reached to turn the page.

"Latin is now a dead language," Theodosia continued. "No one speaks it anymore."

Tilda was silent for a moment. "Grandmaum, dead now, she. Told me she speak like her own mother in Africa, but now nobody understands. That be dead language, too." Stunned, Theodosia could only stare at Tilda and, for the first time, the girl fully returned her gaze.

So intelligent, mused Theodosia. *If Mary Wollstonecraft can believe women have souls, I will go a step farther. I believe Negro slaves have souls as well.* It was a thought Theodosia knew she must keep to herself.

"Tilda, in Rome, many years ago, people owned slaves like today here at Clifton. When they defeated southern Italy, they captured slaves by the hundreds. There is much poetry justifying slave loves in Latin. In fact, many wrote about free men enslaved in love by slave women they owned! At that time, too, some masters took advantage of their slave women, and as long as it was kept quiet, people looked the other way. Listen:

"'There's no guilt, believe me, in loving such a handmaid...and... Agamemnon burned for a captured maiden during his triumph.'"

Theodosia turned to her slave girl, ready to explain the text, but was startled to find Tilda's head lowered and tears flowing, thin silver streams down a face the color of earth.

CHAPTER 41

⟡⟢

The summer of 1803 found Theodosia once more at Richmond Hill, but this time she had persuaded her husband to accompany her. Her joy at returning to New York was marred by the appearance of her former home. Its grounds were a riot of floral color but there was no order. The landscape was overgrown and unattended.

Burr, Theodosia, and Joseph retired to the library after a plain dinner and ordinary wines. Empty bookshelves and sparse furnishings attested to Burr's continuing pecuniary problems. He told Theodosia that Natalie had given birth to a girl in January, hoping to distract her from his embarrassing distress. "Maybe the new Little Miss Natalie will take a shine to our boy here."

Just then Peggy, bending to hold a tiny finger, helped her precious charge toddle into the room. "This child is so happy, Miss Theo! Smiles and just melts your heart. Like you used to do."

Joseph took the child onto his lap where he wiggled and arched his back, eager to be down and show off his new walking skills. Burr stopped his familiar pacing and urged his grandson to toddle in his direction. "A fine lad you are indeed! Not surprising, of course, considering your heritage."

He picked up the child, lifted him high above his head. "Grandpa, say Grandpa my fine boy." He lowered him to eye level. "Grandpa, *Grand - pa.*"

The child merely gurgled.

"Well, you will greet me soon enough, little man. I do not like to see you so pale, but a few months of northern air will invigorate you. By fall, we could be reading Shakespeare, and maybe starting Latin."

Joseph stepped quickly to Burr's side, taking the child from him. "My God, Colonel Burr, he is but fourteen months old — just a baby."

"Education can never start too early, Joseph. Theodosia was reading at age three, but only because I began teaching her letters at...."

Theodosia interrupted, patting the seat beside her. "Papa, you have forgotten. Surely, you allowed me to be a baby for a year, or maybe two.

Come here; sit with me. Your grandson has totally consumed you."

"Ah, Miss Prissy, you know you are always first in my affections, and first to hear my plans."

He did not stay seated long. Moments later he jumped to his feet again and said, "Hear this! It seems the Federalists are eager to pick up what Mr. Jefferson is so determined to cast away."

"You speak of yourself, Papa."

"None other. Soon, it is rumored, the United States will buy vast lands in the West, solid Republican territory. The Federalists are panicked. They will be grossly outnumbered."

A knot coiled inside Theodosia's abdomen as he continued.

"The Federalists may form a new nation. But first, I must become Governor of New York and lead it into the new confederation. Become its President!

"Papa!" she gasped. "This is just what Jefferson has accused you of, pandering to the Federalists."

"Ah, but I shall run as an independent."

Joseph was incredulous. "Sir, General Hamilton will never allow you to become Governor of New York. And when you lose, you have lost all. Neither party will claim you."

"Lose?"

"Yes, lose, sir, be defeated! It is possible, you know. Your political life will be in shambles."

Burr's voice shook with anger. "Focus on defeat and one is beaten, Joseph. Burrs do not accept defeat."

Joseph was silent momentarily then he spoke slowly, firmly emphasizing each word. "It appears to me, sir, and I mean no disrespect, that what you cannot accept, is reality!"

The two men glared at each other. Their silence was more unbearable to Theodosia than ugly words. She tried to shut out everything but found no respite — only her mother's voice.

He is spirited...like a high-strung horse needing a tether. I have been that for him, Theodosia.

She jumped to her feet. "Stop! Stop this at once!"

The men remained squared off. Burr made a fist and told Joseph, "Do not forget, sir, that you are in my home." Then he abruptly left the room.

After a while, Joseph spoke first. "I cannot understand him, Theo.

It is fortunate we leave within the week. I have reached the end of my tolerance."

The couple summoned their servants, who began packing for the trip back to the South Carolina Lowcountry. Theodosia had always been consumed by sadness when she bid farewell to her father, but this visit had caused her so much consternation she was eager to be gone.

Papa and Joseph disagree on everything. And this latest idea — deserting the Democratic-Republican Party and subjecting himself to the wrath of Hamilton — is madness. Joseph is right. Papa's credibility will be lost, perhaps forever.

CHAPTER 42

Washington, D.C. October 16, 1803
I was very happy to find myself here, for we had been near taking
quite a different route.

Burr smiled as he read Theodosia's lively description of an accident
they experienced on the journey.

The carriage harness broke and the horses panicked. One of the
animals unknowingly saved us by throwing his hoof over the carriage
tongue, bringing us to a jarring stop. Otherwise, the poor world would
have been deprived of the heir-apparent to all its admiration and glory.

She also wrote that she thoroughly enjoyed a visit in Washington
with Dolley Madison.

Mrs. Madison is still pretty; but oh, that unfortunate propensity to
snuff-taking.

Back home at Clifton there was good news. Natalie and Thomas
Sumter had set sail from England to Charleston in a ship christened *The
Two Friends.* Theodosia was convinced the name was a good omen. She
and Natalie would soon be able to spend precious time together again.

Also, much progress had been made on the restoration of The
Oaks, their plantation house. Joseph and Theodosia took a brisk ride
to see it, he leading on a path that twisted through dense underbrush
changing from green to red-gold. Crisp, wind-funneled leaves crack-
led under the horses' hooves. Theodosia felt better than she had since
the birth of her boy.

Swinging a leg over the pommel of the sidesaddle, she urged her
mount to full speed and left her husband in pine needles and dust.

"Theo!" he admonished her, then broke into laughter. "Just when
I think I know what you will do...."

"It is difficult to straddle this silly saddle," she shouted back to him, "but it is worth the discomfort to ride like the wind!"

Joseph urged his horse forward and they raced to the house. It was not large or ornate but the workmen had improved its appearance inside and out since the Alstons last visit. The new landscaping was pleasing. Inside, Theodosia ran her hands over the walls in amazement — they were as smooth as glass! No one else on the Waccamaw River had plastered walls, the very newest trend.

Clifton. November 8, 1803
Dear Papa,
We have visited the Oaks since our arrival. The walls are newly plastered. How soon do you think we can safely move in?

While waiting for her answer, she traveled to Charleston hoping to be there for Natalie's arrival. Her anticipation turned to restlessness as the days went by and *The Two Friends* did not arrive. Theodosia dressed the baby warmly, and — accompanied by Tilda and her son's nanny, M'aum Hattie— she walked daily to the water and searched the harbor.

Finally, Theodosia could wait no longer. She asked Tilda to pack and go searching around the taverns of Charleston for their errant driver. Enough waiting! She needed to check on the progress of her plantation renovation as she was counting on her family celebrating Christmas at The Oaks. But a letter from Burr awaited her at Clifton, dashing those hopes.

Washington, D.C. December, 1803
Your house will not be a fit or healthy residence for your boy before the middle of April or first of May. The walls may, to the touch, appear dry in three or four weeks, but shut up any room for twelve or twenty-four hours and enter before it be aired, and you will meet an offensive, and, I believe, pernicious effluvia; an air totally unfit for respiration. This is the air you will breathe if you inhabit the house. I could, perhaps, show chemically how the atmosphere of the closed rooms becomes thus azoic, but I prefer to submit to the test of your senses.

Much against her wishes, Theodosia, Joseph, and their son moved in with brother John Alston and wife Sally at nearby Hagley Plantation. Although she found life more informal and fun with a younger woman as mistress of the house, she was riled to be once more a guest in an in-law's home.

CHAPTER 43

~~~⚭~~~

H er irritation was short-lived for no sooner had she settled in at
Hagley than word came from Charleston that Natalie's entourage from France had arrived. She summoned servants and returned
to Charleston, where she would occupy the townhouse Colonel William had recently deeded to them.

It was a handsome brick home on Church Street with elaborate
interior moldings and a towering three-story staircase. Her little boy
delighted in standing in the entry hall and looking upward into the
swirling space until he staggered, pleasantly dizzy and full of giggles,
into her arms.

Theodosia was the happiest of hostesses. She and Natalie were
together again, and for the first time since her marriage, she was
entertaining in her own home. Colonel Alston had earlier sent over a
contingent of slaves to see to the Sumters' needs. They were unpacked
and eagerly waiting the Alstons when they arrived.

"Oh, my sister. My sister!" Natalie embraced Theodosia, kissing her
face over and over in the French manner. "You are thinner and still
so beautiful, Theo. I am happy. So happy!" The two spun about like
children, breaking apart only to hold and cuddle each other's babies.

Soon they were caught up in the whirlwind of Charleston society
at the height of the social season. It began every year in late fall. The
Georgetown planters moved to their Charleston homes, celebrating
weddings and attending musicales, masquerade parties, soirees, and
debutante balls.

Though always accompanied by what seemed to Natalie a small
army of servants, the two young women felt free as they moved
through the holiday-decorated streets, made the rounds of parties
in homes that wore festive necklaces of pine garlands and glowed
pediment-to-street with candlelight.

But too soon it was time to leave Charleston and return to their
plantations for Christmas.

"You must come to The Oaks as soon as we are able to move in,"

Theodosia told Natalie as they departed. Joseph wanted to spend Christmas on the Waccamaw even though they remained guests at Hagley. The Sumters were eager to see the High Hills of Santee area in Stateburg southeast of Columbia, and nearby Home House, the plantation that Sumter's father had prepared for them.

Theodosia wrote to her father in December:
The people of Charleston paid Natalie every possible attention. Mr. Sumter is very affectionate and attentive to her, and he was polite to me. I like him. He is an amiable, good-hearted man with talents to render him respectable.

Theodosia and Natalie each had a good husband and a baby as they had dreamed of as girls, but their youthful fantasies excluded the realities of separation, isolation, and compromise. However, Theodosia, renewed by the bustle of Charleston activity and precious time spent with Natalie, returned to her husband's beloved home determined to be a more amicable member of the Alston family. Love asked for her very best effort. Duty demanded it.

CHAPTER 44

∽⚬⚬∼

Finally in March 1804, three years after Theodosia and Joseph married, the renovation of The Oaks was completed. It had dragged on for so long Theodosia had sometimes feared this day would not come.

The spirited Alston clan traveled the ten miles from Hagley to The Oaks in Joseph and Theodosia's new carriage. Peet skillfully guided the horses, singing at the top of his lungs, periodically joined by Tilda, her mother, Mae, and M'aum Hattie in a second carriage.

We will have quite enough assistance with only these four faithful people, whom I have come to love so dearly, Theodosia had written to Burr. *The women will share the roomy new kitchen house. Peet has been promoted to butler and overseer and will have his own cottage just outside the main house.*

Another lively group followed the two carriages, filled with more than fifty slaves who would work the fields. Some rode horses, others drove wagons overflowing with possessions and supplies. Most of the children were on foot.

Joseph entered the house first and Theodosia followed, carrying their son. She set the child down on the polished heart pine floor in the hall, and he began to explore, laughing and chattering. He was an intelligent and charming boy with dark Burr eyes, strangely prodigious in a cherubic face framed by golden curls.

Theodosia handed him a small framed portrait of her father. "This is Grand-pa, sweetest. Grand Pa. Can you say Grandpa?" The boy stared at the image, struggling hard to imitate his mother. "Ga...Ga, Gampy!" Pleased with himself, he broke into his sunniest smile.

Theodosia scooped him up in her arms. "Gampy, indeed. Your Gampy is Aaron Burr. You are Aaron Burr Alston!"

She pointed to Burr's portrait. "Gampy."

The child touched his own face, laughing. "Gampy!"

Theodosia persisted. "You are Aaron Burr Alston...he is Gampy."

Shaking his head emphatically, the child returned to the portrait to his mother. "Me, Gampy, too!"

His father joined them, and Theodosia proudly reviewed their conversation.

"He knows his name is the same as Papa's, but he cannot quite say Grandpa. He wants them both to be "Gampy!"

Joseph was not taken with the nickname, but he gave into it when he saw his son's excitement. He managed a smile and slowly removed a letter from his pocket. "Speaking of 'Big Gampy....'"

Theodosia snatched the letter and read out loud.

Richmond Hill, New York. March 28, 1804

We are busy here with the Governor's race. If you would be busy, you might have taught A.B.A. his ABCs before this. God mend you. By now, he should be acquiring a knowledge of natural history, botany, and chemistry, as well as language.

CHAPTER 45

I n New York, eight men left their dining table and filed out to an adjoining parlor. Alexander Hamilton accepted a snifter of brandy and reached in his pocket for a cigar.

"Dr. Cooper, this election is crucial not just for New York but for our union. If Burr is elected, it will be in serious jeopardy! The little bastard wishes to be King of Something, at any cost!"

"Strong words, General," answered the doctor. "Burr receives much support from your Federalists."

"Only the conservative faction, sir," Hamilton retorted. "And I am truly ashamed of them. I can assure you the majority does not agree."

"Well, General, you have certainly done your part to spread the news. Not a day passes that I do not see you quoted in the papers, thoroughly thrashing Colonel Burr. If half of what you say is true, we have a monster in our midst."

"Dr. Cooper, I am a courageous man, but as yet I have not been bold enough to put in print all I know about Aaron Burr. He represents everything that is evil; he is truly despicable. He...."

Hamilton lowered his voice to a near whisper. There was more, so very unspeakable in Hamilton's mind that his companions had to move close to hear it.

The next morning, William Van Ness was appalled as he read his copy of the *Albany Register*. He did not wait to finish the article, but called for his horse and covered quickly the distance between his home and Richmond Hill.

Burr opened the door himself. "William! Come in; come in; a pleasure as always!"

Van Ness shoved the *Register* at Burr.

"Perhaps not, Aaron, when you see what I bring you. General Hamilton has called you despicable. Already there are outrageous opinions about just what he meant. I have heard discussions in the street as I traveled here. Read the letter from Dr. Cooper. These statements were made in important company, Aaron. It is a disgrace."

Burr read the letter as the two men retired to the library. When he finished, he sighed and seemed sadder than usual. Resigned.

"General Hamilton has accused me of private misconduct, lack of integrity, and readiness for treason. But now I believe he speaks of dishonor, William. It will cost me the election."

Van Ness agreed. "Possibly. There is scarcely time to refute the rumors that already abound."

"If I lose, William, I will challenge him. Honor demands it. If that time comes, will you take the letter to him, my friend?"

Sadness creased Van Ness's face. He nodded.

"And if we should take up arms against one another, Hamilton and I, will you accompany me, serve as my 'second' on the field of honor?"

"For nothing but save loyalty, Aaron. All else in me rejects it. But you know I will."

CHAPTER 46

Burr was soundly defeated in the gubernatorial election, and he blamed Hamilton's surreptitious disclosure to Dr. Cooper. His bitter disappointment boiled out in his first of several letters to Hamilton.

"The first offense requires the first apology," he said to Van Ness, "so go, take this to Hamilton, and we shall see if Hamilton comes to his senses. Such as they are."

Richmond Hill. June 18, 1804
General Hamilton, you must perceive, sir, the necessity of a prompt and unqualified acknowledgment, or denial, of the opinions you expressed to Dr. Cooper.

Van Ness delivered the note to the Grange, Hamilton's home. The next day, Nathaniel Pendleton, a friend and legal colleague of Hamilton's rode out to Richmond Hill with the reply.

The Grange. June 22, 1804
Your letter, in a style too arrogant, made an unprecedented and unwarrantable demand. I have no answer to it.

Burr countered in two days.

Richmond Hill. June 24, 1804
A definite reply to my letter is requested. The necessity for an interview will not be diminished by anything short of an apology.

Burr read Hamilton's next reply to Van Ness aloud by candlelight in his library, his words echoing in the almost-empty room:

The Grange. July 1, 1804
Sir, I cannot imagine to what Dr. Cooper may have alluded nor can I

recall the particulars of that conversation. To the best of my recollection, my remarks consisted only of comments on your political principles and views, and what might be expected if you were elected Governor. Your obedient slave, Alexander Hamilton.

Van Ness stared through a dusty window into a moonless night wondering how things had come to such frightful discord.

Burr fingered the parchment for a long time. With a wry smile, he stood and walked over to his gun cabinet, opened it, and removed a pistol. His fingers slid up and down the short barrel then moved to the elaborately carved handle.

Van Ness watched him for a time, and then, unable to shake the unbearable tension, his gaze shifted once more to the window. All he saw was blackness. "Aaron, let me go to Pendleton. Between us, we can perhaps resolve these differences."

"Nonsense, William. You are too sensible a man to entertain such an idea. This statement of Hamilton's...."

Van Ness interrupted. "Very few are even certain of what he said, Aaron. Let it lie. You will come out the victor in principle."

Burr shook his head. "You are my social equal, the only friend I have who can properly serve as my second. But if I have to, I will choose another. Never mind you have already given your word."

Van Ness was no match for Burr's sentimentality, however slight, and for the plea in his unwavering eyes, dark as slate and every bit as cold.

"My heart protests, Aaron, but my words will stand."

CHAPTER 47

Later that evening in New York, Burr visited the Queen's Head Tavern on the corner of Broad and Pearl streets. He liked frequenting the place where George Washington said good-bye to his officers in December 1783, even though he had not been invited to the ceremony.

That evening he was there to attend the annual meeting of the Society of the Cincinnati, founded by Continental Army officers twenty-one years before. Only men who had served as commissioned officers in the Continental Army or Navy during the Revolutionary War were eligible for membership. Its founders chose the name Cincinnati because of Lucius Quinctius Cincinnatus, a Roman statesman and general who epitomized patriotism. George Washington had been the Society's first president, and now it was Alexander Hamilton. Burr was just two seats away from him at dinner.

Following the meal, one of the members had a request. "A most memorable evening, my friends. Before we close, will General Hamilton do us the honor of singing 'The Drum'?"

Hamilton chortled. "A certain prescription for indigestion, my friend. But...if you insist."

He rose, cleared his throat, and sang in a clear tenor.

We're going to war
And when we die,
We'll want a man
Of God nearby.

When his song was finished, Burr's seat was empty.

CHAPTER 48

Richmond Hill, New York. July 10, 1804
Dear Joseph,
I have called out General Hamilton. We will meet tomorrow. If it should be my lot to fall, I shall live in you and your son. I commit to you all that is most dear to me — my reputation and my daughter. Aid Theodosia in the cultivation of her mind. Let her acquire knowledge of many languages and all branches of natural philosophy. In time, all this will be poured into your son. If you should differ with me as to the importance of this, suffer me to ask it of you as a last favor.

Burr sealed his letter into an envelope with wax and began another one. This task was harder. He agonized over every word.

I am indebted to you, my dearest Theodosia, for a very great portion of the happiness which I have enjoyed in this life. You have completely satisfied all that my heart and affections had hoped or even wished. With a little more perseverance, determination, and industry, you will obtain all that my ambition or vanity had fondly imagined. Let your son have occasion to be proud that he had such a mother.
Adieu. Adieu.

As Burr wrote, the Alston women — Mary Motte, Mary, Charlotte, Maria, Sally, and Theodosia — were on an outing, walking along the beach under colorful parasols. A group of children ran ahead of them, herded by Tilda and several others. Little Gampy, as Aaron Burr Alston had come to be known to all, struggled to keep up with the older children, often falling behind when he stopped to examine objects brought to shore by the tide.

Theodosia was preoccupied, plagued since the loss of Burr's election by unrelenting anxiety and feelings of helplessness. Burr had made light of his defeat, but she knew better. His long-festering hatred for Hamilton was swelling to near-rupture, and there was nothing she could do.

She lagged behind the others, gazing out to sea. It comforted her to look at the Atlantic Ocean and know it reached all the way to New York, curved into the furrow of its harbor and lapped against the edges of the lawn at Richmond Hill. Her hands trembled as she shaded her eyes. Her legs felt numb and weak.

Little Gampy toddled to her and wrapped his arms around her knees, but she appeared unaware of his presence. The other women stopped and looked back, perplexed as they often were by Theodosia and her mysterious moods.

Despite the exercise and fresh air, Theodosia tossed fitfully most of that night. When first light slipped into the room and fell across her face, she awakened from a troubled semi-sleep with a piercing cry. Joseph took her in his arms and held her hard against him.

"Theodosia, dearest, what is it?"

"Papa!" she screamed. "Papa! My God! My God!"

She could not see the thin haze hovering above the Hudson River or the oarsman maneuvering a skiff silently through the mist. Nor could she see Van Ness sitting at the back and Burr standing at the bow facing squarely what the day would bring.

The mist lifted slowly, and Burr saw Hamilton's skiff cutting through the same waters, the rising blood-red sun behind him. With Hamilton were Pendleton, his second, and Dr. David Hosack, a physician whom Theodosia had entertained at Richmond Hill.

Both boats neared the New Jersey Palisades, the dark, high precipices Theodosia admired. Burr's boat reached the shore of Weehawken first. He and Van Ness scrambled up a steep cliff to a rocky ledge, accessible only by foot from the shore. Just 6 feet wide and 30- to 40-feet long, it was an often-used dueling spot.

Burr and Van Ness walked to one end, Hamilton and Pendleton to the other. Dr. Hosack centered himself between the two.

The adversaries and their seconds turned to face each other. Burr raised his pistol slightly and rubbed the barrel. Hamilton moved his pistol to eye level, lowered it, reached into his vest for his glasses, wiped the lenses with his handkerchief and put them on. He nodded to Pendleton.

Both men raised their weapons.

Van Ness's voice was clear and steady.

"Are you ready?"

Hamilton replied with cold composure.

"I am, sir."

Burr responded.

"I stand ready."

"Pre-*sent!*"

Theodosia shuddered in her sleep. She dreamed of a loud crack and two simultaneous shots. She also saw Hamilton fall to one side and clutch his abdomen, moaning softly, the doctor rushing to him, kneeling and unfastening his belt and his pants, exposing a gaping, bloody wound.

The sun climbed higher in Weehawken as Burr took a few tentative steps toward Hamilton. Van Ness stopped him, guiding him toward the ledge's rim. Burr allowed himself to be pulled along but his eyes remained on Hamilton until, as he descended, the sharp edge of the precipice severed the consequences of the duel.

Hamilton was still but conscious. Pendleton gently elevated his head and bent close to hear his labored words. "It is a mortal wound, Pendleton."

Below, Burr's oarsman was already in position. The men climbed into the skiff, and with Burr still fixated on the ledge above, they crossed the Hudson River, now blazing with light from the rising sun.

"Papa!" Theodosia continued to cry. "Papa! My God! My God!"

CHAPTER 49

November 1804

In the newly decorated parlor of The Oaks, Joseph and Algernon shared an early-morning cup of tea before riding out to the ricefields.

Algernon was concerned for his brother and Theodosia, knowing she was not physically strong. He suspected she was distraught about the news that trickled in from New York over many weeks.

"How is she, Joseph?"

"Not well, Algernon. We still have not talked about the duel, but she knows. Letters have come, and the newspapers. I don't know what she reads, but she has said nothing. She seldom eats. Her sleep is fitful."

"What is the latest news from New York?"

"General Hamilton is a hero in death. Most feel the duel was fair, but the public has demanded a villain, and as the survivor, Colonel Burr has the distinction. Listen to the words of this song, which is being sung in the streets of New York:

Oh Burr, O Burr what has thou done?
Thou hast shooted dead great Hamilton.
You hid behind a bunch of thistle,
And shooted him dead with a great hoss pistol.

Algernon grimaced, shaking his head. "T'would be humorous if we were not so negatively affected. A despicable thing, dueling."

His brother nodded his agreement. "Indeed! General Hamilton's own son was killed in a duel, and his daughter completely lost her senses after that. You would think he would have avoided this at all cost. He not only accepted the challenge, but he might have actually fired, as well as Colonel Burr. Some say Hamilton took the first shot; others say he threw it away. Others say Burr fired first. No one will ever know the truth."

Joseph stood and put down his cup. "But what difference does it

140

make? One man is dead, another a fugitive. It appears both men fell on the so-called 'field of honor.'"

Peet, promoted by Theodosia from field worker to house servant at The Oaks, entered the room with a letter. "Fo' you, suh."

Joseph saw it was from Burr and read it aloud:

You will find the papers filled with all manner of nonsense and lies; even accounts of attempts to assassinate me. I assure you, these are fables. Those who wish me dead prefer to keep a very respectful distance. I walk and ride about as free as usual. I was in Philadelphia, hoping passions would subside in New York where I have been indicted for willful murder!

"My God, I cannot believe it!" Algernon exclaimed. "Is there more?

"Yes...he goes on:

I had warnings of an indictment in New Jersey as well, so I left Pennsylvania and have joined my friend, Pierce Butler, on St. Simons Island off the coast of Georgia.

"Brother, can you conceive of it? The Vice President of the United States a fugitive from justice?"

Footsteps drew the men's attention to the staircase. Theodosia descended slowly, gripping the banister. She was in bedclothes, unaware her breasts were almost totally exposed. Her hair was unkempt, a dull-rust rivulet over her face, her eyes dull, sunken, and ringed with dark circles.

Algernon glanced away as Joseph rushed to rearrange her nightclothes. He led her to a chair and helped her to sit. Her lips were parched, her voice thin and barely audible. "A fugitive, dear God. Oh, Papa."

She sighed as she twisted her hair through her fingers. "He killed him, then? General Hamilton? I feared he would challenge him, Joseph. He could not bear the defeat in the election and the empty future that lay ahead. He could not resist retaliation."

Joseph nodded. Theodosia reached for a fan from a table nearby. "Burrs must be occupied, or they burn inside."

She slowly moved the fan back and forth across her damp and flushed face. "There are many kinds of duels, dear husband, dear brother. From without, from within. Which is worse, after all? To quickly kill a visible enemy, or like myself, to battle and surrender over and over in an inner war?"

She covered her face with her hands. "Oh, Joseph, had I been there, perhaps...."

"No, Theo!" he said. "You could have done nothing to prevent this."

She sagged against him. "Joseph, what will become of dear Peggy and Alexis?"

"Your father has freed them, dearest. They have left to make their own way."

"Freed them? Oh how I wish I could find them and ask how it feels to be free."

Joseph helped her up the stairs and into her bed.

Later that day she tossed feverishly while Tilda mopped her brow. Theodosia heard voices — some strange and menacing, others familiar. Troubled wakefulness bridged bouts of merciless dreams.

Your anxieties about me indicate that you are not well, she heard her father lament. *I fear that the climate, or some other cause, has affected both your mind and your body.*

"Papa," she moaned

"Missus...." Tilda said.

"Peggy, oh, Peggy!" Theodosia cried.

Tilda was frantic. She urged her mistress to stand and helped her outside, hoping a walk might restore her. But Theodosia continued to hallucinate, staring at an apparition of Peggy standing beneath a huge oak tree. A dense mist clung to Theodosia as she spoke in a voice that seemed to come from a great distance.

"When you sees happiness in this world, grab onto it, hold it tight. Hold your freedom, too, girl. It will keep you strong."

Tilda steered her mistress back inside the house and into her bed. Still lulled by the voice she thought was Peggy's, Theodosia's restless thoughts left her and allowed her to sleep. She dreamed of a time when she worried only about her lessons, proper menus, a choice of gowns, and stabling Wind in time to be prompt at the dinner table with Papa.

She smiled as she waked.

Oh, the duel was a dream, just a nightmare after all. There was no eruption of loathing. No journey of vengeance to the high Palisades. No death of hopes and honor.

But consciousness brought reality. Pain seared her heart as completely as it had when she learned that Burr killed General Hamilton. She had never before known such helplessness. Now she seemed unable to help herself; that was unforgivable enough.

But if she could not lead Burr from this path of destruction it would be inexcusable. There was solace only in oblivion. She slept again.

CHAPTER 50

Burrs do not admit defeat.

The mantra that destroyed the future for Aaron Burr sustained Theodosia, and she gathered strength. Copious letters from her father eased her mind. Sometimes several came at one time. She was weak and spent a great deal of time in her bed, but she was again inspired to write in her journal:

The Oaks, South Carolina. December 1804

Papa seems to thrive in Georgia and writes that he plans to visit the Floridas for several weeks. I so wish that he had stopped here when traveling south, but it was not to be. I suppose it was somewhat out of his way, but it is agony knowing that he passed somewhere within a day's journey to me and we had no reunion. Impatience was his excuse as he had received an invitation from Major Butler at St. Simon's. Joseph says that Papa wanted to arrive before the Major changed his mind, but I would hear none of that!

CHAPTER 51

Fall 1804

Theodosia tied her hair back with a yellow ribbon and patted a space beside her on the bed. Gampy snuggled eagerly into her side, curling contentedly into the crook of her arm as she read to him.

"Four letters from Big Gamp today! He says all is well at St. Simons, that they have plenty of milk, butter, fowls, pigs, geese, and mutton."

"Mutton?"

"That's a little lamb, sweetheart, all grown up. Now listen to this:

"I am constantly discovering new luxuries for my table. I have offered a reward to anyone who will bring me an alligator, which I mean to eat!"

The child broke into gales of laughter as Theodosia said, "He plans to eat this alligator in soup, in fricassees, and in steaks. He says he knows how much we would want to help him with this meal."

Gampy made a sour face and shook his head.

"Where is Big Gamp?"

"Not so far from here, in Georgia. He wants me to tell you about Mexico. It's a place to the south owned by another country far away across the ocean called Spain."

Joseph appeared at the doorway and stopped to listen.

"Our country may go to war with Spain soon. General Wilkinson — he's the Commander of the *wh-o-ole* U.S. Army — has talked to your grandfather about helping him take Mexico away from Spain and make it a part of our country!"

She stopped to hold the child closer, charmed by his wide-eyed amazement. Neither had noticed the frowning Joseph, still in the doorway.

"He says he could become the leader of the new state, and that he would want us to be with him."

"Like a king and queen?" Gampy asked, wriggling with excitement.

"Well, he is thinking of something like that, I suppose."

The child jumped from the bed, clapping his hands. He snatched a small book from the bedside table and tried to balance it on his head. Theodosia began to worry. *A kingdom? Is that what Papa is thinking?*

Sinking back against the pillows, she remembered snuggling beneath her own mother's arm that last time. She knew that loving a man who is not always rational is a difficult thing. She heard her mother's voice instructing her, *"You must...." Mama, just what did you ask of me?*

Gampy was beside himself trying to snare her attention with his dancing and shouting. "My crown, Mama, my crown!"

The boy saw his father and ran toward him holding the book on his head. "Papa, look at me!"

The book fell, and the child picked it up and handed it to him. "My crown, Papa. Crown me, Papa! Make me a king, just like in a book!"

Joseph returned the book to its place.

"That's right, son," he said firmly. "It's a story, not real life. Your kingdom is The Oaks Plantation, right here on the Waccamaw. And speaking of our kingdom, young man, there's a nip in the air and the crop is in. Plenty of time today for a ride."

"Can I go, Papa, please? May I, Papa?"

"It seems a good idea, especially, of course, if Mama will come along. What says Theodosia?"

She rose quickly. "A ride! Oh yes! The air should do me good, I think. No humidity. And finally, no insects!"

Joseph and Theodosia rode into their fields with Gampy between them on his pony. Shorn of its rice plants, the ground was flat. They could see the river, and if they stood in their stirrups, the ocean. The creeks, thick with rotted marsh grass, drained listlessly toward the Waccamaw River. Only a few weeks before, torches burned late into every night so that the slaves could see how to shelve the newly cut rice sheaves.

"The field slaves cut the rice with sickles," Joseph explained to his son. "Then they laid the stalks on the stubble to dry for a day or so, tied them in sheaves, and stored them in the barnyard."

"I remember." Gampy responded. "I could see the barn lanterns from my room."

"Ah!" Joseph recalled falling asleep as a boy in a room blazing with light. He got up early to watch the changes in marsh, creek, river, and ocean as the lanterns' fading reflection gave way to a mauve sky. A gentle breeze often whispered through the marsh grass, and he could forget the sun would soon suck its green away. It never failed to exhilarate him.

Returning from the fields, the Alstons heard the sounds from the threshing areas where the rice kernels were hulled and polished by hand. The slave women pounded the particles with wooden mortars and pestles, singing in rhythm with their hammering.

Brother, you shoulda been dere.
Yes, my Lord.
Sittin' in da Kingdom. Hearin' Jordan roll.

CHAPTER 52

⁓⁓⁓

The weather was cool when they returned to Charleston. This, combined with a planned visit inland to Natalie at the Sumters' Home House, further revitalized Theodosia. When Burr wrote he would be joining Theodosia there, she was thrilled.

"Tilda, I must have a new outfit. Red. Not scarlet, but darker — the color of wine, like Colonial William's Madeira! Will you cut the pattern, dear? I shall go to the wharf and see what fabrics the ships have brought. Velvet would be nice, don't you think?"

"Trim with black ribbon, missus? A big hat, match de dress. Shiny black ribbon bow on de side."

"Oh perfect, Tilda. But put away the pattern paper and come with me. We shall choose fabric for you as well."

"How gwine make it?"

"How? Are you asking that of me, the one called 'masculine' because I know nothing of sewing and cooking?"

"N'om. Don' mean how to make it. I mean...how you want mine to be?"

Theodosia took Tilda's hands in hers, a gesture that had terrified the slave girl when they met. Now she was accustomed to the gesture, warmed to it even. Her eyes shone like polished black river stones when she realized Theodosia wished her to design her own dress.

"Tilda, you make it just as you want. The color you want, the fabric you love, in a style that will make you look even more beautiful than you are already."

The two made their way through dust and foul puddles on Market Street in Charleston, an area rimmed with meat vendors. Vultures hoping for a meal hovered above the blood-splattered men. One of the butchers heaved a hindquarter of beef onto a worn wooden table. *Whack!*

He severed a thigh from the foreleg with a large cleaver, and a gull dipped just overhead, screaming with excitement. The man threw a piece of blue-white sinew into the air, and the gull grabbed it and flew quickly away, escaping the vultures. Theodosia shuddered and increased her pace.

Two ships had docked that day, and the market was a parade of excited women, determined to find not just cloth for dresses and bonnets, but hair combs, fans, shoe buckles, and perfume. Tilda chose gold silk and decided to trim her dress in black ribbon. Some of the slaves would be jealous and hateful to her, she knew. *But I be gwine to Home House! House girls there be scaid'a me, cause I from Off'n dress up fancy. Missus and me, we gwine look grand. We is grand.*

CHAPTER 53

~~∞~~✑~

Duty-bound even in disgrace, Burr wished to return to Washington and the Senate. But for now he had the promise from friends in Savannah of a sturdy horse that would take him to the High Hills of the Santee River in South Carolina.

Theodosia set off for the same destination with Gampy and a carriage filled with their belongings and gifts for Natalie and her little girl, "Nat." She and Tilda sang raucously during the three-day trip, joined by Gampy and sometimes the driver. As evening approached, they tempered their voices and sang sweet lullabies to the little boy until his eyes fluttered heavily. Finally, his golden curls sank quietly to Tilda's shoulder.

Upon arrival, Theodosia and Natalie saw each other simultaneously: Natalie framed by a wide window at Home House, and Theodosia waving frantically as her carriage bumped and swayed up the driveway. Tilda grabbed her mistress's arm fearing Theodosia would jump from the carriage before it came to a stop.

Soon Natalie and Theodosia hugged and squealed like children.

"I was unable to accomplish any of the chores I planned for today," Natalie exclaimed. "I have spent hours at the window instead!"

"I saw you there," Theodosia said, "like a beautiful portrait, framed in blue by the drapery!"

Natalie ushered her guest upstairs and into the guest quarters while Tilda tried to disengage Gampy from her skirts and persuade him to take the hand of Natalie's little girl.

Burr arrived several days later, and to Theodosia's dismay, his visit was short, only six days.

"I refuse to end my office in defeat, skulking off like some beaten animal," he vowed to his daughter soon after their reunion. "I will preside over the Senate as I am eligible to do this last time, and in March, when my term as Vice President is nearly over, I shall resign."

The Sumters had a grand dinner that evening, and Burr was quite taken with the Southern women. He toasted them in his usual courtly manner. "Men I have ever found treacherous, but women? Ah, they can be counted on to sustain in adversity, giving a charm to life without which it is not worth possessing."

The men raised their glasses to the pleased group of women around the table. Fine crystal pealed like tiny bells as the servants placed fresh wine glasses beside the dessert plates.

All were enthralled by Burr's majesty, thrilled to be in the presence of the man who spoke so eloquently and was, after all, still the Vice President of the United States.

"So let us drink," Burr continued. "Though one may be poorer for drinking good wine, he is, under its influence, much more able to bear poverty."

Burr had no idea at this point just how poor he was. Word had not reached him that his creditors had confiscated Richmond Hill with all its furnishings, and John Jacob Astor had purchased it for only $25,000.

Later there was dancing to a string quartet, and some of the guests walked out onto the porches to enjoy an Indian summer sunset. Natalie took Theodosia's arm and led her through the house and upstairs to a balcony, away from the music and the "oohs and ahhs" of her visitors. "God's boldest artist is at work," she whispered.

"Ah, yes," Theodosia agreed as the two stood quietly in a seamless bowl of yellow. "It is as though someone with a paintbrush as large as the moon is using the sky as his canvas."

Theodosia soon whispered, "Natalie, look at us, at our gowns and the skin on our arms. We are bathed in gold!"

Natalie took Theodosia's hand. "Theo, this is a good omen. Our friendship has always been like gold — precious and enduring. I pray that we will reunite often as we grow older; that our children will become friends. Some of them, perhaps, even mates!"

"I cannot recall a happier moment in my life," Theodosia said. "When we are lonely, let us always think of it. We could not be unhappy, remembering this time."

The sun dropped quickly beneath the horizon and a dark cloud coiled over the brilliance that had bathed them in amber moments before. Theodosia seized Natalie's shoulders, trembling as she often did when the fever and gnawing pain that often ailed her returned.

Natalie gently took her hands. An owl called out loudly in the tall pines behind them. "Theo, dearest. Your hands are like ice."

Theodosia shuddered. "The Negroes say the owl is a death bird."

"Theo, you have been too long alone. Listen to me. We are young. You must get well. And when we remember this time, this moment, we will know we have each other, and we will, always."

The owl cried out again. Natalie shuddered, suddenly less confident about her prediction. Perhaps there had been no good omen.

She was right. Circumstances the young women could not portend spoiled their hopes of ongoing reunions. Thomas Sumter Jr. was offered a diplomatic post in the Portuguese colony of Brazil. They left for Rio de Janeiro in 1809, and Natalie did not return to South Carolina for eleven years. The devoted "sisters" never saw each other again.

CHAPTER 54

Theodosia returned to the Waccamaw saddened by her goodbyes to Burr and Natalie and exhausted from the overland trip from Stateburg to the coast. She had always been happiest at dawn. Now, as winter closed in, a cold wind whipped the long tendrils of moss into a frenzied dance, cones fell from the tall pines, and she found herself unwilling to leave her bed. Her torpor worsened when she heard of the loss of Richmond Hill.

The home had been her anchor, her refuge, a treasure chest of memories from her childhood: her happy growing-up years and courtship. As a very young woman she had entertained royalty and dignitaries at Richmond Hill. Since her marriage, it was a place of retreat to refresh her energies and spirit.

She thought of the gardens, the mammoth trees, the rush she felt when she looked over the Hudson, exhilarated by its ongoing clash with the tides, soothed by the great green hills of New Jersey beyond. And the stables. *Oh, Wind, did they take you, too?*

She would never ride again to her special place along the Hudson River. Sorrow intensified her physical distress. An attack of "inflammatory rheumatism" assailed her, followed by a fall in which she injured her spine. She was bedridden for three months, her body almost motionless but her mind spinning her into a fever of anxiety.

Tilda was uneasy, too. She feared her mistress might give up and lose the vitality that was her trademark — the spark the mayor of New York jokingly said could blow up a ship.

"Missus, you gots to walk. Here, hol' my hand. I keep you up."

The women walked slowly on the grounds of The Oaks, but Theodosia saw little.

She leaned heavily on Tilda, who sang:
> There is balm in Gilead,
> To make the wounded whole;
> There's power enough in heaven,
> To cure a sin-sick soul.

"Peggy!" cried Theodosia.

Tilda tried to hustle her mistress back to the house, but Theodosia was rooted to the spot, her mind projecting images no one but she could see.

"Peggy! Oh, Peggy!"

Theodosia, secure in her sweet vision, noticed little of her surroundings. Her face dripped perspiration, and Tilda dabbed at her cheeks.

Gampy, returning from an outing with his nanny, M'aum Hattie, joined them, ecstatic to see his mother out of bed. He jumped about and cried out to her, but she barely noticed him. He picked up a stone. "Watch how far I can throw, Mama!"

He pitched the stone, leaping with glee.

"Good throw, Mas' Gampy," Tilda said. "Made your mama proud."

The day was unusually humid for winter, but Theodosia pulled a shawl close about her. "It's so cold, Tilda."

Frowning, Tilda felt her mistress's brow. With a sudden urgency, Theodosia turned to face her and grasped her arms with trembling hands. "Tilda, this is important."

Gampy raced here and there, choosing more stones to throw.

"Go way out, Mas' Gampy. Lotsa good stones on the bank yonder," Tilda called out to him.

The child laughed and ran swiftly toward a rice paddy in the distance. Theodosia tottered, held tightly to Tilda and tears spilled down her cheeks.

"Tilda, say nothing of this to anyone. Something whispers to me that my end approaches."

"Missus' no! Don't...."

Theodosia interrupted. "I feel I stand on the brink of eternity. I must tell you these things before I leave you."

Tilda shook her head. "No, Miss Theo...."

"Do not be frightened. Listen to me. When I am gone, remind Master Joseph of his love for little Gampy. Tell him he must love him for me also. Death is not welcome to me. My loved ones have made me too fond of life. Tell Master Joseph to let my father see my son sometimes. I beg him to be kind towards him whom I have loved so much. Pray see to this."

Gampy's hair glowed in the sun as he dashed about continuing his search for just the right pitching stones. Farther along, he found a dead sea bird, its neck twisted, and its white wings spread wide. He stooped to look closer, confused and sad. He stroked the bird's head, caressed its body and wings, and moved its body slightly as though he could make it more comfortable.

Theodosia slumped toward Tilda. Then she gathered strength and stood erect, taking hold of Tilda's shoulders, staring intently into her face.

"Tilda, this may seem strange to you, but it is important. I beg to be kept as long as possible before I am buried — and do not allow me to be stripped and washed, as is usual. I am pure enough to return as I am to dust. Why, then, expose my body?"

She grew more agitated. "Pray see to this."

Tilda nodded, but Theodosia was not placated. "I hope for happiness in the next world, for I have not been a bad person in this one."

"Shush, missus. It be all right."

Both women wept now, struggling to compose themselves as they saw Gampy in the distance, his chubby legs pumping eagerly toward them.

Theodosia ended her plea quickly so that he would not hear. "Tilda, please, pray that someone will remember me!"

CHAPTER 55

In March 1805, two days before his term as Vice President expired, Burr formally resigned as President of the Senate. He moved through the crowd on the Senate floor, stopping here and there to greet old friends as they took their seats, mounted the podium with confidence, arranged his notes and began his address.

"I have come this evening, gentlemen, to bid you farewell. I know I must have, at times, wounded your feelings. As for myself, however, I have no injuries of which to complain. I thank God I have no memory for injuries."

He put down his notes, and spoke extemporaneously, his dark eyes boring into the audience.

"This house, I need not remind you, is a sanctuary, a citadel of law, of order, and of liberty. It is here that resistance will be made to the storms of political frenzy and the silent arts of corruption. And if the Constitution be destined ever to perish, which God avert, its expiring agonies will be witnessed on this floor."

His unexpected candidness moved many to tears. The newspapers finally had positive things to say about Aaron Burr. Theodosia's determination to recover was boosted by his improved public image. She walked daily with Tilda. The cold of the winter seemed to re-energize her and brought some relief from her symptoms.

"The Washington papers are calling his resignation speech the most dignified, sublime and impressive ever uttered," she told her husband. "The whole Senate wept!"

"Well, we know, of course, that he can charm," Joseph replied. "And I know that irresistible charm runs in the family!"

Theodosia's short laugh was obligatory. She was too worried for joking.

"Joseph, we know the press is erratic. Papa must leave politics now while his reputation is at last partly restored. He could come live here as a retired statesman; live like his esteemed Lord Chesterfield. Help me convince him, Joseph! Please! Public life can do nothing but harm Papa now."

Joseph laughed.

"Ha! Chesterfield himself was not more Chesterfieldian than Aaron Burr fancies himself. But it is not just his perfectionism that worries me. Two restless Burrs may be more than this man could handle! But even if I thought I could, it is too late. Remember Commander-in-Chief Wilkinson? He is urging your father forward in his plan to conquer Mexico."

"But Joseph, I hear there is no longer threat of a war with Spain."

"I know, Theo."

"Conquering Mexico for the United States is one thing. But if Papa still has ideas of forming his own nation in Mexico, and if any of the country goes with him, some will say...."

"Most will say it, Theodosia. Treason."

CHAPTER 56

⁓

The Oaks, South Carolina. April 23, 1805
So much of the last few months have been a blur. I recall little of it, actually. I was so feverish that perspiration dampened my sheets constantly, and Tilda changed my bed linens several times a day.

Poor Gampy. His mama lay in bed and had no energy to be up and about with him. I remember the women coming to The Oaks. Mother Motte and Sally. Mary, too, I think, and all of their dear little ones.

They sang just outside my bedroom door. I remember but one of the songs. Sally's little Mary Ashe sang, "Leave My Heart With Thee," in the loveliest voice, so bell-like, clear and pure. Tears came to my eyes, and I was relieved to be feeling something after weeks of experiencing no emotion at all.

True melancholy is not, I believe, only sadness, but rather a profound numbing of the soul. Far more frightening than sorrow. I was separated from anything that mattered to me before. I was in every sense, alone.

Laudanum is partly responsible, I imagine, and I suppose I was given much of it at times. Before the numbness set in, I would weep a great deal, sometimes because of pain, other times for relief from a terrible nervous anxiety.

But then my soul suffered a paralysis. I felt that nothing could move, though, of course, my heart kept beating, and I breathed in and breathed out. I was prisoner to a lack of will to live so profound that nothing seemed worth any effort at all. I had neither the strength nor the intelligence to reconnect. I was nobody at all.

Theodosia spent as much time as she could at the Castle on the beach at DeBordieu. The ocean seemed to heal her, distracted her from the fear she might be terminally ill. She felt stronger, her appetite was restored, and she walked for miles along the edge of the waves, often removing her shoes when alone, reveling in the feel of velvet-soft sand. She lifted her skirts and let the cool salt water break over her ankles. The retreating surf carried off her tension and pain.

She took M'aum Hattie, Peet, and Tilda to the beach, and she alone cared for Gampy. Every day Peet hauled in nets bulging with shrimp from the creek, and sometimes the women peeled them for hours. Peet taught Gampy to catch and boil crabs and how to pick out the sweet white meat. All of them fished and enjoyed meals of flounder and bass.

Tilda and Peet picked wild strawberries and poke salad plants and gathered firewood to keep the cottage cozy. He shored up the old structure, taught Tilda and Theodosia to brandish a hammer, and together they patched up places where chilly gusts from the sea found their way inside.

Except for Joseph, the Alston family could see no reason to leave their comfortable plantation lives for a primitive cabin where frightening storms sometimes appeared with little warning. Joseph visited the Castle as often as he could get away, bringing fresh eggs, hominy grits, and ingredients for breads.

He refused to be drawn into conversations with relatives about his wife's penchant for the shore. She was a mystery, even to him — an enchanting conundrum of enthusiasm, candor, intelligence, and deep passion. He was blessed with her love; he felt no need to justify anything about her.

CHAPTER 57

While Theodosia was growing stronger at the Atlantic shore in the fall and winter of 1805, Burr was traveling surreptitiously on another body of water, the Ohio River, on his way to the Gulf of Mexico. He commissioned a houseboat, an "Ark" as he described it, sixty feet long by fourteen feet wide, with a dining room, a kitchen with fireplace, and two bedrooms.

Always at its bow by sunrise, he blinked in surprise one hazy morning in West Virginia thinking he might have imagined the lush island that stretched out before him like a water-locked Garden of Eden. He squinted into the early-morning mist as his vessel glided closer. It was no mirage.

A magnificent home adorned the islet like a jewel atop an opulent crown. Burr was enjoying his adventure aboard his primitive yacht, but he craved luxury and lavishness no less. A long dock sliced into the river from the island, and he signaled his captain to head in that direction. Here he met the congenial Irishman Harman Blennerhassett and his wife Margaret. They invited Burr to stay for dinner on Blennerhassett Island.

Burr was pleased with the meal of quail and dove served with an impressive selection of wines. As he relished the food, he looked about him and concluded this place was the ideal spot to gather recruits for his purposes. It offered seclusion and an easy journey by water southward toward the Gulf.

Although he had lost his wealth and political power, Burr had not given up on his plan to conquer Mexico. His persuasive abilities remained strong. Not only had he discovered a beautiful and perfectly located center of operations for his enterprise, but also his instincts told him the Blennerhassetts would support his scheme and help him gather further recruits. Now he had only to travel to the east again and convince Joseph and Theodosia that his mission was on solid ground. He had good timing on his side. The season's rice crop was not

promising, and Joseph's zest for politics seemed to have waned as well.
Warm spring weather in 1806 brought hordes of family members to the seashore, so the Castle was no longer Theodosia's hideaway. Colonel Alston imposed a dress code. Even though they were at the beach, the family wore their finest apparel to dinner, and children were not allowed at the table.

Servants swarmed over the cottage all hours of the day, cleaning, washing clothes, and running after screaming children. Theodosia had no haven at the Castle and no place she wanted to go now that Richmond Hill was gone.

Black flies flew in from the marshes like storm clouds, forcing everyone off of the beach. The family, crammed into the cottage, was growing increasingly petulant from lack of privacy.

The servants produced yards of dusty netting from the attic, covering every window and draping every bed to keep out deadly mosquitoes, but it only darkened the rooms and made all seem dreary. The insects seemed more determined than ever to find their prey.

Several family members became feverish, among them little Gampy who, already thin and pale, developed a high fever and a swelling under his chin. Theodosia wrote Burr, who consulted with doctors in Pennsylvania. She traveled there and found healing for him at Bedford Springs. Joseph joined his family in late summer in Philadelphia, relieved to find them well.

Burr also began his campaign to win over Joseph and Theodosia. He had written them of his plans months before, but now he could describe the details face to face.

"Establishing a vital new community in Mexico will use all of our best talents," he said. "There you will be free of all your present distress. We will be a royal family!"

"But, Papa, with no war with Spain...."

"Ah, that is no matter at all, *ma chére*. None at all. Mexico shares hundreds of miles of border with America, and we should be in control. General Wilkinson and I can easily assemble troops and take over this backward little country. When it becomes a part of our nation, it will need strong leadership — a governor, a leader."

"A king!" Gampy piped in.

"Well said, my lad, nothing less!" his grandfather exclaimed.

The Alstons' health concerns and fears about their finances had worn them down, which insured a quick victory for Burr when lobbying for their support. With the promise of a generous contribution,

Burr returned to Blennerhassett Island in high spirits. Eager for their new life, the Alstons rushed back to South Carolina full of hope and anticipation.

CHAPTER 58

〜〜

"You be needin' this, Miss Theo?" asked Tilda, holding up a long coat.

"Pack it, Tilda. I have no way of knowing what autumn weather is like in the West this time of year. Pack clothes for all kinds of weather. For you, for me, and for Gampy."

Joseph came in from the fields to assess their progress. "It is gratifying to see you so energized, Theo."

"The future appears bright to me now, Joseph — a new land, new people, our family together. You and me, Gampy and Papa! Oh, do come with us now, Joseph. Papa says the Blennerhassett's home is a mansion!"

"What's a mansion, Mama?" Gampy asked.

"A huge house, darling, like Clifton. Only the Blennerhassett mansion is not a plantation. For now, it is the headquarters of Big Gampy's project."

Theodosia tried on a plumed hat and modeled it for her husband's approval, twirling about until she fell dizzily into his arms.

He held her for a while. "I would question the wisdom of this journey except I know you will be well treated by the Blennerhassetts," he said, "and I will join you in just two months."

"You are finally in favor of Papa's plan, aren't you, Joseph?

"Enough to invest in it, Theo, and no small amount. Aaron's letter allayed my fears and convinced me he only wishes to add the wealth of Mexico to the United States. This is a chance for better health for you and Gampy; a fresh beginning for our family."

They wept as they kissed. Tilda, her arms laden with clothing to be packed, stepped into the door and quickly backed out. She was frightened about the journey and quite miserable. Though she had not the courage to ask, she had fervently hoped Peet would be included in the trip, but there was not room.

Joseph walked with them to the carriage. "Write me, Theodosia, and you, too, Little Man. Big Gampy will help you form your letters."

Joseph watched the carriage until it disappeared down the drive and wished the next two months were already over. He missed his boy and Theodosia already and dreaded the family's reaction to his decision.

Theodosia had begged him to wait to do so until just before he would leave to join them on the Ohio River. The rice crop would be in by then. Disappointing as it would be, the pressure of the season would be over. The fearful time of the fever would be gone. Timing would be better then, she thought.

But Joseph knew there would be no good time for what his family would interpret as a monumental betrayal. It would amount, in their eyes, to domestic treason and blasphemy to the religion of tradition. He wanted it over and done.

CHAPTER 59

A veteran of several trips back and forth to New York, Theodosia was accustomed to rough roads, uncomfortable beds in taverns and hours of boredom as the scenery barely changed from one long hour to the next.

But the trip to the West was more difficult. Often the roads were almost non-existent. Rivers had to be forded, and sometimes water came into the carriage, dampening the travelers' clothing and sagging spirits.

"Gampy, stop whining and wriggling about. Be still! And, please, just for a while, be quiet!" Theodosia admonished him most of the time while on their journey. She never imagined she could be so cross with her son and felt guilty for her sharp reprimands. Not only did she have to contend with the child's restlessness, but also Tilda's near hysteric anxiety.

Tilda was so fearful Theodosia was often unable to help her at all. She expected to see a "h'ant" around every curve.

"Just what are 'h'ants'?" Theodosia asked her.

"Fixuhs."

"Fixuhs?"

"Fixuhs, h'ants. Spirits from Africa. Dat why at home, we paint blue round de doh."

"The door?"

"Yes'm. Paint blue. Keep out the h'ants...." She shivered, her voice falling to a whisper as if the "h'ants" were eavesdropping.

"Now always be movin', we. H'ants follow. My sista gwine over to Hagley and h'ant follow her in de woods. Her baby be born with a caul."

"Oh, Tilda, whatever is a caul?"

"Caul a cloud ober de eye. Chile wid caul can see h'ants and warn folk."

Suddenly she shrieked. "Lordy!"

Both women jumped as the carriage rounded a curve. Above their heads a flailing rope of twisted vine swayed in the wind. A great forest loomed ahead, an eerie green canopy that stretched as far as they could see.

There was no peace for them in the evenings. Taverns were far apart in the countryside, and the travelers often rode through half the night before finding a place to sleep. The food was cold by then and the beds were typically lumpy and sour. They seldom got the rest they needed.

Once a ragged band of Indians on horseback followed them an entire day. Tilda, more frightened than ever, could not speak, even when asked questions by her beloved Gampy.

"Why are they following us, Tilda? Why do they wear feathers? And look! There is paint on their faces! Red and yellow. Oh, and on their arms and legs, too. Why, Tilda?"

Tilda sat rock-still, staring straight ahead.

"They are called Indians," his mother answered. "Don't bother Tilda now. She isn't feeling well."

"Why don't we have Indians in South Carolina, Mama?"

"Well, we did, ah, we do. There are some, I think, upstate. But, well, they've left where we live, son. Someday I will read to you about it. "Waccamaw" is an Indian name. The Indians named our river."

Gampy liked having the Indians trail them. He sneaked a look out of the back of the carriage as often as his mother would let him, and eventually he mustered up enough courage to wave to them. One of the young braves lifted a hesitant hand and waved back. Shortly afterward, they turned off on a side trail and disappeared into the forest.

The mountainous terrain they encountered from time to time shook the carriage until Gampy became nauseated. Tilda covered her head with a shawl and refused to look outside for hours. Only the thought of meeting Burr at a tavern close to Blennerhassett Island kept Theodosia from falling into despair.

Finally they reached the rendezvous. Theodosia climbed down shakily from the battered carriage and fell into her father's arms. After a long embrace, Burr turned and hoisted his grandson high above his head and whirled him around. "Oh, my fine boy, I have waited with such impatience for this very time!"

The tavern had a welcoming fireplace, and the aroma of food, properly cooked, wafted from the rear kitchen through the main room. The accommodations were good for a change — even those for Tilda and the driver, who had often slept on straw with the horses. The journey almost over, Theodosia slept deeply and awoke eagerly for the final day of travel.

They stored the carriage in a riverside settlement and boarded a sloop to Blennerhassett Island. The four of them stood on the forward deck, straining for a look at the estate. Gampy saw it first.

"Look, Mama...it's the mansion! Just like you said!"

The house sparkled in the late-afternoon sun, a graceful structure, two-storied with curving wings. A meticulously landscaped lawn curled about it. In the distance were pastures, orchards and vegetable gardens. A stand of massive trees formed a mosaic backdrop of hardwoods dappled with the beginning of fall color, evergreens thick with long needles and fat cones.

Gampy jumped from the sloop as soon as it touched the wharf. Burr gave a hand to Theodosia and Tilda, and the awaiting servants unloaded their boxes and trunks.

Margaret Blennerhassett, isolated from civilization, had anticipated this day with much excitement and preparation. She accompanied her husband to the dock. Theodosia watched their every move, hoping this woman would fill her longing for another female friend.

The Blennerhassetts were a handsome couple, each with fair Irish complexions. Alongside them scampered their two small sons. When the visitors began the short walk to the house, the children ran forward to greet them. After dinner, Burr paced, holding the Blennerhassetts, Theodosia, and Gampy spellbound.

"We have the nation's *crème de la crème* in sympathy with us — the Swartwouts and soon-to-be-Mayor Willet in New York City; General Jackson in Tennessee. Independent and worthy individuals will people our colony on the Washita River, and its society will be remarkable for its refinements. From there, we shall watch for an opportunity to march into Mexico where I shall become Emperor."

He bowed low before his daughter.

"And you, my fair one, will be Lady of the Court; Gampy will, of course, be my heir, and your worthy husband will be the Head of Nobility."

The crisp fall days passed pleasantly for the women and boys. Burr and Blennerhassett recruited a group of "confederates," backwoodsmen from the area intrigued with the cause. Often they huddled over brandy, cigars and maps in the library discussing a voyage down the Ohio to their new settlement on the Washita River.

The women became quite fond of each other and enjoyed their time alone with the children. But Margaret feared Theodosia would be summoned to the new land first, and she dreaded parting from her. When the weather was kind, they took brisk afternoon walks.

"Miracles have happened here," Theodosia told Margaret during one of their strolls. "I feel alive and energetic, but content at the same time. A combination of healthy air and good company!"

"'Tis lovely here, yes," Margaret agreed, "but so lonely before you came. You brought my mind alive again. But we'll continue to be together. We must! God willing, we will!"

CHAPTER 60

Blennerhassett Island. October 15, 1806

I feel invigorated here on this lovely island, and each morning I rise anticipating a day of good energy and a calm mind.

Margaret and I enjoy breakfasting outside when the weather is pleasant, and if it is blustery, we sit before a cozy fire, and we sip our tea and plan our day. That is, if we wish! Sometimes we let it unfold as it will.

Here there is no flock of servants, so Margaret and I share the light work with Tilda and a lovely Irish housemaid.

We conduct lessons with the boys until lunchtime, and then we resume until we take tea. The men are almost always either closeted upstairs in the drawing room with their copious maps and charts or out and about in the community recruiting followers. I miss Joseph terribly, but the days pass swiftly and in such a pleasant manner that I find no discontent.

Margaret and I often walk, sometimes in the early morning, other times after we have had supper and read the boys the nighttime stories that they love. We make up tales for them, and then we turnabout and listen to the fiction from their own imaginations.

What fun that is for all of us! Gampy thrives, both in health and in state of mind. Constant company keeps us cheerful and satisfied.

I do have one recurring thought that troubles me. Was Papa serious about the ridiculous titles he talked about the first evening we were here?

Is he truly thinking that he would be called an emperor?

And I the Lady of the Court? Gampy a future emperor? And I can barely keep from laughing aloud when thinking of Joseph as the Head of Nobility!

I should ask Papa, I suppose, and end my ruminations, but if I am honest with myself, I must confess that if he said he is serious, it would end the carefree time I am finding so precious.

And so I play the ostrich and continue to be well, relaxed, and content. In fact, I could perhaps be persuaded to give up any idea of being Lady of the Court and reside, with Joseph and my boy here on the magical isle of Blennerhassett for the rest of my days!

CHAPTER 61

⧫

Joseph came as promised, arriving in late October. His welcoming celebration was lavish. Theodosia and Margaret spent days in planning and helping to prepare a special dinner of wild game stuffed with apricots, baked guinea squash, four kinds of puddings, and pies made of peaches, apples, and cherries.

Their first evening together was festive. Several of the "confederates" joined the festivities, lingering for much longer than Theodosia and her husband could bear. The couple slipped away at midnight, eager to be alone.

They loved and talked way into the night, oblivious of the mutterings of restive doves and the liquid sounds of the moon-dappled river as it slid peacefully by. Joseph described his family's reaction to the news of relocation: Colonel William, incredulous; Mary Motte, non-committal; Lady Nesbit lashing out, saying, "Stupid brother. This entire affair smells of dishonesty, of grandiosity. You are terribly naïve to be taken in."

The other sisters and brothers were quiet in their disbelief and disappointment. Joseph said hasty good-byes before more conflict could erupt. Happily for Tilda, he traveled with Peet, his favorite servant.

But the Alstons' time at Blennerhassett was short-lived, and Margaret's hopes dashed when the press sounded an alarm. In early November, the district attorney in nearby Frankfort, Kentucky accused Burr of engaging in an enterpirse contrary to the interests of his country. Burr was ordered to answer the charge. Then, as now, politics were often personal and vindictive. The district attorney had hated Burr since his duel with Hamilton and now had, he thought, an opportunity to ruin him.

"We go to Kentucky," Burr announced to his daughter and son-in-law. "Tilda, assemble all belongings for Mr. and Mrs. Alston, Gampy, and yourself and Peet. Pack for a long stay." He assured the Alstons that this was a mere inconvenience, and they reluctantly prepared for the short journey.

Burr, a legal genius himself, hired the young Henry Clay, who had just been elected to the U.S. Senate from Kentucky. The district attorney was granted a grand jury hearing, but he brought no witnesses. Charges were dismissed, but two days later, he again requested and was granted another hearing. Burr spoke in his own defense, and Henry Clay declared that he "did not entertain the slightest idea of his guilt." Again, Burr was vindicated, and his supporters celebrated with a festive ball.

Theodosia believed their worries were over, and Burr did nothing to dissuade her. But he knew this unrest was only the beginning. He had heard rumors before they left Belnnerhasset Island that Wilkinson was wavering, and he knew how determined Jefferson was to bring him down. If he should fall, he would not drag down those he loved best, his reason for insisting the entire family travel back to South Carolina with all of their belongings.

He delivered his message quickly, urgently. There was no time for agonizing. He broke the news to Theodosia a few days later on a cold early December morning: "You must travel back to South Carolina."

The day was raw, but Theodosia's excitement left her impervious to the cold. Burr's sudden pronouncement wiped out the weeks of rest and distraction in an instant. She shuddered with a powerful chill that shook her entire body.

Burr's voice was harsh: "Do not agitate yourself, Theodosia."

Her retort was equally hostile: "Papa, this is unacceptable. You said we would soon go down the river to New Orleans, then to Mexico. I see no reason for us to return to the Waccamaw."

"This is a short-term delay. For the moment there is nothing you can do here," he said.

Tears sprang into her eyes, and she struggled to blink them away.

"Theodosia, I barely recognize my daughter. You appear to have aged overnight. Look at yourself."

He took her arm, but she turned away, seeking relief from his ranting.

"I wish to have everything arranged when you join me in Mexico," he continued. "And, at this moment, you do not appear fit to be Lady of the Court. Cease this sentimentality and prepare for our farewell in the morning. Go home and await the clangor of trumpets. This separation will be our last."

Joseph knew there was much local outrage about the dismissed charges of treasonous activity. He was more than ready to take leave of Kentucky and led Theodosia away to begin preparations before anger erupted again.

Burr and Blennerhassett returned to the island and soon went down the Ohio River to pursue their baffling scheme. They had assembled a flotilla of only 13 boats, manned by a pitiful "navy" of 60 men. The few recruits who joined along the way moderately swelled their ranks.

Languishing along the Ohio, Burr was not yet aware the nation was in a frenzy. He knew, of course, some thought his actions were treasonous, but he was confident he had few enemies. He did not know General James Wilkinson, the man who Theodosia had described to Gampy as "Commander of the *wh-o-ole* U.S. Army," had folded. Frightened by the charge against Burr in Kentucky, he withdrew his support from the project. He wrote to Jefferson, hoping to save his own skin.

CHAPTER 62

❧≈✦≈❧

Thomas Jefferson opened his mail in a sunny and spacious room on the southwest corner of the White House surrounded by empty china coffee cups and an odd assortment of other items. He was too busy to be bothered by the clutter, unaware of the incongruous combination of official papers and carpenter's tools on the long table where he worked.

Flowers, plants, maps, books, globes, and charts lined the floor-to-ceiling shelves. Overhead his pet mockingbird, free from his cage as it usually was, dipped and darted. Just outside the window his caged bears roared as they tumbled in play, but the President ignored them as well. The letter consumed him, and his face contorted in shock as he finished. He pounded on the desk, rattling the cups and causing the tallest pile of paper to hit the floor.

"Merciful God! That bastard!"

The startled bird shrieked and tried to escape through the closed window, its wings flapping noisily against the glass. The commotion brought in a slave.

"Mas' Jefferson, suh?"

"That little son of a wanton woman! Always able to sway people toward his devious schemes!"

"Suh?"

"Aaron Burr. He must be stopped at any cost. Get me a messenger and the fastest horse in Washington. General Wilkinson says that Burr is attempting to separate the nation. A militia must be assembled to halt this treason!"

Jefferson ordered a troop of mostly inexperienced militiamen to be organized quickly. Soon the shouts of men anticipating the thrill of combat could be heard from the waters surrounding Blennerhassett Island.

Boat after boat went ashore on the island, and the men spread like ants over the grounds. When all had come on land, they regrouped and waited for their command.

"Rea-a-a-a-d-y...charge!"

The soldiers found the wine cellar early on, and the attack lost its focus quickly. Some used their pistols to break off the tops of bottles. They took great gulps and passed the bottles around. Beset by the paranoia of intoxication, they hunkered down on the cellar floor.

"Let's hear it for the traitor!" shouted one with a hiccup. "T'weren't fer him we wouldn't be partaking of these fine spirits!"

A comrade answered with slurred words.

"Can't drink to treason, Jake. A toast to treason will not pass my lips!"

"Well, the wine, it seems, slips by your lips without a problem!"

An officer stood and waved his arm, signaling it was time to get back to war.

"Ho...the rest of you! What shall we drink to?"

"Death to the traitors! But thanks be to God it was not before they harvested their grapes!"

"Up the stairs, men. Our duty must be done! Death to the traitors!"

Clamoring drunkenly to their feet, they moved up the staircase and poured into the house, some falling and others tripping over the ones who had passed out. A man ripped down the ornate draperies in the dining room. Another raked an entire wall of pictures onto the floor with his arm and joined in a jig with his fellow combatants on top of the frames, crushing the glass to shards.

Outside, other militiamen trampled shrubbery and pulled vines from the house shouting, singing, and laughing.

An officer bellowed above the fracas.

"Enough, enough! It is time to move in on the enemy!"

Weaving and tripping, the group wobbled up the stairs leaning heavily on the banisters and one another. A man removed a portrait of Mrs. Blennerhassett from the wall and kissed the replica of her prominent cleavage.

The officer continued in his attempt to gain control in the midst of elegant furniture lying twisted and broken on wine-stained rugs.

"Have we done it, my men? Are the traitors destroyed?"

The group stared at him with slack faces. One finally spoke, looking from side to side.

"Traitors? Where are the traitors?"

A breathless soldier burst into the room. "The boats are gone, sir. They ain't here. Gone down the Ohio, I'm told."

The men exchanged sheepish glances. The "traitors" had indeed left, except for a few "confederate" stragglers who had missed Burr's boats.

CHAPTER 63

In some places, the Ohio River was a narrow stream, choked with floating chunks of ice. The flotilla Burr manned meandered slowly past tiny Fort Massac, where the soldier on guard squinted toward the river and shook his head in disbelief.

A scraggly convoy of boats, each one different, floated slowly down the river. Some had laundry hanging from the sides, and one had a goat as a passenger. A guard wrote in the log:

December 31, 1806. Colonel Burr, former Vice President of the United States, passed here with about 10 boats of different descriptions, navigated with about six men each. Nothing suspicious could be seen. They looked as though they might be going to a market.

Later, another boat slipped away from the island, its passengers, save one, silent. The captured and released confederates were now rowing Margaret Blennerhassett in search of her husband. She was far from silent.

Sitting in the stern, she looked back at her ruined house and grounds. When she could no longer see them, she cupped her face into her hands and wept long and loud. Startled by her wailing, a rabbit scurried into the thick, winter-ravaged bushes that flanked the shore of the Ohio.

CHAPTER 64

E ventually, Burr's rag-tag flotilla reached Bayou Pierre, near Nat-
chez, Mississippi. Burr stood at the bow of his boat, surveying
the landscape and thinking it looked much the same as Theodosia's
Waccamaw River home.

As the crew secured lines on a wharf at Bayou Pierre, an officer
with an armful of papers approached him. "Are you Colonel Aaron
Burr, sir?"

Burr nodded.

"By the authority of President Jefferson, you are under arrest for
treason against the United States."

"And on what does he base this accusation?"

"Evidence from General Wilkinson, sir. He is the Commander-
in-Chief of...."

"I know who he is," Burr snapped.

The soldier removed more papers from a satchel and began to read.

"General Wilkinson revealed to the President your letter stating
you plan to separate the western states from the Union...to invade
Mexico and create a royal government...."

"Enough, enough!" Burr commanded. "Jefferson has undoubtedly
found me guilty before a jury has had the opportunity!"

Burr paused. Resigned, he sighed. "Fine. Where do we go, young
man?"

"Richmond, sir."

Burr's face was expressionless, his eyes cold. Behind him on a
nearby staff, a United States flag waved.

During the next two weeks, Burr spent many sleepless nights,
first in a makeshift prison, then in various roadhouses and private
residences as the soldiers transported their prisoner northward to
Virginia.

At about the same time that the Alstons completed their own rough
passage and arrived at The Oaks, Burr was traveling through the
northern part of South Carolina. The group stopped for food and

water in the village of Chester, and Burr seized upon a window of opportunity. He leapt from his horse onto a rock in the center of the square.

"Amnesty!" he cried. "I am Aaron Burr, your former Vice President! I am being held against my will on false charges."

Town folks gathered around.

"What are these charges?" a resident inquired.

"Foolish accusations that I am engaged in treasonous activities. Foolish and false...."

Another man interrupted.

"I have heard, Mr. Burr, that you planned to form a new nation in Mexico, and you have persuaded hundreds to desert America and go with you."

"Not true," shouted Burr. "I wish to add the riches of Mexico to our country."

The soldiers had circled around Burr and began to close in on him. His voice rose with desperation.

"Please! My son-in-law, Joseph Alston, serves in your state legislature. I implore you, give me refuge!"

His guards drew their guns, seized Burr, and forced him into a carriage. He was no longer allowed a horse. Now in North Carolina, the carriage swayed and bumped along a rocky path as he pulled his ragged cloak about him and stared through the mud-splattered window at a high gold moon.

At The Oaks, the same winter moon bathed the slave street in thin light. In their space above the cookhouse, Tilda and her mother, Mae, warmed themselves before a dying fire.

Earlier that day, Joseph had sought Tilda's advice. "I have read today's papers and the news is not good," he confided. "Miss Theo's father was arrested in Mississippi and is being taken to Richmond, Virginia, to stand trial for treason."

"Treason, sir?"

"Many believe he betrayed this country."

He could see the girl still did not understand.

"Tilda, it is possible he was not faithful; that he told trusting people things that were not true...things that would make him feel important, but would hurt this country. Colonel Burr is a prisoner. He is going to be tried and perhaps punished severely. How should I tell Theodosia?"

Tilda understood betrayal and punishment. She was treated well, but her people had stories. Tales of treachery, captures, and brutality.

"Jes' tell her, suh. Tell her, straight out. She be strong. She be wantin' to know."

Tilda and Mae heard Theodosia's cry and knew there would be no rest this night.

"He done tol' her fo' true," said Tilda, rushing up the stairs to her mistress.

Theodosia sat trembling on the side of her bed. She motioned Tilda to sit beside her.

"Miss Theo?"

"Begin to pack for me, dear Tilda. We need to go through all of my ball gowns; I will need most of them. Formal clothes for Mr. Alston as well. A few weeks hence, and we will be going to Richmond, Virginia."

CHAPTER 65

Following several days of silence, Theodosia finally received a letter from Burr.

Richmond, Virginia. April 6, 1807

You have read to very little purpose if you have not realized that such things happen in all democratic governments. Was there in Greece or Rome a man of talent, virtue, and independence who was not the object of vindictive and relenting persecution?

Now, Madame, I pray you to amuse yourself by collecting and collating all the instances to be found in ancient history which you may connect together, if you please, in an essay, with reflections and comments to send to me.

Energized by news from her father, Theodosia began to finalize her travel plans. When the second letter arrived she was all but ready.

Richmond, Virginia. July 6, 1807

If you come, some good-natured people here will provide you a furnished house near me. In the meantime, I expect you will conduct yourself as becomes my daughter and that you manifest no signs of weakness or alarm. Remember...no agitations. No complaints. No fears or anxieties on the road, or I renounce thee.

Theodosia told the servants to start loading the carriage. Her husband would accompany her, but she pushed away all thoughts of their separation from Gampy. She simply could not bear to think of it. The child grew and learned so quickly that she dreaded the time she would not be with him.

On departure day she walked to the carriage with steady steps, but when she stooped to hold her little boy, she swayed, and Tilda stepped forward to bolster her.

"Tilda, watch over him. Take him to the beach house. If the fever returns...."

Tilda pulled at a string around her waist, smiling confidently.

"Don' worry. Dip string in turpentine. Tie a knot eber time boy feels a chill. Fo you know, be well, he! Bile him up berry ob dogwood, take away de fever."

Theodosia humored her. "Do these things, Tilda. But ride for the doctor also. Promise me?"

Tilda nodded and pulled Gampy to her.

"Big Gampy says no agi...agi...ta...." he attempted.

She smiled and smoothed his curls.

"No agitations. And he is right! Burrs are strong! And you are Little Master Aaron Burr Alston!"

He held up five fingers.

"Not little, Mama. I am this many!"

"My heart child, you have spent all of those years in my arms. I shall miss you so."

He stood very straight and hoped she wouldn't see the tear he quickly wiped from his cheek with the back of his hand.

"Try to be happy, Mama. Even without me."

A brief look of terror crossed her face, and she kissed him a final time, forcing herself to mount the steps into the carriage. Alston embraced his son and climbed in beside her. They waved and threw kisses to Gampy as long as they could see him standing bravely beside Tilda with one hand waving and the other blowing kisses. The carriage reached the King's Highway, and the driver urged the horses into a trot. Another journey to Burr had begun.

CHAPTER 66

B urr's trial began on August 3, 1807, and after Theodosia's immediate arrival, it became the social centerpiece for Richmond. Every evening there were elaborate parties. She planned and presided over many of the festivities, determined her father's image would not be tarnished by this latest accusation.

She and Joseph hired Luther Martin as Burr's defense lawyer. Martin cared not a whit about what anyone thought of him. His voice was harsh, his dress shabby, and his peers described him as "liquidly convivial." It was he who provided comfortable quarters for Theodosia and her entourage during their stay in Richmond. He proclaimed his infatuation with her openly and took every opportunity to be at her side.

At a social gathering he approached her, balancing a brandy snifter in one hand, a cigar in the other, all the while staring at her décolletage.

"Dogs of war." He exclaimed. "Hell hounds of persecution! That's what Jefferson's henchmen are."

His cigar ashes, inches long, crumbled and slid down his wrinkled evening weskit. Cursing, he brushed them off. "Excuse me, madam. I would not offend you."

Theodosia laughed.

"No one who defends my father with such passion could offend me, Counselor Martin."

He popped his cigar into his mouth, its ashes still trailing downward. "Good. We will prevail!"

He guided her to an open window.

"My worst problem is that it takes me an hour to get a decent drink in this town. The Eagle, The Swan — all the best bars are full of troublemakers. Come and see."

The two looked down at Brick Row, famous for its taverns. Tents and wagons lined the streets. Gentlemen in fine suits, ruffled shirts, and silken tassels mingled with backwoodsmen, farmers, and mountaineers. Roughnecks in buckled breeches shoved each other off the sidewalks, shouting, spitting, smoking, and wiping sweat from their brows.

"Thousands have moved into the city to be close to the trial," Martin said to Theodosia. "They are camping out in August, if you can believe it, and it being 95 degrees and better! Dogs of war, I say! Sons of dogs! Excuse me, Madame — hounds of persecution!"

Two fighting men fell into a gutter, and others were mud-splattered trying to pull them apart.

"Called him a damned traitor, he did!" shouted one of the fighters. Martin tried to pull Theodosia away, but she shook her head and continued to watch in fascination.

"Burr ain't no traitor!" the other hollered. "That bastard Wilkinson, he's the traitor! Told crazy lies to Jefferson!"

"Believe everything you read in the papers, you dammed fool!" spat his adversary. "Burr was takin' us right into war, and you'd be the first one to tuck your yellow tail and run!"

The two were at it again, rolling in the mud, but soon lost their audience when a man wearing a turban picked his way along the filthy street, swinging his hips and holding high the tasseled end of an absurd Turkish sash.

"Oh damn that Colonel Burr," he declared in a high voice. "Such a coward. We should just...." He twirled the sash and continued, "Just... well, I cannot think of anything bad enough for that awful man!"

The fighters ceased their wrestling and gaped at the spectacle. The crowd erupted into laughter.

Theodosia leaned from the window to better see the man, who by that time had resumed his strut down Brick Row.

Martin reveled in this chance to touch Theodosia. "Madame," he began, taking her elbow. "That is General Eaton, and one would think the defense had hired him. His silly denouncements win us friends every day!"

Still holding her elbow, he escorted her to the dinner table.

"Come. Don't, ah, excite yourself. Do let us leave the General to do his good work! Dinner is served." He seated her at the head of a long table, his hands lingering on her shoulders as he pushed in her chair.

The treason trial lasted just short of a month. Burr was found not guilty.

The celebrations escalated, and Theodosia lifted her goblet for the first of many times.

"To my father's innocence!"

"Hear, hear!" her guests cried as Martin, listing slightly, stood and proposed a toast of his own. "To our hostess! For her loyalty! And her endless round of parties! Theodosia Burr!"

All stood, cheered and drank. Martin, seizing the opportunity to move about a bit, leered as he found a better view of Theodosia's cleavage.

Joseph stepped between the two.

"I join you in your high regard for my wife, Theodosia Burr Alston. She, like yourselves, finds the rumors of treason and conspiracy mere fantasy, created by those who hate and envy Colonel Burr and fanned by an overwrought press."

He lifted his goblet.

"To my wife's discernment, and yours."

Later, as they prepared for bed, Theodosia released her hair from its elaborate coils and began to brush it.

"There is no look of health here," she complained. "No shine, and look, even the color has faded like everything else."

She ran her fingers through her hair and leaned closer to the looking glass. "Look, a grey hair. And here is another!"

Joseph went to her, took the brush from her hand, and drew it gently though the length of her hair. "Ah, Theo, you imagine things. I see no grey, but I will love you even more if someday I do. Your tresses will be like velvety bricks touched with whitewash."

He was silent as he began to undress for bed. How should he begin to tell her it was time for them to leave?

Theodosia went to him, helped him unfasten the tiny buttons on his shirt.

"We have done all we can do here, Theo," he began. "We must return to The Oaks."

She was horrified. "All we can do! Joseph! You know there is to be a misdemeanor trial. We must see this through to the end."

"Theodosia," he answered wearily. "We have no idea when that trial will begin. We have spent our time, energy, and a fortune being here. At home, we have, I hope, a rice crop — and a son. I will return to South Carolina tomorrow. I expect you to accompany me."

Leaving Burr's supporters to rejoice and find entertainment on their own, the Alstons departed against the wishes of an exhausted Theodosia, and in predictable opposition from Burr. He kissed his daughter perfunctorily when she bid him good-bye and returned to his books, offering no praise for her efforts to save him.

The journey home was especially difficult for Theodosia. She was depleted and sad, remembering their precipitous departure and Burr's indifferent farewell. But she thought about holding Gampy in her arms, and her heart was lighter.

Before they arrived home, the jury found Burr not guilty of the misdemeanor. But a shadow lay over the celebration at The Oaks. There was a possibility that Burr could be sent to the West and again be tried for treason.

CHAPTER 67

Several months after the Alstons returned home, Theodosia and Gampy rode on the edge of the ricefields watching the slaves reap another harvest of Carolina Gold. The boy had absorbed his father's passion and watched the cutting over of the fields with interest, listening intently to the mellow resonance of Negro voices. The melodious calls relieved the monotony and physical discomforts for the workers during days of hard labor.

Theodosia could feel a trace of fall. Soon a wake of yellow and red leaves would spin behind them when they rode, and fallen foliage would curl into brittle piles and crunch under the horses' hooves. Their outing took them to the Waccamaw, still a lazy black thread yawning for fresh water below a haze of dragonflies. They rested their mounts and watched the slow-moving water.

"Tell me more, Mama, about the trial," Gampy said.

"No more, there is no more," she said. "I have told you absolutely everything."

"Tell it again, about Old Brandy Bottle!"

Theodosia laughed. "You must not repeat that! It is a silly nickname for Counselor Martin. He is a fine attorney, and I am sure he has won the second case for your grandfather, brandy bottle and all."

They returned to The Oaks in time to see a messenger approaching. Theodosia snatched his proffered envelope and read aloud to Gampy from a letter sent from Richmond dated October 23, 1807:

"Celebrate with me the result of this second fiasco. The depositions gathered proved no clear-cut evidence of misdemeanor. Once more, I am 'not guilty.'"

Theodosia squealed like a child and raced into the house, leaving her horse grazing without restraint. Her son followed.

"Joseph! Joseph!" She found him in his study. "Oh, Joseph, the most wonderful news! There are to be no more trials! Papa's ordeal is over. Finally over!"

He took the paper and read it; then he shook his head.

"I wish this were the end of it, Theo. Jefferson will not give up so easily."

"What do you mean?"

"Your father can still be indicted in New York for Hamilton's death. And even more likely, he and Blennerhassett may both face legal action out West."

She winced.

"Honor is inside, Joseph, not a garment to be worn and tossed aside. We must go to him and persuade him to come back here with us. We helped him during the trial. We cannot let him be ruined now."

Joseph walked slowly around his desk and stopped inches from Theodosia, his arms folded tightly across his starched white shirt. "Theodosia, my time, not to mention my patience, has run out. If your father wishes to come here, he is welcome. But he alone must be responsible for the things he has done."

Like a high-strung horse. Sometimes needing a tether. Now it must be you.

Her mother had said more, but the words eluded her, as they always did. Theodosia took a step backward. "He does not always see things clearly. I must go to him, Joseph. You may do as you see fit."

He turned from her, returned to his desk, and was silent for a long moment.

"Theodosia, even if I wished to join Aaron now, I cannot afford economically, morally, or politically to do so. I did not wish for you to know this, but I feel now you must. Mr. Blennerhassett is threatening to publish a book about your father's activities. In it, he will claim that I participated in treason."

She gasped, "Can he be stopped?"

"Yes, 15,000 dollars will stop him immediately, Theo," he answered her with a cynical laugh. "That's 15,000 of our dollars!"

"That is blackmail!"

"Of course! I have chosen to ignore it at this point, hoping it is an empty threat, but I cannot ignore my conscience. Surely you can see I cannot take the side of your father. I cannot put myself in that position."

"*Will* not," she shot back.

He shrugged. "You are right. I *will* not be involved any longer. Your father is not an evil man, Theo, but he has shown poor judgment. If you join him now, I must question your judgment as well."

There is truth in what he says, she thought, *yet how can he expect me to desert Papa?*

She rushed toward the door, but before leaving, she turned toward her husband, folding her arms hard against her chest.

"No matter what happens, Joseph, I remain honored — always — to be the daughter of such a man."

CHAPTER 68

❧❧❧

A cold winter on the Waccamaw matched the cold mood that prevailed at The Oaks. Gampy tried his best to be amusing but soon gave up. The entire Alston family assembled for Christmas celebrations. Charlotte and Mary had anticipated spending time with Theodosia but found her distant and withdrawn.

"Mary, I cannot bear her silence. She is like a stone," Charlotte said. "Is it something we have done?"

"Oh, Charlotte, dear Theodosia has always been moody. And she worries about her father."

"Yes, but she seems to not want our company at all."

The two turned to watch Joseph tentatively approach his wife with a glass of port. She stared at him full-face, raised a hand to reject his offering, turned her head and walked away. Across the room Maria winked at them and mouthed an obvious, "I told you so."

Burr decided to go abroad until opinions about him settled down. There, he wrote to his daughter that he could live as he once had. He would socialize with intellectuals and move about without seeing hatred in the eyes of passersby. He had just enough money for one passage, but wished her to join him in Europe as soon as he collected some monies that were owed him for legal services he had provided through the years. He wrote to her that his foes were disinclined to pay him. Perhaps she would be more successful in collecting his debts than he had been. But first she must return to him in New York.

Theodosia anxiously awaited further instructions. When she received the name of the rooming house in New York where they would meet, she prepared to go overland once more.

Would he be there first, or was she to endure a long wait? She read in the papers that emotions still ran high against him. Would he be injured on his journey from Virginia to New York City? She was too proud to voice her despair to the only source of comfort she had — her husband.

CHAPTER 69

※

The Oaks, South Carolina. February 15, 1808

Except for fear and despondency, my steadfast but unwelcome companions, I am completely and frightfully alone. This is the result of my decision, of course. It is I who am determined, against the will of my husband, to go to my father.

Papa tells me that he wants the monies owed him so that he might bring me to Europe, but I know the real reason. He has no source of income, and when he arrives there, he will be at the mercy of those he knew when he had power and finesse. Many of his debtors in New York turn their backs on him, still thinking him guilty of treason, but perhaps they will be willing to pay me.

It has cleaved me in two. I am wife to a good man and mother to a beautiful child, but I am obsessed by a duty that is possibly unjustifiable. I pray that there is some wisdom in my going, but I fear that I might have lost all ability for rational self-appraisal.

Oh, how blessed I was when I was confident and physically strong. Wisdom has not come to me with age as I had expected. I am determined to go forward with a decision that I regret, grieving for what I am leaving behind before I have said farewell. But if I stay and Papa should die, poor, disgraced, and alone in some foreign land, I should be devastated as never before. No amount of repentance could restore me.

I so fear the journey. The sheer physical effort often seems beyond me. And what of my precious little boy? He will be well cared for, of course. Tilda and Joseph do all they can to see that no harm comes to him. But he will need his mother's arms. I know him so well that I feel his slightest discomfort immediately. I kiss his knees when he falls, sing him to sleep, and wake him each morning with a kiss.

I agonize, but my decision is made. I will restore to Papa the money that is due him. In time, his old friends will welcome him back to New York. His mind will be at ease, and he will be free to join us and enjoy a gentle old age in Charleston, on the Waccamaw, and at the Castle in DeBordieu. French. He will love it.

CHAPTER 70

Theodosia left in early spring, alone except for her gaunt old driver. Just before departure, she held her son lightly for a moment and put him down then brushed her lips to Joseph's cheek. Once out of their sight, she doubled over in anguish, pressing her damp forehead to her knees, praying for tears of release. But this pain was too great for tears.

Turn back, please turn back. But they were only thoughts.

The trip grew more intolerable as they plodded northward. The mellow early spring she had enjoyed in South Carolina gave way to cold rain and occasional snow flurries as the days turned into weeks. New York had never seemed so far away.

The driver drank heavily at the taverns and often was unable to begin the day's journey until well into the morning. Their progress was agonizingly slow and increasingly uncomfortable.

The journey from Richmond northward was arduous for Burr as well. In Baltimore he was forced to hide from an angry mob of men who gathered to hang him in effigy. More curious than cautious, he stood in an alleyway shivering with cold, watching as a bonfire cast bobbing shadows over the cobblestone streets.

A man placed a noose around the dummy's neck, heaved the rope, and cheered as the crude representation of Burr swung out. The mob joined in the celebration, jeering and cheering.

"Justice for the traitor...justice for the murderer. Justice, we say! May Burr's soul burn in Hell!"

The men hit and spit on the dummy as it swung back and forth. Suddenly one of them pointed into the blackness of the alley.

"Hey...ain't that Burr yonder?"

The mob grew silent as every eye searched.

Burr turned and slipped into the shadows. The men chased him, cursing and shouting. Those who entered the alley collided with each other as they hit a dead end. They swore louder as they left, foiled by the wily Burr.

He was ready to leave his country and shed his past. In time, he believed, anger would cool and bitter memories would be forgotten. He had been foolish, but he was no fool. Aaron Burr had known for some time he had run out of safe places.

CHAPTER 71

◦≈◦≈◦

Dressed in a long black cloak, the man turned up his collar against the wind and tugged at the wide brim of his hat until it hid his brow. As he approached the peeling doorway, a woman answered his knock.

"Mr. Edwards?"

Burr nodded. "Yes, Madame."

She stood aside, and he entered the rooming house, averting his face as he removed his hat. He kept his cloak wrapped around him as he climbed the stairs. In a few days time, she answered another knock.

"You are expecting me, I believe? I am Mary Ann Edwards."

"Ah, yes, come in, my dear."

With silent steps, the thin young woman disappeared up the stairway and soon found, for the first time in weeks, a comfort of sorts in her father's arms. They would have only one evening together. After dinner, they sat in Burr's room. A great fire burned in the fireplace, but Theodosia could not stop shivering.

"I fear for you, Papa. The sea journey, foreign countries, exile."

"Nonsense, Theo! This is an adventure. Memories fade quickly, and soon I can return. In the meantime, who knows? In England, Europe, there are men of vision. I will tell them about my venture. You and I may yet lead a bold new nation!"

She pressed her cheek to her father's shoulder, knowing it was futile to try to dispel his delusions. They sat together before the fire all night, knowing there would be no sleep.

June 7, 1808 began with a moody sky and a brisk northwest wind. Musicians played chanteys as sailors readied the *Clarrisa Anne* for her passage. In a rare moment of tenderness, Burr wiped the tears from Theodosia's face with his handkerchief.

"You are my daughter, Theo. It is weakness to mourn, but wisdom to look ahead with courage. When you collect the monies I am owed, you shall join me. We will be wined and dined by those we entertained at Richmond Hill. Do not buy a thing before you travel. I will dress you in the latest Paris fashions!"

They embraced silently. She fled quickly, so he would see no tears and she could no longer hear the muscians.

Oh, the story winds do blow
And the raging seas o'er they flow.
While we poor sailors are toiling in the tower below
And the landsmen are lying down below
And the landsmen are lying down below.
Three times around sailed our gallant Ship,
Three times around sailed she,
And when she was going the fourth time around,
She sank to the bottom of the sea, the sea
She sank to the bottom of the sea.

Finally, she stopped for breath and looked up into a cloudless sky.

"Grant him safe passage," she pleaded, "and be with him, now that I cannot."

CHAPTER 72

⁓⁓

From a second-floor window, a woman peered out, straining to see who had knocked at her door. "It's her," she whispered.

Her husband sat at his sewing table, wrestling with a thick piece of leather. "Who?"

"Ah, the Burr woman, er, Alston."

"God in Heaven! Aaron Burr's daughter?"

The knocking persisted. "Shall I let her in?" the woman asked.

"In our Lord's name, no! She's wantin' the money."

"T'was before the duel when he drew up the will, George. We do owe the debt."

"Yes, to him and everyone else, it seems."

He stood and shook the thick leather. "I owe for this sorry hide, Mildred. When I've made it into breeches, I'll hope to sell them, so I can pay the butcher, then the doctor, if any is left. So it's not that scoundrel Burr I'll be paying now. Get away from that window!"

She jumped back, but not so far that she couldn't watch Theodosia walk slowly along the street with her head bowed, lifting her skirts above the murky puddles.

As Theodosia walked, she pictured her husband's face, then her father's.

Why did you abandon me when I need your counsel and tenderness? My heart cries out to Heaven. Reunite us before I die.

Burr trained her to look forward not back, to display courage in every situation, but she was close to the end of her will and endurance. Painful arguments with herself ravaged her body and kept her mind spinning in endless circles. Self-doubt grew like a cancer.

Am I able to save him? Or might it be true, as Joseph said, that my father can't be restored? Joseph, oh my husband. So concerned for me always. Years ago I wrote to you from Richmond Hill, assuring you that where you were, there is my country, and in you were centered all my wishes. Oh how far I have erred from that declaration. Is that my feeling now? I know not my own heart.

She thought about it and decided her feelings remained steadfast.

Yes, my dearest Joseph, you remain the center of my wishes still, but I have chosen to leave you for this duty. Do you embrace our boy for me? He has you, your family, Tilda, and his beloved nanny, M'aum Hattie. But is he happy without me?

She reflected upon the time when her mother became ill. The hushed voices and the doors closed against her. Peggy could not fill the void. Not even her father. She shuddered as the memories came back, feeling, remembering the helpless longing that was with her after the death of her mother. Gampy was certain to be suffering in just the same way.

Wherever I turn, anguish assails me. Alas, I do live, but why? I am of little service in this world to anyone.

CHAPTER 73

～◇◇～

Joseph and Gampy rode in the ricefields and watched the field hands. Some were cutting rice stalks with sickles known as rice hooks while others lay the grain on the stubble to dry. Father and son dismounted.

"Rice is shipped all over the world from Charleston, son," Joseph explained.

They soon were joined by Adam, Peet's father. His skin was the color of walnuts, his hair grizzled through with white under the battered straw hat he tipped in deference to his owner. "Good day, Marse' Joseph, Marse' Gampy."

Gampy kicked at a clod of black earth, embarrassed to be called "master," especially by Adam whom he had followed about since he was a toddler.

"Adam!" he cried. "I have not seen you for so long!"

"Harves' time, Marse' Gampy. Won't see me 'til all the leaves fall, prob-ly! Rackin' starts tonight!"

"Rackin'?"

Adam held up a stalk of rice.

"These here be racked up in de barn...stacks and stacks. Be burnin' torch lights all night. Can't quit till we racks all we cuts today. Got whole half-acre, me. Happy when Sunday come!"

"Carolina Gold, son," added Joseph. "This has survived snakes, moles, rats, maggots, blackbirds, crows, ducks...even the clever little rice birds! Remember last spring? You could barely see the sky for the rice birds!"

"Carolina Gold! A survivor. Mama said Big Gampy is a survivor."

"Thanks to her, that is true," his father said.

This puzzled Gampy, but his father was saved from an explanation. They heard a horse approaching. Squinting into the sun, they saw Lady Maria Nesbitt riding toward them, dodging the stacks of rice.

"Good day, my brother, and good day, Littlest Burr, my most handsome nephew. Tilda told me I might find you here."

196

"Good day to you, Maria," Joseph said.

"We are concerned, Joseph. Father, Charlotte, all of us. You deserve a wife at your side, and Gampy needs a mother."

"We manage quite well, Maria."

She sniffed, and Joseph glanced away to hide his annoyance. He watched Adam slicing through the tough stalks, his mellow voice rising and falling with the rhythm of his rice hook. "Jesus! Uh! Savior! Uh! Look down, Jesus!"

"You may feel that you manage, Joseph," Maria continued, "but how long has it been? Three months? Four? I have lost track. And how many more will it be?" Her voice softened. "Bring the boy to me at Clifton. I will read him his lessons and give him the attention he is entitled to."

Gampy stared at the ground, downcast, and afraid he would be turned over to his least-favorite aunt.

"He reads Latin and Greek under my supervision, Maria. He studies arithmetic, history, and biography. We do not need your help or your pity."

"Well you have it, whether you wish it or not! I am sorry for you and for your boy, practically an orphan. Your wife, if one could call her that, should be ashamed!"

Before her brother could answer, she cracked her crop, turned the horse, and rode swiftly away.

Tears filled the child's eyes. "I am not an orphan, Papa!"

"Of course not!"

"I want to see Mama. Sometimes, I lie in bed at night and try to remember her face." His voice broke. "And I can't, Papa. The harder I try...." He stopped and lowered his head.

Joseph stooped and pulled him close. "I know, son, I miss her, too. She will be coming soon." Joseph gazed into the distance as though he saw her riding toward him, knowing he could barely hope what he said was true. If he could believe that she was making her tedious way home, he would lift his son high and twirl him about until they fell laughing into a tangled heap on the sandy soil. Then they might gallop furiously away, their horses churning the fallen leaves into a brilliant trail of gold. They would ride until they met her. But he guessed that her work was not done and worried that it may never end.

CHAPTER 74

Theodosia wondered if the dampness between her breasts was from the heat or a fever as she made her way slowly toward the entrance to the White House. The persistent pain she had known ever since she gave birth to her son was hot in her belly, and she stopped to mop her forehead. She was very thin, her eyes sunken, her skin and hair lusterless.

She had written to her father from New York before leaving for Washington.

Pelham, New York. January 3, 1809
How I long to go home. Your financial concerns give me much anxiety, but as yet, no one has paid. My heart feels your suffering more than its own afflictions. I had hoped long before now to have resolved your problems. Now I believe that you should come home.

She was expected at the President's residence and was shown into a high-ceilinged parlor, furnished elegantly in American Empire style. The cheerful, lemon-yellow walls failed to lift her spirits. She sank onto a loveseat and smoothed her hair with a trembling hand.

The rustle of stiff crinolines heralded the approach of Dolley Madison, who soon burst into the room, filling it with her energy, the bodice of her turquoise and gold gown stretched to the limit over her breasts. Her fingers sparkled with multiple rings, and though her hair was meticulously styled, constant motion loosened the neat chignon, setting curls free to bounce and spin like a halo gone wild.

Theodosia stood with some difficulty and smiled as the two women embraced and settled side by side. She began talking before the conversation could be trapped in pleasantries.

"Mrs. Madison...."

The older woman interrupted.

"Look at you. So beautiful! Though you could use a little fattening up!" She laughed and patted her ample bosom. "I suppose you could take instructions from me."

Theodosia forced a smile and pressed on.

"Mrs. Madison, you must know that my father was in danger after his trial in Richmond, even though he was found not guilty. Jefferson and others fanned the flames of doubt and hate that his enemies still harbored."

Her damp hand trembled as she reached for Mrs. Madison's.

"For his safety, he left the country but I think now that passions have quieted and the only impediment to his return is the indictment that still exists in the West. Only President Madison can restore him to me and his country. Please apply to him for a removal of the prosecution now existing against Aaron Burr."

Dolley Madison was serious now, concerned not just for Theodosia's physical health but also for her state of mind.

"My dear...."

Distraught, Theodosia moved closer. "Papa is driven from his friends, from an only child, at an age when others are reaping the harvest of past toils. Those who owe him money are disinclined to pay because of the prosecution."

"Theodosia, you must listen...."

Theodosia was unable to stop herself. "Please! Mr. Alston does not know I am making this request. If it be wrong, attribute it to the zeal of a daughter who is separated from an adored father."

Mrs. Madison reached for Theodosia, held her as she would a daughter.

"Dear girl, I have known you since you were small, such a pretty, accomplished little girl. Then you lost your mother and had to grow up so quickly."

"Yes, and Papa had such high hopes for me, and his wishes were mine as well. I want to be remembered for important things. But now it appears there is little, perhaps nothing, left of me."

Mrs. Madison continued to hold her. "Ah, my dear, I often wonder the same. What, if anything, will history record of me? Perhaps, if we are remembered at all, it may be because we loved so completely and that we were loyal to those we loved."

She brushed back wisps of damp hair from Theodosia's forehead. "You are much admired for these things, Theodosia. But my dear, loyalty has its limits, and when you love someone, that person must treasure what you have given them and never use it to further his own designs. You know, don't you, what your mother wanted for you?"

"She wished for me to watch over Papa. Keep him in check, so he would not ruin his chance for greatness."

"Oh, no, my dear! Her foremost wish was that you not succumb to his control. She may have hoped you could restrain him as she had, but she knew that was impossible for a daughter. I visited her there at the last. She told me she prayed you would be strong enough to fight for yourself."

"So I haven't failed her?"

"Oh, my dearest Theodosia, if you were my daughter, I would tell you, you have done far more than expected. And I would tell you, too, Aaron Burr is past saving!"

Theodosia waited for anger to surge through her, but instead, she felt relieved. When she could speak, her voice was soft, but steady.

"Thank you, Mrs. Madison. You have been most gracious to receive me."

Both stood and Dolley Madison showed Theodosia out herself. She watched Theodosia from the window as she made her way slowly down the walkway of the White House. Only when Theodosia was out of sight did Dolley turn from the window, open a drawer and remove a gold snuffbox. Looking behind her to be sure she was alone, she furtively shook a bit of acrid powder inside her lower lip. "Poor, poor darling. Robbed of her youth, and now, she is like a pitiful old woman in the prime of her life."

She rolled her plump, bejeweled hands into fists, raised an arm, and shook it toward the ceiling and beyond.

"Damn him, anyway!"

She paused, then repented. "Excuse me, Lord."

She looked up. "But you would agree, would you not, God? He has about ruined her. So damn him! Yes, God. Damn Aaron Burr!"

CHAPTER 75

Washington, District of Columbia. March 7, 1809

I now know that my "independence" is an apparition. I am transparent, a witless prisoner, no more in command of myself than a slave.

I have been captive to a promise given long ago, hazily and only partially remembered, and until now, misunderstood. My past appears to me as a wasteland, and my future may be equally bleak.

But as I write this, it becomes quite clear what I must do. I will end the war within me that has rendered me useless to him whom I have so long loved, and if there is forgiveness for me when I ask, it will suffice. If there should be love left, my heart shall swell until it fills my ears with the sound of its beating: Joy! Joy! Joy!

Theodosia slept, waking often, startled, disoriented, and wondering where she was. She never asked the driver how far they had come. She had more patience when she did not know. He was often catnapping anyway, his head listing, swaying with the motion of the carriage as it bounced along the rutted roads.

There was plenty of time for reflection. She felt as though she was taking the first deep breaths of her life, and the relief her conversation with Dolley Madison had brought seeped through her veins like warm honey. She had been so blind! But there was time for recompense. She was weak and tired, but determined to find a life that made use of her talents and contributed to the happiness of Joseph and Gampy. *That is, if forgiveness is forthcoming. Oh it must be; it has to be.*

She could tell when they reached the Carolinas. The roads were more primitive, and the spring vegetation along the roadway was already sun-blistered. When the driver turned the rig into the long driveway leading to The Oaks, three uncomfortable weeks had passed. She smiled at the droll live oaks and their cloaks of silver moss and brilliant green sprigs of resurrection fern creeping along their branches.

Resurrection fern. Maybe a good omen.

Inside the house, Tilda was polishing silver, always watching at the window for activity. When she saw the carriage, she leapt up, ran to the window and shouted, "Marse' Gampy, Marse' Gampy! Somebody comin'!"

Gampy rushed in and shouted with joy as he recognized his mother's carriage. When it stopped out front, he was already outside waiting, but suddenly he was hesitant. He opened the door of the carriage for his mother but stood stiff and erect as she stepped down. She looked tired and drawn.

"Gampy, my darling." She took a step toward him. He stayed where he was. She took another step and put her arms around him. "My precious boy."

She brushed his hair from his forehead. "You have grown so. Could it be possible? Nine years old, and you are almost as tall as Mama!"

Gampy struggled to keep his emotions in tow, but his eyes filled with tears, and he looked away. She dropped her arms. "I know it has been a long time.We have to get to know each other again."

She saw her husband on the front stairs. Now it was she who was hesitant. Joseph stood quite still for a time before approaching her, and the three stood in an awkward circle.

Finally, he asked, "Theodosia, you are home?"

"It sounds like a question."

"It is."

"Do you still want me?" she asked.

They were silent. Gampy fidgeted until his father spoke.

"We do. We both do. Welcome home."

CHAPTER 76

⁓⟡⟡⟡⁓

In the long, lonely months without Theodosia, Joseph had made two pledges to himself. If she returned to The Oaks and abandoned her fruitless attempts to restore Burr's fortune and honor, he would provide a retreat for his family away from the climate that brought the fevers, a haven he prayed would bring them together again. He also would put into motion a life change he believed would be challenging and fulfilling for Theodosia and Gampy. But Theodosia had to be part of the decision.

The era of the great rice kings was ending; he could see it. His interest in state matters escalated. He now served as Speaker of the House of Representatives and found it gratifying, feeling he had ideas that could make a positive difference in the life of South Carolinians. He wanted to be their Governor. He felt this would please Theodosia.

The young capital city of Columbia thrived and attracted a lively culture to satisfy the interests of the politicians and their families. She would enjoy making acquaintances, and when she had rested from her travels, they would entertain. They would take only a few servants, not enough to impose a great responsibility.

But he kept silent, savoring his secrets until winter's end. Spring brought a thawing, the softening of hard feelings, a rebirth of spontaneity, and a resurrection of love. The time was right for disclosure.

Without warning on an April day, he ordered two of his largest carriages brought around to the front. He had instructed the servants what to pack. He gently propelled Theodosia and Gampy outside as well as the servants who were to go along on this journey, the first the Joseph Alstons had taken together in a very long time.

The activity brought color to Theodosia's cheeks.

"You must tell me, where do we go? How long will we be away?"

"It's a surprise, Mama," Gampy told her. "Papa said if he tells us, it is no longer a surprise!"

"Up you go! And away we go!" Joseph said.

"I cannot stand this suspense!" Theodosia said as the carriage left

The Oaks and turned north.

"Stand it you must!" Joseph told her. "Listen to me. You used to love a commotion more than any person I have ever known. Prepare yourself for the biggest bustle of your life. I promise you will not be disappointed."

The roads toward what was called the backcountry of South Carolina were always rough and sometimes disappeared altogether, necessitating a search through a forest or across a stream to find a continuance. A great swamp, far larger than any other in the Lowcountry, had to be forded but this did not dampen the spirits of Joseph Alston.

Gampy was taken ill before the three day trip to Greenville was complete. Theodosia could feel the heat of his fever through his clothes as he slept with his head on her shoulder.

"Joseph, he grows more feverish," she told her sleeping husband. "When do we arrive at our destination? He needs a doctor."

Tilda came forward from the rear of the carriage and felt his brow.

"Fever again, fo sho, Missus. While you gone, he come down wid it, lots times, he did. Don' you worry, Miss Theo. Soons we git dere, bile him up berry ob dogwood. Take away the fever."

Theodosia anxiously fanned the boy.

"Dogwood berries, indeed! Gampy needs a doctor."

She shook her husband's arm.

"Joseph! The boy is burning up with fever! When do we arrive?"

Joseph roused and touched Gampy's cheek. "Theo, the fevers come and go. Tilda seems to be able...."

"I want him seen by a doctor, Joseph! When do we arrive?"

"This time it is not serious, Theo. Within the day, he will be fine. You'll see."

Tilda untied the familiar string around her waist. "Remember, missus? Turpentine on the string; tie a knot when he has a chill. We git where we gwine, he be well."

The landscape swelled into lush green hills. Theodosia turned her attention outside the carriage, trying not to think of the precious time she had missed with her husband and her son. Her family had changed, molding itself into new shapes. Would she ever again be part of the fit? She thought of her father's edict.

Look ahead with courage.

Courage. Courage. Her mantra turned in her head in rhythm with the creak of the carriage wheels. She breathed in great gulps of cool air, spice-scented with pine, and closed her eyes.

They arrived at last, and Joseph shooed everyone out of the carriage except Gampy and Theodosia. For them, there would be an exquisite prolonging of suspense.

"Now close your eyes, Theo, Gampy. Close them tight!"

Theodosia squeezed her eyes shut, and Gampy, improved and lively once more, covered his face with his hands.

After a few intolerable minutes, Joseph allowed them to step outside. "Turn around three times, both of you. Then you can open your eyes!"

They obliged.

Theodosia saw a small village below the high hill where she stood. Church steeples rose above modest homes and wide level streets. Residents of the village scurried about, busy with the day's activities — women with market baskets, men riding to blacksmith shops, leather tanners, and carriage makers.

She turned slowly, spellbound by the land on which she stood. The ground atop the hill was level, and all about her were trees and wild flowers.

"I will build a home for you here, my Theodosia," Joseph announced. "For you, for Gampy and for me. We will spend the summers here."

Theodosia began to whirl about.

"Cool, clear air! And, I would imagine, water one can drink without boiling! Joseph! Gampy!" She took their hands and pulled them into a frantic circular dance until they dizzily fell to the ground.

When she could stand again, she brushed the grass from her gown. "Joseph, how can we summer here? The rice crop? The servants at The Oaks?"

"I have more surprises, Theodosia. With your blessing, I should like to pursue the office of Governor. I have in mind a good overseer to supervise the plantation. Here, we will be as close to the capital as The Oaks!"

Theodosia's face was radiant as she contemplated her new home high on this hill overlooking the charming new town of Greenville. She closed her eyes, imagining her house.

It could be a replica of Richmond Hill. Smaller, but with the same soaring portico that would afford a wide view of the hamlet. And she would have Ionic columns and two piazzas, although she could safely call them verandas here in a place too new to be pretentious. She would have horses, ride, and explore new territory. Alone!

Joseph as Governor! Me as First Lady of South Carolina! A bit less grandiose than the Head of Nobility and Lady of the Court, but they are real titles. They suit us – my precious husband and me.

"We must give our home a name," he said. "What do you think of Theoville?"

CHAPTER 77

B lessed by favorable weather, Theoville flourished in the rosy soil of the upcountry and grew in one short year into Theodosia's dream of a smaller version of Richmond Hill. The Alstons moved into their new house in the summer of 1811.

Greenville was an energetic settlement on the Saluda River in the foothills of the Blue Ridge Mountains. Some citizens of the Lowcountry raised their noses at the mention of the backcountry of South Carolina, believing residents there to be crude and without culture. But Theodosia found pleasant friends in Greenville and rejoiced in her son's good health. She wrote to her father in Paris that the climate agreed perfectly with her, and Gampy remained well at Theoville. His bilious fevers seemed to have left him.

"Mama!" he cried. "Mrs. Morgan has brought berry jam. She said it is fresh, made just yesterday. May I have some, please?"

She pulled him to her, thankful for the color in his cheeks. Sunburn, not fever. She had shed the shroud of omnipresent gloom that had weighed her down for so long. She felt light and energetic, and she almost forgot the days of worry and pain.

A neighbor, Mrs. McBee, appeared at Theodosia's doorstep early one morning with a covered basket. "I saved the plumpest 'un for ye," she declared with a rolled Appalachian "r." Curled in a blanket was a tiny black-and-tan spaniel puppy with large round eyes and a wet black nose.

"A King Charles spaniel, he is," Mrs. McBee informed Gampy proudly, "and he is yours young man."

Gampy was beside himself with joy. "Then he should be named for a King. George the Third. He's the King of England now, right, Mama?"

Theodosia nodded.

"Then we will call him George, George, George!" he cried.

"Quite a mouthful," Theodosia answered with a laugh. "Let's see, George tripled. How about Trip?"

Gampy liked the name. He lifted the puppy from the basket and carried it into the yard to let him try out his wobbly legs.

In Greenville, Theodosia continued to relax and enjoy herself. President Madison had not responded to her request to remove the prosecution against her father, but she seldom thought of it. Burr's letters were cheerful, and she thought him content.

Paris, France. July 1811

For many months, I have been asking for a passport so that I may return to you. It is uncertain when I may be permitted to leave the country. I send you a little book for Gampillus. When I am settled in New York, you must send me the boy. I shall superintend his studies. If he is to do nothing but drive servants and plant rice, the present plan may do well enough.

I had to sell all the pretty things I had bought for you so that I might eat. But don't cry, dear little soul, Pappy will buy thee more.

She began to detect bleakness amid the frivolity in Burr's letters. But she had no idea of just how difficult life was for this émigré, trapped in his self-imposed exile. He was wandering the streets of Germany, practically penniless, depending on the occasional hospitality of a few old friends. He traveled to Paris, but his situation was no better there. A personal and political enemy was the minister to France, and the American consul in charge of passports was one of the prosecutors during his treason trial. For many months, his pleas for a passport were ignored.

Finally, Burr managed to secure some money and a passport. He booked passage to the United States, landed in Boston, and traveled to New York in early June.

About 800 miles to the south, at Waccamaw Neck, Gampy hoped the envelope the messenger brought contained good news about his grandfather. He found his mother with quill in hand, poring over record books. Hearing his footsteps, she asked without looking up, "Gampy, my sweet, is that you?"

He stood silently with his hands behind his back.

Shaking her head, she continued. "Slavery, a terrible injustice, son. I hope when you are grown you will never...Gampy, what are you hiding? You are up to something, Mr. Gamps! What have you behind your back?"

Tantalizing her, Gampy very slowly he pulled the letter from his back pocket. "Um, this is dated March 25, 1812," he said. "Ah, it is written, let me see...." He paused. "Oh yes, it comes all the way from London."

She rushed around the desk. "Give it to me!"

"Patience! That is what you tell me, Mama!"

She tried to grab the letter but he ran. She chased him until she was winded. "All right, son, you win! If you will not give it up, please read it to me. Quickly!"

"Big Gampy has left London for Boston. He says...the rest is all funny words and numbers, Mama."

She snatched the letter. "It is our code." She read, breaking into a great smile of joy.

"What's a code?" he asked.

Distractedly, she answered, "Sometimes Big Gamp writes to me in a secret language. If anybody read his letters, they would not understand them."

Always curious, Gampy began, "But why...?"

Her joyful cry snuffed out his question.

"Oh, Gamp, he is here, on this side of the ocean. He was to disembark in Boston and travel to New York, and he says, if it is safe for him to travel, he will come to us this summer!"

They hugged each other, she crying, and Gampy shouting gleefully. "After four years, we'll see Big Gampy again. Will he know me, Mama?"

She hugged him tighter. "Of course, darling, you are his little Lord Chesterfield. He could pick you out in a crowd of hundreds."

CHAPTER 78

Theodosia stood beside her husband's carriage as servants carried his luggage from The Oaks.

"Must you leave again, Joseph? Surely the politicians in Columbia have long since made up their minds that you must be the next Governor."

He drew her to him. "You have already astounded the citizens of every county, but they might yet harbor doubts about me. There is much discussing and planning left to do. But for now, I wish you to prepare to leave for Theoville. June is too late as it is. You should have been gone long before now."

She lowered her head, biting her lip. "Papa could be on his way to South Carolina now, Joseph. I had hoped not to go until he arrived."

"I command it, Theo," Joseph responded. "You know the fever is not to be reckoned with!"

She moved to Gampy's side. "I shall begin to pack, Joseph. When you return, we shall talk of leaving. Safe journey."

"You are not thinking clearly, Theodosia. Your father will not come here and risk the Lowcountry summer, and neither should you. I would prefer you leave immediately."

He kissed the top of Gampy's head, then reached toward Theodosia but abandoned the gesture. She had already turned toward the house.

The temperature climbed, and she suffered in the heat, longing for the cool relief of Greenville. Conflicted feelings returned to torture her. She heard nothing more from Burr. *Was he en route? Had there been an accident? Were old enemies hounding him as he traveled? If he made it to The Oaks and found her gone, would he have the strength to travel to Greenville alone?*

She had not forgotten how relentlessly the fever stalked, and she pressed her cheek to Gampy's forehead several times a day. He remained cool, and she was thankful.

A week after Joseph left, a sound pierced the night, shrill as the scream of a woman in distress. Tilda and her mother had been arguing in the cookhouse as Mae mopped her neck and arms, stirring a heavy pot in the fireplace. A tiny smirk of a moon peeked through the thick haze of a breathless night.

"Don' need to be cookin'," Tilda chided her mother. "Got the cold chicken for day next, we."

The owl screamed, and the women froze.

"Screech owl, Tilda," said Mae, rushing to the window and flapping her handkerchief. "Getta way, death bird."

But the bird shrieked again.

"Be close, he," Mae whispered. "Means somebody gon' die. He'p us, Lawd."

The women dropped to their knees, and Tilda began to chant.

"Oh come down, Lawd, come down. Come down, Lawd, come down."

Theodosia, roused by the bird's cry, hurried into Gampy's room and touched his brow with her hand. "Oh, God, no!"

She ran from the room, down the stairs, and outside to the cookhouse, finding Tilda and Mae still on their knees. "Come quickly. Master Gampy is ill. Please, come!"

At Gampy's bedside, the slave women shook their heads as they felt his hot skin.

"The shore," cried Theodosia. "We must get him away from the marsh. The ocean breezes will restore him. Quickly, please!"

Tilda ran quickly to rouse a driver as she tied the familiar string about her waist. Mae carried the boy, deep in his feverish sleep, and laid him across the seat. They rode towards DeBordieu, Theodosia holding Gampy's head in her lap, pressing her damp handkerchief to his forehead.

The driver carried the boy to the front porch of the beach cottage and placed him in Theodosia's arms. She rocked him, humming a song he loved as a baby.

Sleep my child and peace attend thee, all through the night
Guardian angels God will send thee, all through the night.

Moonlight illuminated the surf. Theodosia's arms grew numb, but she held her child close to her heart as the tide flooded, ebbed, then flooded again.

At dawn Tilda crept to her side, stooped, and felt the boy's brow.

Theodosia continued to rock him. "He is cool now, Tilda."

Tilda frowned and felt for the child's pulse. Tears spilled over her face, and she bowed her head. "Miss Theo. Oh, Missus. Angels done took our baby."

Theodosia's hollow eyes stared at the moon.

Did Missus hear me?

"Let me tak' 'im now. Wash 'im, dress 'im pretty," Tilda said.

Theodosia clutched the boy closer. "Are you crazy? Do not touch him! Get away!"

Tilda turned and left the porch. The sun rose over a flat sea as Theodosia sat, rocking the body of her son. Joseph soon arrived, dismounting quickly as the servants assembled. "The messenger reached me. Is he...?"

Tilda's face answered the question that had ridden with him every tortured mile.

Following Tilda, Joseph walked unsteadily into the house and out onto the porch.

His wife still held the body of his son. Joseph stood motionless for a long time looking at them. Theodosia did not meet his gaze.

His voice was harsh. "The mountains, Theodosia! Why did you not go?"

He cried out like a wild animal, a sound that rose above the roar of the ocean. "Wh-h-h-y-y-y?"

She looked at him, her eyes flat and dry. "You know the driver is a drunkard."

"We both know the driver was not the reason, Theodosia."

She turned her face from her husband, gazed again at the ocean, rocking slightly, not resisting when he took Gampy from her. Joseph stared into the still white face then buried his own into the boy's neck. He turned from Theodosia and carried his son into the house.

The next day, the Alston family, their slaves, and friends along Waccamaw Neck clustered around a freshly dug grave in the family cemetery. Theodosia and her husband stood apart.

The slaves of The Oaks raised their voices in a powerful hymn and were soon joined by the voices of slaves from adjoining plantations who had come for the funeral. Some were overcome with grief and sat down, but all continued to hum together, and those who stood swayed in unison and sang:

Deep riber
My home is ober Jordon
I wanta cross ober
into Paradise.

Theodosia, her dark eyes clouded with the ashen color of grief, showed no emotion. Charlotte, weeping, looked at her with compassion, but Maria shook her head in disapproval. *How could a mother not shed tears for her son?*

Only dry despair lived in the place where Theodosia had taken herself. Self-castigation would not allow her the relief of tears.

I have returned to that dark time, before Mrs. Madison's soothing words. I learned the truth but I relapsed, just as surely as if I had the terrible fever again. There is no balm for this fever but forgiveness, but perhaps I have no right to it again.

Colonel William and Mary Motte wept openly as the polished pine coffin was lowered into the sandy earth. The servants continued to sing as the crowd filed out of the cemetery. Charlotte walked at Theodosia's side, holding one arm, and Tilda slipped quietly to the other, bearing her up. Joseph walked a few feet ahead.

In the days that followed, Theodosia lay on her bed, her knees drawn up almost to her chin. Once she managed to get to her desk and wrote to her father, hoping the letter would reach him in New York.

The Oaks, South Carolina. July 12, 1812

A few miserable days past, my dear father, a letter from you would have gladdened my soul. But there is no more joy for me. The world is blank. I have lost my boy. My child is gone forever. May Heaven, by other blessings, make you some amends for the noble grandson you have lost.

Members of the Alston family who had not gone to the mountains had moved to the Castle at DeBordieu, but Theodosia could not think of returning to the place where she had lost her son. Neither could she leave The Oaks where her precious son was buried. She had only to sit up in bed, and she could see the tiny cemetery framed in twisted summer vines. She remembered the tombstone there that had touched her so.... "All that could die of this beautiful child, lies here."

She lay virtually motionless in her bed day and night while Tilda tended to her, washed her and coaxed her to take just enough food and water to stay alive. Joseph knew she would not leave in spite of the danger of summer illness, and it mattered little. He had no fear of death now, only the thought of living for the rest of his life with this unrelenting pain.

He ordered the servants to remove every piece of furniture, every toy, book, and article of clothing from Gampy's room and take them to the slave street to be divided among those who could use the items. He had a narrow bed and a night table brought in and began to sleep there.

Fall came and winter followed. Outside of Theodosia's bedroom, dead leaves swirled downward and a cold wind twisted and coiled the long trails of Spanish moss that clung stubbornly to the live oaks.

Theodosia found no peace, even in sleep.

"Gampy! The ball! Just there by the wall."
"I see it, Mama. Ready now? Catch!"

She woke with her arms held high, joyful, until she remembered the agonizing truth.

CHAPTER 79

A s the Alstons grieved for their only child, the United States declared war on Great Britain for the second time. This "forgotten war" lasted two years and assured American independence once
and for all.

South Carolina was not directly affected, as the pivotal battles
occurred in Baltimore and New Orleans, but because of this War of
1812, duty compelled the new Governor Alston to assume his obliga-
tions quickly and be vigilant. Winning the election had brought him
no joy. Nothing did.

On Christmas he rose early. Moving like an old man, he forced
himself to make several trips downstairs, placing gifts under the
scrawny Christmas trees the sorrowful house slaves had decorated
with candles and berries.

Dressed in their "Sunday best," they were hiding in another room
waiting to shout the traditional "Christmas Gift" that would announce the official beginning of the day. But there was little spirit in
their cries and even the children stood in an orderly line to receive
their gifts.

Tilda joined the group late. "Missus be sleeping...."

Joseph interrupted. "Let her rest."

He had given up hope of her rallying or their marriage surviving
and had spent days planning the best way to send Theodosia to New
York.

After breakfast, Joseph knocked at her door; though there was no
answer, he went in and stood by her bed. "Theodosia, I have made
plans for you to go to your father," he said abruptly. "You leave in
four days."

She struggled to sit up as he continued. "I have not been able to
secure a responsible coachman, so you will go by sea. On the *Patriot*,
a swift pilot boat docked in Georgetown. I have asked Tilda to pack
your things."

Theodosia was out of bed now, standing unsteadily, pulling her dressing gown about her. "Joseph, you must go with me."

"You have withdrawn from the world, Theodosia!" he answered with a sharpness that sliced through her melancholy. "We are at war with England, and though it seems to mean nothing to you, I am the governor now. By law, I am not allowed to leave the state in time of war."

Before she could reply, he had turned and left the room. He made it only to the hallway before he gave way to sobbing, biting his fist so that he would make no sound.

Shaken, Theodosia paced, raking her tangled hair from her face. *Has he stopped caring?*

She had to know. She went quickly to her desk, spilled the contents of drawer after drawer until she found her journal. Writing had always helped her understand her thoughts more clearly. She reached for her quill.

The Oaks. December 27, 1812

Just before I lost my boy, I lapsed, forgot my promise to end the battle inside myself. To love Papa as ever, but leave him to his own devices, even if they were folly. My first loyalty, I had pledged, would be to my heart, and that which was dearest to it — my husband and my child.

I paid dearly for my wavering. Had I not waited for Papa in the heat as the fevers struck and festered, Gampy might be in my arms. And then I chose to mourn alone, and worse yet, sentenced Joseph to the same isolation.

But there is love, so much of it, in me for him. And, I believe there may be hope and courage left in us both. Once as I traveled in the North alone, I feared that Joseph might have ceased to love me and could not forgive. I asked and was given, without reservation, both devotion and absolution. Perhaps it is futile, but I will ask again.

That night Joseph retired early in his son's tiny room and was, as usual, restless. *Three more nights,* he thought. *Then she will be gone, maybe forever.*

He tossed from side to side, reviewing his decision. *Once Theodosia is with Burr, far away from this place that may forever bind her to sorrow, would she ever return? Is this even what I wish?*

Since Gampy's death he had been torn, desperate to share his grief and to hold and comfort Theodosia. At other times, he turned from her to hide his fury. *If only she had just left the Lowcountry in time.*

I should have taken them to Greenville myself and much earlier. I was so preoccupied with being elected, but now that I am Governor, it means nothing.

He looked out at the moon, a pale circle in the black sky, disappearing from time to time in a mist of swift clouds that drifted northward. The way Theodosia would go.

Quickly and quietly on bare feet, Theodosia slipped down the hall. Fearing if she knocked he would tell her to go away, she opened the door. "Joseph?"

He sat up, and she went to him, kneeling beside the bed. "Joseph, my husband, what is to become of us?"

He refused to look at her. "Nothing is left of us that I can see. Go to your father, Theodosia. I cannot help you."

She rose and sat on the edge of the bed, touched his bare shoulder. He flinched.

"All these months I have pondered, Joseph. Please. You are blameless." She leaned against him, and he felt her tears hot against his skin. "I am at fault. Waiting for Papa. Always Papa. I cannot, will not, be bound to him any longer, Joseph. I have done my best as a daughter. If you hold in your heart even a tiny bit of affection for me, I could try again to be your wife."

They were both quiet. Then Joseph turned and took her in his arms and pulled her into the tiny bed beside him. "Theodosia, we are both to blame. I should have accompanied you to the mountains." He held her closer. "Oh, my God. It has been so long."

Later, she pleaded with him, "Please, my sweet husband, don't send me away."

"My Theodosia, the thought of separation seems unbearable, but you must go to your father. He is expecting you, and you have been long separated. When this unpleasantness with England is over, I will come for you. We shall begin again."

She nestled close, fitting herself tightly against him in their small space. "I am thinking of the letter that Papa wrote before the duel. He said he was indebted to me for a very great portion of the happiness he had enjoyed in this life. Such a remarkable blessing for me, a daughter who is proud to have such a man as her father. It is right that I go to him now, but know each day when I awaken, I will think of you first, my beloved. Of you and the new beginning. We are young, Joseph. Perhaps we can have another child."

They lay together until morning when they heard the servants moving quietly about the house. Outside their window, a hardy bird puffed up his feathers against the cold and warmed himself by singing his sweetest song.

For the first time since Gampy died, Theodosia felt a stirring of joy inside her. "Joseph, I should so like a long ride before I leave, but I fear I have not the strength."

"I have strength for us both, my dearest," he assured her. "We shall ride!"

Joseph dressed and went to the dining room, hungry for the first time in many months and was met by a frightened Tilda. "Marse' Joseph, Miss Theo ain't in her bed!"

"She is, ah...she is in Gampy's, ah, my room," replied Joseph, clearing his throat. "Please have Mae set a place for her, Tilda. She will be coming down for breakfast."

"Breakfas' Marse' Joseph? Miss Theo ain't been to breakfas' since...."

"She is coming to breakfast, Tilda."

The girl tried hard to control her mirth, but a giggle spilled out, and she ran from the room.

CHAPTER 80

Joseph searched Waccamaw Neck for the right horse. It must be large and strong but gentle, with a smooth gait. Even so, she would have to straddle the horse if they were to ride together, so he would also need a double saddle. He smiled, envisioning Theodosia in her favorite riding position. Oh, he could make the day a perfect one!

The day before Theodosia was to leave, the animal he had chosen was led to the front door of The Oaks. Joseph emerged in his riding clothes, followed by Theodosia on Tilda's arm. Theodosia squealed like a child when she saw the handsome animal, his dappled coat a stunning tapestry of gray, black, and white, his mane and tail braided and decorated with red ribbons.

Joseph helped his wife mount and hoisted himself up behind her. He held her firmly as they rode away from the house. When he felt secure with the horse's pace, he urged him into his smooth trotting gait. They rode along the edge of the ricefields, Theodosia leaning back against her husband. The field slaves greeted the couple with smiles and waves.

Later, they rode to the sea and trotted along the water's edge, their bodies blending into one shadow in the late-afternoon sun. Theodosia did not want the ride to end.

"I want to ride like the wind! Just once!" she cried.

He held her closer and kissed her cheek. "Theo, I wish to keep you safe, not dump you in a sandy ditch!"

"I will be safe, Joseph! Let us ride. Like the wind!"

She twisted her hands deep into the horse's mane as he slapped the reins, and the animal responded with a burst of speed.

A carriage bearing Colonel William, Mary Motte, Charlotte, and Maria approached the riders in the opposite direction. Mary Motte saw them first and squinted against the setting sun. She could not believe what she saw.

"Is that — could it be — Theodosia? Why, the last time I saw her, she could scarcely lift her head."

Joseph and Theodosia maintained the pace. He shouted a greeting as they rocketed by. "Good day to you all!"

The Alstons were speechless except for Maria. "It is indeed Theodosia! And, oh, my word! She is — she is not riding properly."

Colonel William slapped his knee, threw back his head ,and howled with laughter. "That's the way, my girl!"

Joseph reined in the horse and guided him to the walled family cemetery. At the graveside of their son, they stood hand-in-hand until the sun was low behind the giant live oaks. It leaned into the rim of the low brick cemetery wall and cast for one brief moment a blaze so intense the couple shielded their eyes. Then, as quickly as a life slips away, it was gone.

They ended their ride at The Oaks's dock, watching the sun's afterglow turn the dark waters of the Waccamaw to liquid gold. Theodosia leaned against her husband. Slaves walked home in small groups, talking to each other in song.

Ain't got long to sta-a-a-y here.

Nightfall stole the river's color for a time, but Theodosia and Joseph knew that soon the moon would rise, and the black waters of the Waccamaw would turn to silver. They eagerly anticipated the night, but a farewell dinner waited for them inside The Oaks.

Too soon, they were once more on the dock, boarding the small skiff that would take them to Georgetown. When her luggage was aboard, two servants prepared to navigate the boat from the shallow waters of the creek into the Waccamaw.

"Wait, Missus!" It was M'aum Hattie, running as fast as her cumbersome frame would allow. She held Trip in her arms.

"Need to go, he. Be too sad, you gone."

Theodosia cuddled the spaniel in her arms.

"Why not? The little dog has been ignored for too long. He can sit in my lap on the deck. And he will delight Papa."

The rowing began, and she heard the voices of the slaves singing their good-byes long after the small boat had rounded a bend, and she could no longer see them.

A brick warehouse on the wharf in Georgetown provided shelter for Theodosia as she waited until *The Patriot* was fully loaded and ready for its voyage. Tilda stood close to her mistress, constantly tucking her cape about her shoulders. Joseph warmed her hands with his.

He had previous concerns about *The Patriot* as she had been in service as a privateer, but the captain assured him that her guns were stowed below and she would not be confused with a warship. He also pointed out that she was newly built and well constructed. Joseph hoped this would be a swift trip for the sixty-three-foot schooner.

When preparations were complete, the Alstons and Tilda boarded and stood on deck as *The Patriot* sailed out of the small cup of Georgetown harbor and into Winyah Bay, white caps scribbling alongside. A tiny rowboat with an oarsman trailed behind her. As *The Patriot* neared the Atlantic, she slowed, and the small boat slipped close to her side.

Theodosia and Joseph held tightly to each other. He buried his face in her hair, which had come loose in the wind. "I leave you here, Theo. Every day you are gone will be without life for me. Travel safely."

He forced himself to back away from her, and she held her arms outstretched, reaching for him. He descended a rope ladder and joined his rower in the small boat, turning to look at her one last time.

She watched him until the boat vanished into a milky fog. She felt him still, his arms around her, his head pressed to her face, breathing into the curtain of her hair.

Joseph strained to see Theodosia high on the deck. The keen breeze spun her hair into a deep red glow about her head. *The Patriot's* sails swelled with wind as she came about, straining to be off. Minutes later the little pilot boat had disappeared into a mist.

EPILOGUE

❧❧

The second night out a sudden and powerful storm rocked the little boat, but she gallantly held her course. Below, Theodosia slept on a narrow bunk with Trip cuddled close to her. Tilda lay on the floor beside her on a pallet. The ship heaved, moaned, and shuddered, waking them.

"Be a storm, Missus," cried Tilda. "Oh, Lawd, come down and be with us, yo chirren."

They saw water sloshing against the glass of the porthole and heard the pounding feet of sailors trying desperately to secure the boat. They left the cabin and stood in a hallway just outside their door, listening to the wind and the frantic voices of the captain and crew.

"Lower the sails, damn it. Lower them all!"

"Tryin', Cap'n. Half the sheets broke."

"Women on board, bad luck every time. Takin' on water, Cap'n. Bad."

Later in the night the *Patriot* began to list. It continued to pitch and roll as the winds howled, stirring up gigantic white caps. A sailor saw the women in the hallway and ordered them back into their cabin, where they sat together on the tilted cot.

"Tilda, do they know?" Theodosia asked. "Do they know how I love them?"

"Who, Miss Theo?"

"My husband, my father, do they know? And Gampy, did he...." Her voice broke.

"They know, Miss Theo. Had to know. Love with your whole heart, you."

"Do *you* know, Tilda? Do you know that I love you, too?"

Tilda nodded, and Theodosia held out her arms to her. The girl hesitated, then quickly slipped inside her mistress's embrace.

"My mama tol' me white peoples think slave folks got no soul. I b'lieved it 'til you come, Miss Theo. Then I knowed diff'rent. You showed me my soul. My heart, too."

She put a fist over her heart, then opened it, extending her hand

222

to Theodosia.

"Feels my heart. Feel it go to you."

"And will they remember me?" asked Theodosia.

"Oh, yes. Fuh sho, they will," answered Tilda.

Theodosia's eyes filled with tears, as she took Tilda's hand. The two held each other tightly as the water seeped up to their knees. The little spaniel shivered in Theodosia's lap.

The *Patriot* rode low in the water, listing harder. Tilda began to pray.

"Good Lawd who made wonders in the deep...."

Theodosia joined her, resigned now, her voice calm.

"Thou who has raised up a stormy wind and lifted up the waters of the sea, be with us."

The surf hammered the hull of the *Patriot* and churned up waves that broke high over her decks. Long white patches of foam streaked the sea along the direction of the wind, and the edges of whitecaps crested into quaking mounds of froth.

By daybreak the storm had passed and the waters were calm, sparkling in the sun's first rays. There was no boat in sight.

II

Small waves curled against the breakwater at the tip of Manhattan Island. Aaron Burr stood at the rail, looking across the harbor toward the sea. His hope lived even in the face of a more likely reality. Often he visited the harbor at first light, searching for the sight of a little pilot boat preparing to dock and a frail young woman with dark eyes like his own standing at the bow, searching only for him as she had so many times.

He began to walk slowly and was stopped by a man with a face like a weasel, his ragged cloak twisting about his thin frame in the raw wind.

"Aaron Burr?"

Burr eyed him suspiciously.

"I am he."

"Got news for you 'bout your daughter."

Burr studied the man with his piercing gaze.

"What is it?"

"Wouldn't you be givin' a poor man a coin for his trouble?"

Burr sighed, reached into his pocket, and put a coin in the man's hand.

"Well?"

"Dominique You. A pirate. Heard of 'im?"

Burr nodded.

"Go on."

The man hesitated, relishing in Burr's suspense.

"Dominique You captured your daughter's ship, took her captive. They been in Barbados for three months now."

Enraged, Burr raised his arm as though he was going to strike the man.

"Get away from me, fool!"

The man covered most of his face with the dark cloak and slunk off into the darkness.

Burr shouted after him.

"She is *dead!* She perished in that miserable little pilot-boat! Were she alive, all the pirates in the world could not keep her from her father! Do you not understand? *She was coming back to me!*"

III

At The Oaks, Alston sat at his desk, quill in hand, trying as he had been for days, to write a letter to his father-in-law. So far, he had been unable to complete one sentence that suited him.

In the past, the Waccamaw had inspired him, but now he could not even look in the direction of the river. Each day at dawn, the wide water drew the sunlight deep into its blackness and gave back a blush of gold that tinted everything around it, a spectacle that had always delighted him. But now it would only renew the raw memory of a recent morning and Theodosia's departure.

He left the house, walking along the river to the Alston family cemetery as he did every day. The gate creaked as he opened it and entered the brick wall that encircled the random scattering of headstones.

He had not ordered a marker to cover his son's grave and left it to his family both to see to this and to compose the wording that would commemorate both Gampy and Theodosia. His stepmother had asked him what he wished to have carved on the gravestone.

"Whatever you wish," he had answered, immediately aware that his curt answer had hurt her.

What possible difference do words on a stone make? Soon enough the carving will be covered with moss, and in time, it will disappear altogether.

As he left, the rusting iron gate protested with its familiar screech and a nesting cardinal scolded him for startling her. Alston watched her flutter from shrub to tree and back again, until she was finally convinced that he meant her no harm. She pressed her plain brown body into the nest, still eyeing him with a yellow stare.

As he began to walk, he noticed Peet had also been watching the mother bird. The slave turned and strode away quickly, but not before Alston saw the tears on his face.

"Peet!"

The tall brown man stopped, but he did not turn around.

"Peet?"

His back still to his master, Peet's answer was almost inaudible.

"Yessuh?"

Alston caught up with him, realizing how long it had been since they had spoken. He had ignored him really, not giving a thought to this man who was suffering his own terrible loss. He wanted to put an arm about his shoulder, invite him inside his house to talk, to remember. But propriety prevented him from this kind of intimacy.

"Peet! Ah, how have you been?"

The question was lame, he knew. The big man turned toward him and the space between them grew awkward.

"Doin' all right, suh. All right."

An impulse seized him. There was something he could do for Theodosia. A real memorial, not just words on a stone that would crumble. He envisioned her face lighting up. He was certain that it would, if somehow she could know.

"Peet, I am going to give you your freedom."

Peet lowered his head and soon, without a sound, he began to weep.

"If you wish, I can arrange passage to New York for you. Colonel Burr will see to it that you have what you need. There are communities of freedmen who will help you start a new life."

Peet's eyes met his master's, and Alston saw his acceptance and gratitude. He knew that Peet would leave and prosper. For the first time since Theodosia left, he felt the tiniest trace of pleasure, so long absent that it startled him.

Alston's steps were brisk as he returned to his desk. Words came easily now, whole sentences that pleased him. He finished his letter to Burr quickly.

He reviewed it and was satisfied. Yes, his feelings were conveyed exactly.

The Oaks. February 25, 1813
My Dear Aaron,

I hear, too, rumors of a gale off Cape Hattaras early in January. I fear there is no more hope. My boy, my wife, both gone! This, then, is the end of all the hopes we had formed. I have realized the truth of her death. The world has become blank to me, and life has lost all its value.

There were times, perhaps, when you and I vied for her love. Now I know that there was no need. Her affection sprung from some infinite source.

And now it is only you who can understand my feelings. Only with you, it is no weakness to feel my loss. Here, some did not value them as they deserved—my boy, his extraordinary talents and character. And Theodosia!

My family seems to consider mine the loss of an ordinary woman. Alas! They know nothing of my heart. They have never known anything of it. I have been an actor, sustaining my little hour upon their stage. But the man who has been deemed worthy of the heart of Theodosia Burr, and has felt what it was to be blessed with her love, will never forget his elevation.

Joseph Alston finished his term as Governor of South Carolina, performing his public duty with dignity. Broken in spirit, describing himself as "too unconnected with the world to take much interest in anything," he died September 16, 1816, at age thirty-seven, four years after Theodosia's disappearance, probably from the same mosquito-borne illness that took his son. He is buried beside Aaron Burr Alston in the Alston family cemetery, now part of Brookgreen Gardens, Georgetown County, South Carolina.

Aaron Burr, stoical and reclusive, maintained a small law practice in New York and died on Staten Island in 1836 at age eighty. He is buried in the Princeton Cemetery, Princeton, New Jersey.

Theodosia Burr Alston is indeed well-remembered. Her fate remains a mystery. Many stories concerning her capture by pirates continue to circulate until this day, but most believe that she perished at sea aboard the *Patriot* in early January, 1813, off Cape Hattaras, North Carolina. She was twenty-nine.

POST SCRIPTS

I t is my hope that *Duel of the Heart* has inspired you to read more about
Theodosia Burr Alston. To this end, I have provided a bibliography, as
well as a chapter-by-chapter list of additional information about places and
people mentioned in the novel. Should you become a true aficionado, perhaps you will be inspired to take a pilgrimage.

The most helpful material for this novel was found in *The Correspon-
dence of Aaron Burr and His Daughter Theodosia,* edited by Mark Van
Doren. Other valuable sources were *Memoirs of Aaron Burr* by Mathew L.
Davis; *The Rice Princes* by Anthony Q. Devereux; *Wives* by Gamaliel Brad-
ford; *Theodosia And Other Pee Dee Sketches* by James A. Rogers; *Lives and
Times: Four Informal American Biographies* by Meade Minnigerode; *The
Aaron Burr Conspiracy* by Walter Flavius McCaleb; *The Life and Times of
Aaron Burr* by J. Parton; the two Milton Lomask biographies: *Aaron Burr:
The Years from Princeton to Vice President* and *Aaron Burr: the Conspiracy
and Years of Exile; The Great Conspiracy* by Donald Barr Chidsey; *Aaron
Burr* by William Wise; *Ordeal of Ambition* by Jonothan Daniels; *Within the
Plantation Household* by Elizabeth Fox-Genovese; *Interview with Honor*
by James F. Risher, Jr.; *The Gadfly* by Addison Lewis; *The Wide World of
Aaron Burr* by Helen Orlob.

Nicholas Michael Butler's comprehensive history of the St. Cecilia Society,
*Votaries of Apollo: The St. Cecilia Society and the Patronage of Concert Music
in Charleston, South Carolina, 1776-1820,* provided a wealth of information
about its early concerts. Peter McGee helped me to obtain what I needed
from Butler as well as Carol Jones of the amazing Charleston Library Society.

More recent and easily accessible books include *Burr* by Gore Vidal; *Theo-
dosia Burr Alston: Portrait of a Prodigy* by Richard N. Côté; *Duel* by Thomas
Fleming; *Aaron Burr: Conspiracy to Treason* by Buckner F. Melton, Jr.; and
Burr, Hamilton and Jefferson: A study in Character by Roger G. Kennedy. I
highly recommend *Fallen Founder, the Life of Aaron Burr,* (2007) by Nancy
Isenberg for a sympathetic view of the ever-enigmatic Colonel Aaron Burr.

CHAPTER ONE

The lower tip of Manhattan now bears little resemblance to the bustling
seaport it was in the 1700 and 1800s. If one knows where to look, he or she
might glimpse a bit of history along the rapidly gentrifying streets, but an

insatiable progress has eliminated most landmarks of the oldest part of New York City.

Richmond Hill was located where Charlton and Varick streets now cross in western Greenwich Village. Its entry gates stood at the intersection of Charlton and MacDougal streets. The mansion later became home to Vice President John Adams.

CHAPTER THREE

Although it is not known where Theodosia's mother is buried, several sources believe it was in New Jersey. Some believe she was buried at the "Episcopal Cemetery," which was just three blocks from Richmond Hill, bounded on the south by Clarkson Street and on the north by Leroy Street in Greenwich Village. However, my research determined no burials had taken place there when Theodosia Prevost Burr died.

I think it likely Mrs. Burr was buried at, or near, The Hermitage, her childhood home in Ho-Ho-Kus, New Jersey. She married Aaron Burr at this site in 1782. The 18th-century stone house is on both the State and National Registers of Historic Places and is located on almost five acres of lawn shaded by ancient trees. The 14-room Gothic Revival home was remodeled from designs in 1847-48 for Elijah Rosencrantz, Jr. by architect William H. Ranlet and incorporates portions of the original dwelling.

The Hermitage is owned by the State of New Jersey and operated by the Friends of the Hermitage Inc., a private, non-profit corporation founded in 1972 to restore, maintain, and interpret the site. The website is www.thehermitage.org.

CHAPTER FIVE

James Madison and Thomas Jefferson founded the Democratic-Republican Party in the early 1790s. It opposed the programs of the Federalist Party, led by U.S. Treasury Secretary Alexander Hamilton. The Jeffersonians feared the principles of republicanism were threatened by the supposed monarchical tendencies of the Federalists, who favored a national bank. The Federalists ended as a national party in 1816. The Democratic-Republicans morphed into our present-day Democratic Party. The Republican Party, as we know it today, was formed in 1854.

CHAPTER SEVEN

A Lady of the High Hills – Natalie Delage Sumter is an excellent source of information about Theodosia's "adopted sister." It was written by Thomas Tisdale and published in 2001 by the University of South Carolina Press.

The neighborhood in which Ms. Senat started her school was the hub of New York City and would later lie in the shadow of the doomed World Trade Center.

Burr's townhouse was on Partition Street, now Fulton Street, in the vicinity of St. Paul's Chapel at Broadway and Fulton, one of Manhattan's few remaining pre-Revolutionary buildings. It is built of schist, the bedrock which anchors New York's skyscrapers. Saint Paul's Church remains a viable presence in lower Manhattan today and served rescue teams for many months after the September 11, 2001 attack on the World Trade Center.

CHAPTER SEVENTEEN

After the American Revolution, several patriotic societies sprang up to promote various political causes and economic interests. Among these were the Tammany societies, founded in New York, Philadelphia, and other cities. The societies took the name of a Delaware chief, Tamanend, who is said to have welcomed William Penn and to have signed the Treaty of Shakamaxon with him.

The Columbian Order of New York City is the only Tammany society to have a long life. It was formed c.1786 and was incorporated in 1789. Divided into 13 tribes, corresponding to the 13 states, its motto was "Freedom, Our Rock." Its rites and ceremonials are based on pseudo-Native American forms, and the titles of its officials are also pseudo-Native American. Although its activities were at first social, ceremonial, and patriotic, the society eventually became the principal upholder of Jeffersonian politics in New York City.

After 1798, the Columbian Order came under the control of Aaron Burr. While it was fighting the political forces of De Witt Clinton, it consolidated its position in the city. Tammany backed Andrew Jackson for President, and after his victories in 1828 and 1832, it became a dominant force, fighting for suffrage and the abolition of imprisonment for debt in New York State.

Although it stood for reforms on behalf of the common person, it was nonetheless increasingly controlled by men of the privileged classes. The hostility of working men toward this "aristocratic" control promoted splits within the Democratic-Republican Party in the city and state. Meanwhile, Tammany steadily gained strength by bringing newly arrived immigrants into its fold.

The immigrants were helped to obtain jobs, then quickly naturalized and persuaded to vote for their benefactors. Because of the willingness of Tammany to provide them with food, clothing and fuel in emergencies, and to aid those who ran afoul of the law, these new Americans became devoted to the organization and were willing to overlook the fraudulent election practices, the graft, the corruption, and other abuses that often characterized Tammany administrations.

CHAPTER EIGHTEEN

The Queen's Head Tavern is now the Fraunces Tavern and stands at the corner of Broad and Pearl streets in New York City. Etienne de Lancey, a rich Huguenot, built it as a home in 1719. In 1762, Samuel Fraunces, a West Indian, bought the house and opened it as the Queen's Head Tavern.

It is one of the city's oldest houses and is famous as the place where George Washington said farewell to his officers on Dec. 4, 1783.

The Long Room in the tavern, where the meeting of the Cincinnati was held before the Burr/Hamilton duel, has Revolutionary War flags and many relics on display today. The Sons of the Revolution bought the building and restored it between 1904 and 1907, and it serves as a restaurant and museum today.

CHAPTER TWENTY-FIVE

In 1801, the domes and wings on the Capitol had not been added, hence my description "chunky."

CHAPTER TWENTY-NINE

The Alston family cemetery with its marker commemorating Joseph and Theodosia Burr Alston and their son, Aaron Burr Alston, is now part of the property of Brookgreen Gardens on U.S. Highway 17 in Murrells Inlet, South Carolina. Tours are available.

CHAPTER THIRTY-TWO

The Miles Brewton House is on King Street in Charleston, S.C. It is the most majestic of an impressive row of old dwellings, and one of the finest Georgian residences in America. Theodosia's father-in-law, Colonial William Alston, bought the house from his first wife's family and made great improvements to its grounds and outbuildings. It is a private residence and not open to the public.

CHAPTER FORTY-FIVE

The brick single house that once belonged to Theodosia and Joseph Alston is on Church Street in Charleston, S.C., and is a private residence known as the Thomas Bee House. Displayed in the foyer is a deed of sale signed by Theodosia and Joseph Alston.

Although the winter and spring months were usually spent at home, some planters chose to travel throughout the United States or abroad. However, the place they visited most frequently was Charleston. In the evenings, the sounds of brass and woodwind instruments, pianists, violinists, and vocalists entertained the crowds strolling or riding in the cool night air and viewing the harbor.

The Georgetown, S.C. elite intermingled with Charleston society by attending weddings, musicales, soirees, debutante balls, dances, masquerades, and parties sponsored by such prominent groups as the St. Cecilia Society and the Charleston Jockey Club. These organizations held their gatherings at such exclusive auditoriums as the South Carolina Institute Hall, Military

Hall on Wentworth Street, and Hibernian Hall and the New Charleston Theater, both on Meeting Street.

Throughout the year, the merchant class reigned in Charleston, but during February, the city was in the hands of the planting class. In this unofficial capital of the Lowcountry, they displayed their wealth in flamboyant fashion.

In 1758 a group of Carolina gentlemen founded the South Carolina Jockey Club, the earliest known club of its type in the United States. This organization was part of a 15-track circuit of jockey clubs that existed in the state during the antebellum period. Colonel Alston was likely to have assisted in its organization. His stable produced top winners; his riders wore red-and-green-striped silk shirts and white buckskin breeches.

It is believed races were held at the Washington Course, now Hampton Park, near The Citadel. The circular configuration of the track surrounds the park today. The "New Market near Charles Town" was adopted as the official sports venue as early as 1759 by the embryo South Carolina Jockey Club. The location was between the two outlets from the city known as the Big Path and the Little Path, now King Street and Meeting Street. The Charleston races occurred by rule on the Saturday, Sunday, and Monday preceding the first Wednesday in February.

The St. Cecilia Society may well be the first concert organization in British America. Formed in 1766 as a subscription association, its founders named it for an early Christian martyr who was regarded as the patron saint of music and musicians. In the spring of 1784, the state of South Carolina recognized it as a corporate entity.

Its membership was limited to 120 gentlemen of the Charleston elite, but ladies were encouraged to attend the concerts. However, its performance series ceased in 1820. Times had changed, and several musical organizations had sprung up. The love of dancing had increased, and subscription dance assemblies became the focus of society.

Of all of the social organizations in Charleston during the antebellum period, the St. Cecilia Society held the most elegant balls. Elizabeth Pringle recalled that during her visit to Charleston in 1850, her family received invitations to three or four balls each week, and the St. Cecilia Society held a ball every 10 days. She wrote that the women in her family always wore French-designed dresses to the St. Cecilia Society dances, which she described as "the most exclusive and elegant balls of them all."

At the balls men and women enjoyed conversation, fine wines, food, and dancing. Popular dances of the era were the waltz, polka, and the maruka, collectively referred to as "round dances." Proper ladies were not expected to participate in the "fast dances," as their constitutions were considered too delicate for vigorous activity.

The St. Cecilia Society continues today as an exclusive social organization and holds an annual ball in January. There, daughters and granddaughters of members may be presented as debutantes.

CHAPTER FORTY-SEVEN

Historians have debated since the famous dinner party at Dr. Cooper's: What did Hamilton say about Burr that was so despicable? His exact words were not recorded, so rumors abounded. The resulting innuendo and gossip put Burr beyond controlling his long-held hate for Alexander Hamilton.

CHAPTER FORTY-NINE

The city of Cincinnati, Ohio, is named for the Society of the Cincinnati. Today, it has about 3,500 members in the United States and France. Headquarters are in Washington, D.C. The society operates a museum and reference library relating to the Revolutionary War at its headquarters.

CHAPTER FIFTY

In the duel, both men reportedly fired a shot, but only Burr's found its mark. Hamilton died the next day. His death was widely mourned, according to reports at the time. A grand funeral took place on July 14, with the oration delivered by Gouverneur Morris, a leading figure at the Constitutional Convention and former minister to France.

On his death bed, Hamilton asked the Rt. Rev. Benjamin Moore, Bishop of New York and sixth rector of Trinity Church, to give him Communion. Bishop Moore at first refused, as dueling was strictly forbidden by the Church; then he relented.

Five of Hamilton's eight children were baptized at Trinity Church. In 1801, three years before his father's demise, Hamilton's eldest son, Philip, was also killed in a duel in Weehawken. Only twenty years old, Philip was buried in Trinity's churchyard. Hamilton's widow, Elizabeth Schuyler Hamilton, died in 1854 at the age of ninety-seven and is buried beside her husband. Hamilton's grandson, also named Alexander Hamilton, was a Trinity vestryman from 1885 until his death in 1889.

A bust of Hamilton in Weehauken commemorating the July 11, 1804 confrontation is in a park near the location of the shooting. Visiting the actual site is prohibited as it is overgrown, and the descent is very steep. A magnificent view of midtown Manhattan across the Hudson River reminds us of the tremendous growth that has taken place in this remarkable city since its early days in the 18th and 19th century.

CHAPTER FIFTY-FOUR

Home House no longer stands, but Natalie Delage is buried on its former grounds in Stateburg, South Carolina. The grave is in "a little chapel, ten feet by twelve" as requested by Natalie, and is one of the few structures that survives from Stateburg's antebellum period. Natalie died on August 10,

1841. She was fifty-eight years old.

CHAPTER FIFTY-FIVE

Had she known what would finally happen to Richmond Hill, Theodosia's spirits would have descended to greater depths. John Jacob Astor moved it to the southwest corner of Charlton and Varick streets in the 1820s to make way for what was perhaps one of the first subdivisions in the nation. Water and gas were brought in to service a number of houses built for resale along Charlton, Vandam and King streets. The house was later used as a theatre, but was eventually torn down.

CHAPTER SIXTY-FIVE

The room that served as Jefferson's study in the White House is now the State Dining Room.

CHAPTER SEVENTY-SIX

The dialogue between Theodosia and Dolley Madison is taken from a letter written in 1809 by Theodosia to Mrs. Madison in which she begged her to persuade President Madison to lift the prosecution against Burr. Mrs. Madison replied by letter, stating her husband would be unable to grant her request.

CHAPTER EIGHTY-THREE

The War of 1812 is often called "The Forgotten War." It lasted two years and brought very little change other than confirming America was truly a nation in its own right. England had attempted to capture Baltimore and New Orleans and failed in both cases. Perhaps the most important result of the war was that it established the efficacy of the American Navy.

CHAPTER EIGHTY-FOUR

The warehouse where it is believed Theodosia rested as the *Patriot* was being readied to sail still stands in Georgetown, South Carolina, near the corner of Front and Cannon Streets.

FROM THE EPILOGUE

II

In 2004, as I set out on a journey I'd wanted to take for many years, my spirits were as bright as the July sun. I was off to the Walpole Library in Farmington, Connecticut, home of that state's Historical Society. I was, at last, going to view the "Nags Head Portrait," a painting believed by many to be of Theodosia Burr Alston. If this is so, it was likely to have been done in Charleston, S.C. between 1810 and 1812; the artist is unknown.

In 1869, Dr. William Pool, a physician in Elizabeth City, N.C., was vacationing in Nag's Head and was called to the bedside of a Mrs. Mann, a seventy-year-old woman who had once been married to a "banker." Bankers were notorious scavengers who lived on the Outer Banks and made their living by looting the many ships that were destroyed and washed ashore by fierce storms. So frequent are these deadly gales, the area is known as "the Graveyard of the Atlantic." Mrs. Mann had no money to pay for Dr. Pool's services and gave him instead a portrait he admired on her wall.

The doctor's daughter, Ann L. Overman, accompanied him on the call and sent the following notarized statement to Charles Felton Pidgin, who in 1904 was writing a biography of Theodosia.

"In the summer of 1869, my father took his family to Nags Head in search of sea breezes. He was called professionally to the 'banker' woman, Mrs. Mann. To all appearances, as they kept no exact dates, she was about 70 years old. I accompanied my father, and entering her rude house, constructed mostly of timbers from wrecks, and thatched with reeds and oakum, our attentions were attracted to a beautiful picture hanging against the rough wall, in dimension 18 x 20 inches, of a beautiful young woman about twenty-five years of age. The house was not clean, and the rafters and portrait were festooned with cobwebs of many seasons. Questioning Mrs. Mann very closely concerning her strange possession, these are the facts she told:

"Some years before her marriage to her first husband, one Tillett, a pilot boat came ashore near Kitty Hawk, two miles up the beach, north; her sails were set and the rudder fastened. Tillett, with other bankers, boarded her. Not a soul was on the boat. They found in the cabin the table set for breakfast; for this they gave the reason that the berths were not yet made up and the cabins were in disorder, yet there was no trace of blood to indicate a scene of violence. From this wreck they brought many things, but so many years had elapsed that she said she knew of nothing left except (what) Tillett, her husband, gave to her. She had an old black trunk opened and showed us two soft black silk dresses and a lovely black lace shawl. The dresses were certainly the apparel of a gentlewoman, small of physique. The dresses were very full skirts gathered into a low-cut bodice, with short sleeves. The contents of an old beaufet (sic) also exposed to our view a vase of wax flowers under a glass globe, and a shell beautifully carved in the shape of a nautilus. My father questioned her closely concerning the details and dates. She said it was before she was married to Tillett, when the English were fighting us on the sea. She knew it was when there was a war, because the wreckers had booty from war vessels, and she had heard the summer folks say so.

"My father calculated the dates to tally. In 1869 she was certainly seventy years old. This would make her fourteen in 1813. She said she was married to Tillett when she was a young girl – more than likely when she was sixteen. The bankers, even to-day, are most singular in their habits, and generally marry, though now by legal and sometimes church service, at fifteen and sixteen. My mother, Mary Savina Pool, examined the dresses and said they were homespun silk. Certainly, I had never seen anything like them. Remarkably well preserved for the long time, but as the banker woman said, they had stayed in the trunk and were aired only on state occasions, possibly half a dozen times since her marriage with Tillett.

"The coloring of the portrait, though very much worn, is still very good. The hair is tinged with auburn, eyes piercing black, lips and cheeks pink. The dress is white. This handiwork of a master is painted on wood, and the mysterious beauty of the face seems to speak from a strange, invisible source, 'Will you doubt me more?' It is held in what was once a plain gilt frame, with but a small beading on the inner edge, those handsome gilt nails having but once, when in the search for some obscure name to prove its identity, been taken from the setting. A tarnished brass ring on the upper edge, by which it may be suspended, completes this most interesting relic from the abandoned vessel."

Dr. Pool spent the rest of his life trying to prove the subject of his portrait was Theodosia. The dates fit; the portrait seems to have first appeared in 1813, close to the time that the *Patriot* disappeared. There are just enough near-facts to intrigue but no hard evidence.

Anna Pool inherited the portrait from her father and sold it to a gallery in New York City. It changed hands several times and was eventually purchased by Annie Burr Jennings of Fairfield, Connecticut. Her niece, Annie Burr Lewis, inherited the portrait; it was bequeathed to Yale University in 1979.

The portrait was smaller than I had envisioned – about 14 ½" X 17 ½". I had seen many photographs of the painting, but here before me was the original, exuding light and energy! The lace atop the bodice was snow white and frothy, and the very low neckline was provocative. The subject's expression is somewhat prim, but I sensed a Mona Lisa-like suggestion of a smile.

I would not describe the woman as pretty. The jaw appeared to me overly strong and slightly undershot. The eyes, though dark, are not large and luminous as many described Theodosia's eyes to be. But perceptions of beauty are not timeless and are intensely subjective. Someone before 1813 treasured and cared for this portrait and to them, the subject was valued and perhaps, even beautiful. To be fair, none of the portraits documented to be of Theodosia look remotely alike. So, perhaps the origin of the Nags Head Portrait will forever remain a mystery.

A thorough examination of the portrait conundrum can be found in Chapter 12 ("The Mystery of the Nags Head Portrait") of *Theodosia: Portrait of a Prodigy,* an extensive biography by Richard N. Côté.

The Lewis Walpole Library is a department of Yale University Library, open to researchers by appointment. Contact them at www.chs.org/library.

III

Duel of the Heart ends with a letter from Joseph Alston to Aaron Burr written on February 25, 1813, and edited only slightly. The reverence and anguish felt by this bereaved husband touched me deeply. Even in his grief, he describes himself as blessed and elevated by the love of Theodosia, not by any definition an ordinary woman.

CHRONOLOGY

1783 - June 21, Theodosia Bartow Burr was born to Aaron Burr and Theodosia Prevost Burr

1794 - May 18, Theodosia's mother dies. Natalie Delage, a young French émigré, moves into Richmond Hill, the Burr estate, and becomes Theodosia's "adopted sister."

1797- Theodosia, only 14, becomes hostess at Richmond Hill, often entertaining alone while her father, now a U.S. Senator, is at the Capital.

1800 – Theodosia meets Joseph Alston, a visitor from South Carolina.

1801 – Feb. 2, marries Alston and moves to his father's rice plantation on the Waccamaw River in South Carolina; Burr is sworn in as Vice President of the United States, Thomas Jefferson, as President; Summer - the Alstons travel to New York, visit Niagara Falls and the home of Chief Joseph Brant Thayendanegea of the Mohawk Indian Nation; Theodosia becomes pregnant.

1802 – May 22, Aaron Burr Alston, called "Gampy," is born; Burr travels to S.C. Theodosia, her health declining after childbirth, returns to N.Y. with her father and baby to recuperate.

1804 – July 11, Burr calls out Hamilton and kills him in a duel; Burr becomes a fugitive, travels to Georgia and Florida and explores the possibility of forming a new nation in the West.

1805 – March 2, his term as Vice President nearly up, Burr returns to the Capitol and formally resigns as leader of the Senate. He heads west and finds a place to headquarter on Blennerhassett Island in the Ohio River.

1806 – Theodosia and "Gampy" travel in the fall to the Blennerhassett home. Return to Waccamaw Neck in December.

1807 – February - Burr is arrested on treason charges in Mississippi and taken to Richmond for trial. Theodosia and her husband travel there and she wins many hearts. Though found not guilty, there is much public sentiment against Burr.

1808 – June 7, Theodosia is in New York with Burr until he leaves the country for a self-imposed exile in Europe. Theodosia spends several months in New York unsuccessfully trying to collect on debts owed to her father and visiting a spa in hopes of improving her health.

1809 – Theodosia returns to South Carolina in the spring.

1810 – The Alstons begin construction on a summer home in Greenville, S.C.

1811 – Alston begins his campaign for Governor of South Carolina. The Alston family and servants summer at their new house in the "back country."

1812 – Alston is elected Governor. May 4 – Burr returns from his European exile. June 3 – "Gampy" dies, probably from malaria or yellow fever. December 31 – Joseph Alston arranges for Theodosia to reunite with her father in N.Y. She sails from Georgetown, S.C., but her ship never arrived at its destination.